Love's Rebirth

To Kate
Best Wishes
& Happy Reading
Asher

LOVE'S REBIRTH

A Tejana Story

Adria Cruz Tabor

To order additional copies of this book, contact:
Xlibris
844-714-8691
www.Xlibris.com
Orders@Xlibris.com
824216

CONTENTS

INTRODUCTION

An unnational territory was born. A mixture of cultures, races, languages, and religions sometimes relating, sometimes segregating, met at that point in time. It could happen anywhere, as history often tells us. *Taysha*, which means "friend" in the Caddo tongue, was the name given to the territory. It was Tejas to the Tejanos or Texas to the Texians. Our story evolved there in the first half of the nineteenth century.

Somewhere in the southwest part of that vast territory was the ranch Hacienda Quinta del Norte, built by Hidalgo Rodolfo Alfonso González de la Fuente for his family. The most treasured member of his ménage was his granddaughter, Ana Dolores Peregrino González.

*A **nation** is a stable community of people formed on the basis of a common language, territory, history, ethnicity, or psychological make-up manifested in a common culture, unity and particular interests.*

—Wikipedia.org

ACKNOWLEDGEMENTS

I gratefully thank my family and friends for their love and support as I endeavored to write this book.

I also owe special thanks for the historical, cultural and literary help I received from the following individuals:

Texas State University emeritus professors and authors, Joleene Snider and Jesús Frank de la Teja; San Marcos Hispanic Cultural Center Membership Coordinator, Cathi Villapando; Reynaldo Pareja, author; Jami Carpenter, editor; and Elly Hengeveld, fellow author.

To the Spiritual Masters,
the Sound and Light of our journeys

CHAPTER 1

No hay rosa sin espinas

Spiritual Magic, in all its manifestations, exists between Earth and Divine Love. Most beings never recognize it, some realize it, a few know it, and fewer yet are born with it. Ana Dolores Peregrino was born with it. To her, it was part of the fabric of everyday life. Thus, it was not strange when she woke up that autumn morning of 1844, feeling butterflies in her stomach and seeing a light flickering at the center of her mental screen, that she knew they were auspicious signs.

Less than sixteen years of age, Ana Dolores Peregrino was a capable nurse. That afternoon, she was the only one helping her foster father, Dr. Moore, at the clinic. In those days, before the annexation of Texas to the Union, the clinic stayed busy because of the occasional skirmishes between Texians and the Mexican militia, as well as to the Indian raids of the *haciendas* and smaller farms and even small towns. It was rumored, though, some of the raids were led by English-speaking men who wanted to get rid of the Tejano property owners, making it easier for them to buy the land cheaply.

Late in the afternoon, Ana heard a commotion coming from the street. Curious to find its source, she opened the door. Dried mesquite leaves blew into the building, followed by a cowboy dressed in blue carrying a wounded woman. Also in came a young child, not more than four years of age. Dr. Moore promptly had the cowboy bring the patient to the examining room, knowing his foster daughter would care for the little boy.

Once Dr. Moore assessed the situation, he called Ana Dolores, who was trying to settle the child in the waiting area with some toys, to help with cleaning the wound and aiding the patient while he removed a partial arrow from her leg.

When she entered the examining room, she almost ran into the cowboy as he came out to check on the child. They stared at each other, as if in recognition. She was afraid he could hear her loud fast-beating heart. She wanted to talk with him, but her desire to converse with him was interrupted by her foster father's urgent voice calling for her assistance.

While she cared for the patient, her thoughts were back with the man in blue. He must have been the reason for her auspicious premonition. She left the dormant woman and stepped into the waiting area to find the cowboy holding and rocking a sleeping child.

As if to explain, he said, "He was crying for his mother."

She asked, "What do you intend to do now? His mother will have to spend the night here."

"I have to go back to find the rest of the family. The boy's father and older brother were killed in the raid, but Mrs. Martin, the lady you are caring for, said her brother lives in the adjacent ranch. My fellow Rangers were on their way there to inform him while I rode here with mother and child."

"Uh-huh," said Ana Dolores, "I can take care of the boy tonight if you want to come back in the morning to get them. I think Mrs. Martin will be able to ride by then."

He was relieved to hear her offer. "I am most grateful. I will be back early to pick them up. His name is Gabriel, by the way."

She put out her arms to take the child from him and asked, "And yours? Your name, that is."

"Please excuse my rudeness. I am Robert Hughes, at your service, Ms. Anita." He placed Gabriel in her arms.

When his fingers touched her, she felt a light current rush up her arm. Hearing her name in the diminutive brought a smile to her face. She thought, *He knows my name? Of course, he heard Papa call me.*

He smiled back at her and tipped his hat as he took his leave. Ana Dolores shut the clinic door and went into the house with the child in her arms.

Waiting for her, her father shook his head at the sight. "I might have known you were going to offer to care for the kid."

The next day at the crack of dawn, Manuela, the house caretaker, picked up the sleeping Gabriel from Ana Dolores's bed and took him to his mother at the clinic just as she was thanking Dr. Moore. She explained that her brother would be back to pay her debt. As usual, Dr. Moore agreed to settle for whatever terms the patient could afford for her treatments.

By the time Ana Dolores came into the clinic, the cowboy had already picked up Mrs. Martin and Gabriel and a bag of breakfast treats Manuela had prepared for their ride. Ana Dolores was disappointed to have missed them, and while everyone thought it was because of the little boy, she was really thinking of the man in blue.

The following Saturday, Ana Dolores decided to go horseback riding and enjoy some fresh air. Her papa was not feeling well and could not go but allowed her to go by herself as long as she stayed close to town, no farther than the river.

She agreed to do so and thought it might be the perfect time to ride by the creek on the west side of town where nature adorned the paths with wildflowers like autumn sage, spider milkweeds, and butterfly milkweeds. Manuela's husband had told her about the Ancient's site by the river that held a spiritual message for those who were lucky to find it. The encounter with the man in blue puzzled her, and she wanted to know its importance. When she got to the riverbank, she dismounted from her gentle companion. As she leaned to throw some freshwater on her face she heard a galloping horse approach.

"What are you doing out here by yourself, young lady?" said the man in blue, getting off his horse and coming closer to her.

———

3

She looked up, and her heart jumped a beat. "Oh, Mr. Hughes, you scared me."

"You should be scared. No one comes this far from town without an escort."

Dismissing his warning, she volunteered, "My friend, a very wise man whose ancestors inhabited this land thousands of years before the white man set foot on it, told me that I could find the spiritual site of sparkling stones called *Tlazolia Occepa* somewhere along here and across the river."

"I know the spot. But it's still a little ways from here, and it will get dark before you can get back home. Besides, it is not always visible to those who seek it. I cannot allow you to continue."

Deciding he wasn't going to intimidate her, she stood up with her hands on her hips and replied, "What do you mean *allow*?"

"Believe it or not"—his eyes squinted from the bright sun—"I happen to represent the law in Santo Tomás at this moment. I am here for your own protection. However, if you really want to go to the *Tlazolia Occepa* site, I will be glad to accompany you, but we would have to start out earlier in the morning."

Ana Dolores relaxed, excited at the prospect of riding with him to the Ancient's site. They rode back together into town to ask for the permission of Ana's guardian for Robert to accompany her on the ride the next day.

Dr. Moore stared at the man from head to toe wondering how he knew him. After a couple of silent odd moments, he remembered the Ranger carrying in the wounded woman the previous week. He couldn't be more than eighteen years of age, had a close shave and neat clothes, which was rather odd—too clean-cut for a Texas Ranger. Despite his age, he seemed like a trustworthy experienced lawman. Knowing Ana Dee would venture outside of town with or without an escort, and after his foster daughter's begging, Dr. Moore reluctantly agreed to let her go the next day.

Robert Hughes met Ana in the early Sunday morning hours. She wore her blue riding culottes, her broad curled-brim cowboy hat, and a blue paisley pickles *bandannoe* scarf—with her initials embroidered on it—around her neck in case she needed to protect her face from the sandy wind.

Robert knew the rocky path along the river well, having visited the site with his mentor on several occasions. He also knew the propitious time of day for the ancient circle of stones to be visible. They rode quietly along the riverbank where the only shade was provided by the bald cypress trees whose extended roots bent their knees into the water. Ana Dolores's thoughts went from excitement about their spiritual destination to shy curiosity about her companion. Robert, on the other hand, was wondering what it was about her that awoke his protective feelings. After a couple of hours, they stopped to water the horses and to eat some of the food from the basket Manuela had prepared.

"I'm sorry, I was sure we would be there by now," Robert said, looking at Ana Dolores. Her self-assured stance bemused him as she reminded him of a curious daring child.

"How did you find out about Tlazolia Occepa?" she asked.

Robert stopped eating, clasped his hands, and said, "Would you believe it if I said that a very wise man told me?"

She gave him a look of reproach. "You mock me."

Playfully displaying a wide grin, Robert answered, "Certainly not. I have a spiritual teacher who told me the real story behind Tlazolia Occepa."

Excited, she put down her *cajeta* candy. "Please tell me about it!"

With a stern look, he answered, "You must promise to keep it a secret." As she assented, he went on. "The spiritual site holds a hidden portal created by the ancient spiritual masters to travel from their spiritual city to the village of Santo Tomás."

Ana Dee's eyes opened wide. "No!"

Robert went on. "Haven't you wondered how Santo Tomás seems to avoid war skirmishes and raids? Its protective aura has been guarded by wise beings. Of course, those spiritual travelers alone know how the portal works, and the site is only visible to a few blessed souls. I understand it has less than a decade left before the portal is permanently closed. If you are lucky and trustworthy, you might be one of the chosen individuals who is able to physically see the site." Satisfied with his explanation, he stood up and brushed off imaginary crumbs from his pants. With an enigmatic smile, he looked across to the other side of the slow-running creek.

Intrigued, Ana Dolores turned to look. Her eyes opened wide as she stood up and yelled, "You see it too? I can see the four rocks sparkling with the sunlight. I think that's it. Let's cross over." She stepped on one of the creek step stones.

Robert grabbed one of her arms and proceeded to help her get across. He said, "Be careful where you step. There might be water moccasins along here."

Ana Dolores jumped back and leaned against him. "I have always been scared of snakes."

Feeling her body pressed against his, Robert couldn't help but say, "If I had known that, I would have mentioned them sooner," and he circled her waist with his arm. He felt his heart beat faster. As she leaned on him trying to avoid stepping in water, her face was close to his. Their lips almost touched. For a moment, they stared at each other in wonderment; and he thought, *Be still my heart*. Her eyes blinked as if waking from a dream. When they reached the opposite riverbank, he reluctantly let her go.

They got closer to the large sparkling quartz stones that formed a square and noticed smaller stones placed in between the four larger rocks, making up a circle about eight feet in diameter. Ana Dolores was exuberant. Her joy was contagious, disarming the brave young scout.

With reverence, she stood in the middle of the circle and proclaimed, "According to Tio Pedro, legend has it that he who stands in the middle of the circle while it is shining will be blessed with true love." She closed her eyes and remained in contemplation, chanting Tlazolia Occepa for a good three minutes while Robert stared at her innocent beauty. As she twirled around the stones in a joyful dance, her blue handkerchief fell to the ground.

Robert bent down and picked up the kerchief, tucking it in his pocket. When she came out of the circle, he asked, "Did you wish for anything in particular?"

Ana Dee answered, "It's not a wishing well. One simply asks for guidance to do whatever God's will might be."

Nodding, Robert smiled. "Your path likens my path."

He picked her up, and without any resistance on her part, she wrapped her arms around his neck. They crossed the creek back to the other side.

As he helped her mount her horse, Lumen, she asked, "What did you mean by 'your path likens my path'?"

Staring into her hazel-green eyes, he said, "We each travel our own personal path. But you and I follow the same road. We are of the same belief."

As they slowly rode together, Ana Dolores commented, "I wish you would be clearer. How do you know about my beliefs? We've hardly had a chance to communicate."

A shadow seemed to hide Robert's countenance. She saw a black warrior wearing beaded necklaces and holding two different spears. Ana Dee squeezed her eyes shut, shook her head, and blinked several times until the apparition disappeared. She found herself muttering the strangely familiar name, "Kagiso." She gave Robert a perplexed look.

In a trancelike manner, Robert answered, "I see you remember me, Princess Isisa." He stared at her and continued. "Sometimes we recognize one another from the soul level. In this life, however, I know about you from our mutual friend, Fray Francisco."

"You know my godfather?"

"Yes. He is my spiritual teacher. I would not have brought you to the sacred site without his knowledge."

Ana Dolores was too astounded to voice any questions. A trusting childlike happy feeling was growing in her, and she knew she was safe with her "warrior."

They rode slowly, their horses closer together.

"I am leaving on a spiritual mission to join a Rangers' troop for some action tomorrow."

In disbelief, her contentment crushed, Ana Dolores spoke. "I don't understand."

"I know, Texas Rangers and spiritual missions don't exactly go together. There will be time for us to communicate, as you say, on a physical level when I come back. In the meantime, remember God's gifts of love rain upon us constantly. We need to learn to recognize them and accept them with gratitude in our hearts. Some might come in the form of hard lessons, but they are love gifts, nonetheless, for our own spiritual growth. God's love comes again and again—that's the meaning of Tlazolia Occepa."

A great sadness enveloped her as they rode back home. She wanted to know more about the Ranger. What was his mission? He was so unlike the *rinches*—the Texas Rangers many feared. She worried about him going to fight. When they got back home, Robert helped her put her horse back in the stable.

He felt Ana Dee's sorrow. Their parting caused him distress as well. So far, they had shared so little and wished for so much more. While he unsaddled the horse, Robert said, "Anita, promise me you'll remember that you are never alone. The spiritual travelers will always care for you." He turned to face her and found tears streaking down her cheeks. He bent down and kissed them away. Neither said a word as he left.

Their paths did not cross again for some years to come, leaving a small yearning in Ana Dolores's heart.

The blessing of the Tlazolia Occepa Circle did in fact touch Ana Dolores's life. To understand its meaning, we must take a look at our heroine's background, the town in Tejas where she grew up, and the families who raised her—the González Peregrino family, the Moore family, and the Ximénez family.

CHAPTER 2

The González Peregrino Family

You don't choose your family.
They are God's gift to you, as you are to them.
—Desmond Tutu

Ana Dolores climbed on her *abuelo*'s knees and gave him a big smack on his cheek then curled up on his lap as he rocked her to sleep.

The child had the *hacendado* wrapped around her pinky. Her mother, Maria Luisa, thought her father had mellowed since his granddaughter's birth, though as the owner of a large estate he didn't give up hope for a grandson to carry his legacy. Maria Luisa did not have the heart to tell him what Dr. Moore had confirmed for her: she would not be able to have another pregnancy. Her husband, Rodrigo, knew; but he was so special. Every day she thanked God for his love.

She said, "Father, let me put my little girl to bed for her nap. It wouldn't hurt you to take a siesta as well."

Hugging the child closer, the old man replied, "You just don't want me to worry while you go out riding with Rodrigo."

"But, Papá—" she started to protest.

He interrupted her. "Nonsense, child, you think I don't know you visit your friend Catherine whenever you can? What you need are more children to keep you busy."

Don Rodolfo rocked with more gusto. *"Anda, hija.* Go ahead, Maria Luisa. Rodrigo will take good care of you. But please take five more riders. The countryside is getting more dangerous each day. Go already, I'll put *la beba* to bed."

Maria Luisa thought her father, Rodolfo Alfonso González de la Fuente, was living in the Old Spain mentality. To her, the old traditions seemed out of place in this wild new land.

As the third son of a rich hacendado in Nuevo León, Mexico, whose family had made their fortune from the silver mines near San Luis de Potosí and then turned to cattle ranching, Don Rodolfo would not have inherited any of the land in Old Mexico. Not wanting to be a priest—traditionally his family's choice—leaving his beloved Maria Dolores, he obtained by concession from Mexico a land grant or *porcion* for six *sitios* or leagues in Nuevo Santander, which later became part of Texas. He was one of the many young adventurers who had been moving north to established villages close to the Rio Grande, a movement set off by Viceroy Escandon as far back as the 1750s.

Don Rodolfo had fallen in love with Maria Dolores at her *quinceañera* celebration, and though she had just turned fifteen, they were soon engaged. He needed to build her a home and a future equal to what she was accustomed to as the daughter of the prestigious Spaniard Joaquin de la Cruz, a well-to-do merchant of woolens and cottons.

So as a young man, Rodolfo traveled north to his new property with barely two dozen head of cattle, half as many horses, and about six good men, whose reward would be the use of a small *parcela* of land each within his property, where they could settle and raise their own families. He made several trips and brought more cattle, horses, other livestock, and *vaqueros* of diverse races, which they categorized as *Criollos* or Spanish descendants born in the Americas, Native Indians, *mestizos, mulattoes, Lobos* or Indian and black, those of various mixed races or *Castas*, and a couple of *Libertos*, or free men of color from Mexico.

By 1808, Rodolfo was able to bring his bride to their new home.

Maria Dolores de la Cruz was raised believing her mother was Isabela Margarita Puente de de la Cruz, who died weeks after giving birth to her. Braulia, a beautiful mestizo woman who lost her baby at birth, became her wet nurse and practically raised her. In reality, Braulia had been her father's mistress who had given birth to a girl child a week before his wife Isabela Margarita bore a stillborn baby girl. Don Joaquin had ordered the midwife to replace the stillborn child with Braulia's baby before his spouse died, letting the poor dying woman believe her child had survived. The midwife had been paid well to keep quiet and do away with the stillborn child. So Maria Dolores became the legal daughter of Doña Isabela Margarita and Don Joaquin de la Cruz. Maria Dolores's real mother, Braulia, did not complain. Her daughter was now legally recognized by her father; and by becoming her wet nurse and nursemaid, she got to take care of her, raise her, and remain with the family.

A year after Isabela Margarita's death, Don Joaquin remarried and had three more children, two of whom were males. Maria Dolores was no longer his one and only prized child. In any case, Maria Dolores loved Braulia like a mother, and they became very close. Around the age of ten, Maria Dolores became curious and asked about Braulia's own family. Braulia said her own child had died shortly after birth and so, affection-wise, Maria Dolores had taken its place. She also said she had no other relatives and her husband had passed away from cholera. At the time, that was sufficient to satisfy Maria Dolores's curiosity. When Maria Dolores's own daughter, Maria Luisa, was born, Braulia took care of her as well, becoming like her grandmother, which in reality she was; and she was called Abuela Brau thereafter.

Maria Dolores had traveled to her new home with her nursemaid Braulia and six two-wheel *carretas* of her precious belongings. It was a rough country; but by the time Rodolfo brought his bride, Maria Dolores, from San Luis de Potosí, he had built a large adobe home covered by white lime, decorative wrought iron bars in its windows, and eighteen rooms around the customary central courtyard. His hacienda, or Quinta Del Norte, as he called it, was truly a Spanish haven.

Rodolfo Alfonso and Maria Dolores were never blessed with a son who could take over the domain Rodolfo had built. Don Rodolfo was convinced he needed to wed their daughter to a good man of Spanish heritage, who knew the value of their traditions and could protect their property. He intended to keep his Spanish blood pure, never suspecting his wife's ancestry.

For two years, since his daughter Maria Luisa's fifteenth birthday, Don Rodolfo had been in touch with his brother in Nuevo León to be on the lookout for a young man of good Spanish heritage willing to come north to marry Maria Luisa. There weren't enough young men of "pure blood" available in the new country. He could not accept the mixing of the races and social status that had recently become more common in the new land.

Don Rodolfo shook those memories from his mind. He took young Rodrigo's hand and welcomed him to his new home. He then introduced his wife, Maria Dolores de la Cruz, whose hand Rodrigo kissed, bringing out a smile to her apprehensive face. The young man was as tall as her own Rodolfo, had an endearing manner, large expressive brown eyes, and beautiful wavy brown hair.

At last, Rodrigo was welcomed by the loveliest girl he had ever set eyes upon. Taking her hand in his, a trifle too long for protocol, he kissed it as he looked into Maria Luisa's large green eyes. Maria Luisa looked at Rodrigo David Peregrino del Toro y León for the first time in her seventeen young years and was relieved by his sweet demeanor. Her prearranged marriage had been a thorn in her heart for the last two years, and she only hoped Abuela Brau had been right in asserting she would fall in love with her intended husband because she had met him in a dream and knew him to be the perfect person for her adored Maria Luisa.

Braulia had been right. You could say two souls recognized each other as their eyes met. It was the proverbial love at first sight.

The hacienda had not had a *fandango* the likes of this wedding festivity before. Don Rodolfo did not skimp on anything. The grand families of the other ranches came from miles away, as well as the prominent people of the nearby village, Santo Tomás. The festivities included traditional Mexican dishes: *tamales, quesadillas, cochinita pibil, uchepos, muk-bil pollo*, venison, duck, rabbit, *ate de guayaba*, as well as many sweetmeats.

Although English speakers were rarely invited to such events, Dr. Anthony Moore and his wife Catherine were the Anglos invited to the ceremonies. Catherine and Maria Luisa were close friends. While Catherine taught Maria Luisa English, Maria Luisa helped her with Spanish when taking care of patients at the town's clinic.

It was unusual at the time for a small village to have a resident doctor, let alone an office clinic. Special circumstances had brought Dr. Moore and his wife Catherine to Santo Tomás.

CHAPTER 3

The Moore Family

The object of kindness is not to return it but to spread it.
—Julia Alvarez

On a hot summer day, as Catherine Moore was taking care of a patient, she wondered why her friend Maria Luisa had not come that day to the clinic she and her husband, Dr. Anthony Moore, ran in town. Maria Luisa was a good student in nursing as well as at learning English. The González y Peregrino family were aware of the cultural transformation in the area, and although they wanted to abide by their own traditions, they also wanted to live peacefully with the incoming dominant Anglo culture.

Catherine Wright first met Anthony Muir at the Bellevue Hospital in New York where she studied nursing and midwifery. He was completing an internship to legally practice under the name of Moore since upon arriving from England, Anthony changed his last name to Moore because others tended to spell Muir as Moore anyway. This caused another problem considering he had a titular doctor's certificate as Muir from Europe. Catherine was immediately attracted to the young man, a good twelve years her senior, who shared his love for science and general knowledge with her.

Dr. Moore confided in her a story of his youth: when he was an adolescent, his great-grandmother on his father's side told him Muir was not the family name, but something that sounded like it. Their ancestors had come to England seeking asylum from religious persecution in Spain. In England, they did well as merchants and were assimilated by their new home's culture. Anthony said the story stayed with him and made him want to know more about his roots. Once he finished his medical studies in England, he planned to visit Spain. He traveled to France and Italy where he attended the medical schools of Montpellier and Bologna respectively. Some of his professors were from Spain, where he intended to go next. He learned about several medical procedures used in Asia and the Middle East and knew he could acquire more of these ancient techniques at the University of Salamanca in Spain.

Anthony Moore never made it to Spain, though, because news of his father's death reached him while he was still in Italy. He returned to England to care for his mother. As a result, he didn't find out any more about his ancestry. By the time his mother passed away two years later, his adventurous spirit was ready to come to the New World. He paid his voyage to New York assisting with the care of ailing passengers on the ship and as an interpreter since he knew three languages.

Although Catherine came from a well-established and traditional English family, Anthony's adventurous free spirit attracted her. He was not a religious man, but he was very spiritual and an avid reader. He meditated daily on writings from St. Teresa de Ávila, to the Tao Te Ching, to the Bhagavad Gita, and many other philosophies she had never heard of. He said he intended to go to the "Wild West" to practice medicine because he felt he could make a difference, and the Spanish heritage of Texas attracted him. She asked if she could join him. He answered she could, but only if they married. She accepted it as his romantic proposal, not a flowery speech, but honest and succinct.

Catherine talked her family into giving them a sizable dowry as a wedding present so they could start a small medical/office-type clinic. She did not tell them where, and it did not occur to her parents to ask. They were just glad she was marrying a good man with a profession. In 1825, shortly after their wedding, Catherine and Anthony Moore traveled southwest to Texas, which was still part of Mexico and where they knew many Anglos were being drawn to with promises of land. Dr. Moore was more interested in the fact that the area had more Spanish/Mexican influence, and under Mexican rule, slavery was not allowed. He abhorred its practice and did not want to raise a family where it was the norm. It should be noted here that although Mexico generally opposed slavery—the 1823 colonization law forbade the sale or purchase of slaves in Texas and specified that children of slaves born in Mexico would be free at fourteen years of age—it did not prohibit the Anglo settlers from bringing slaves with them. A door to slavery was opened while Texas was still part of Mexico.

After weeks of traveling by coach along the route of Camino Arriba, they reached San Antonio, where the Spanish missions, the Mexican military Presidio, and the Canary Island settlers had established a distinctive Spanish-Mexican colony. But Anthony felt he wanted to settle in a smaller town where he could make a difference and decided to keep going south on the Camino Real, or as the locals knew it, Camino Pita.

The carriage came upon the village of Santo Tomás.

CHAPTER 4

Home is not a place . . . it's a feeling.

Santo Tomás was a village built by the gathering of ranchers of the old *porciones*. Its settlers had been granted land by Spain from 1750 to 1810 and by the Mexican government from 1810 to 1836. It was the center where the hacendados could trade and visit and where the hacendados and more prominent citizens had second homes. Their houses were built with frontage to the plaza, where the Catholic church was on one side with a residence for its *cura*. There were also some shops with plaza frontage. The *alcaldia* assigned to the mayor or *alcalde* was on Main Street across from the church. The alcaldia served as city hall, courthouse, property tax office, and for any other necessary legal transactions pertaining to the town and ranches.

It was a pretty plaza, about four acres, with cared-for coppices along the walkways, a nice gazebo in its center, and twelve iron benches spaced within it. The four streets surrounding it were Main, Commerce, Market, and Hidalgo. In each of its four corners and midway between them was a *farol* or oil streetlight, necessary for their evening fiestas. When there was a fiesta, and there were many, all the houses and shops around the plaza lit outdoor oil lamps as their contribution to the festivities. The *conjuntos* or music bands would play in the gazebo and tour the

17

plaza singing for donations to the strolling sweetheart couples and families.

When the Moores arrived at the villa of Santo Tomás, they were well received by Don Juan Acevedo, the alcalde. He informed them of a property on the town square big enough to accommodate their needs. The owners, the González y Peregrino family, were staying there at the moment for the fiesta of Santo Tomás Apóstol, the town's patron. This was unusual because the family rarely stayed in town and hardly ever used their town home. Don Juan introduced the couple to the hacendado and his family. When Catherine and Maria Luisa met, being close in age, they immediately took a liking to each other. The clinic piqued Maria Luisa's interest, and she asked if she could come and help with it. Catherine was delighted by the idea and immediately agreed. Maria Luisa could help Catherine with her Spanish, and Catherine could teach Maria Luisa English and nursing skills.

Thus, the Moores were able to rent one of the more spacious homes facing the plaza, on the corner of Hidalgo and Market Streets, and turn it into a small clinic and their home, making it a mutually beneficial deal for the two families. At the time, very few Anglos were able to reside in the area, but doctors were scarce, and the alcalde was excited to accept the Moores into the community.

Another plus for Dr. Moore's medical practice was the apothecary shop in town, which was unusual for small-size villas. One of the town's hacendados had brought two French apothecarist brothers, named Fournier, from Mexico and placed their shop in the town square instead of his ranch so they would have access to the monks' garden to grow some of the necessary herbs.

To Catherine's delight, the property they were renting would work perfectly, with very few alterations, both for the medical clinic as well as for their home. The building was a smaller version of the González quinta. It had the same layout but fewer rooms. The Moores just had to make the necessary adjustments to separate the clinic area from their living quarters. They were helped by Pedro Ximénez, the house caretaker, with Don Rodolfo's consent.

The year after they settled in Santo Tomás, the Moores were blessed with a baby girl, Elizabeth. Six months later, Maria Luisa and Rodrigo had Ana Dolores.

The Moore clinic and home—on the corner of Hidalgo and Market Street

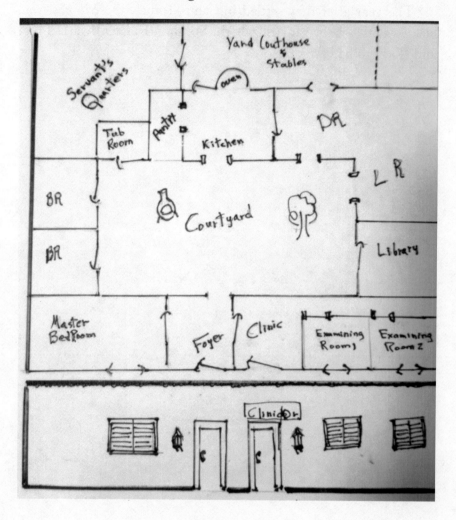

CHAPTER 5

Many people in this country have
paid the price before me
and many will pay the price after me.
　　　　　　　　　　　　—Nelson Mandela

One summer morning in 1831, Pedro Ximénez came into the clinic. "Señora Moore, a farmer from the *mercado* brought a wounded obrero to the doctor's office. He says he wants to see you."

Catherine excused herself from her patient and followed him to the other room where the laborer was being treated.

When he saw her enter, the *peón* said, "Señora Moore, I come from Don Rodolfo's hacienda. We were attacked by the Comanches last night. I saw the fire from my *casita* and was headed to help when the savages shot me and left me for dead by the road."

Catherine asked, "Was everyone killed? Did they take hostages?"

The wounded man explained, "I don't know, señora. My home is at the edge of the González property, a good kilometer away from the quinta, with the other labradores and *jornaleros* who come to work every day. I never got close enough to the house before I was attacked. The farmer brought me straight to your clinic."

21

Catherine turned to Pedro. "Please take care of this man and let Dr. Moore know that I will be gathering supplies to go to the hacienda." She went outside to make the preparations for their departure.

While waiting for her husband, she was approached by a monk dressed in a brown robe, tied by a rope around the waist. "Señora Moore, how is Juan, the laborer from the González ranch?"

Catherine answered, "He will be fine. Just had a bad fall after being scraped by a bullet. My husband and I are getting ready to go to the hacienda."

The monk asked, "A bullet? Not an arrow? Could I accompany you to the González hacienda to help?"

She acknowledged, "Thank you, Father, God only knows what we will find. The Comanches are getting fiercer now with guns coming from Louisiana to raid the Spanish settlements."

"Yes. It is most unfortunate that the Americanos' distrust of Indians disrupted the peaceful relationship that had been growing as a result of the Spanish and Mexican treaties with the Indian tribes around San Antonio."

Not knowing how to respond to the monk's comment, Catherine turned as her husband came out and asked, "Should we not tell the sheriff? Do you think we might need some men for protection?"

Anthony looked at her with concern. "You do know that some of the authorities here want to see the hacendados gone. They are not going to help us. Besides, the raid is over, the Indians won't come back. I hope that some of the laborers were able to assist our friends."

As the three of them climbed onto the cart with medical supplies Catherine and Anthony were able to gather, Catherine was wondering where the monk came from. She had not seen him before although there had been some Franciscan monks remaining from the missions in the area.

As if reading her mind, the monk turned to her and said, "Thank you for allowing me to accompany you. My name is Francisco, and I know the family well. Don Rodolfo was very generous when we had our mission and later in importing medicinal herbs for our gardens.

22

I am his granddaughter's godfather. I live with the monks who grow the herbs for the apothecary."

On the ride from the town of Santo Tomás to the hacienda, which took a couple of hours, Catherine carried on a conversation with the monk while her husband kept his eyes on the reins. "I am curious, Father, I thought all the missions had been closed for a while now."

Fray Francisco answered, "Yes, but our order still helps around the local dioceses however we can. A group of us grow medicinal herbs as well as the vegetables for our local priest and some poor parishioners. Since the northern migration is not as tolerant with our faith, we are not as visible now, but we are still around."

Catherine shook her head. "I am sorry about that. When Dr. Moore and I first traveled to Texas, we had to convert to Catholicism in order to reside here. Things soon changed. Although most immigrants just gave it word of mouth with no intention of practicing the faith, we try to adhere to its dogmas. Maria Luisa and I liked to attend Sunday Mass together. I am so worried about her."

With teary eyes, she and Francisco made the sign of the cross and prayed,

> *PATER NOSTER, qui es in caelis, sanctificetur nomen tuum. Adveniat regnum tuum. Fiat voluntas tua, sicut in caelo et in terra. Panem nostrum quotidianum da nobis hodie, et dimitte nobis debita nostra sicut et nos dimittimus debitoribus nostris. Et ne nos inducas in tentationem, sed libera nos a malo. Amen. Fiat voluntas tua sicut in coelo et in terra.*

By the time they turned into the hacienda's driveway, they were anxious and perspiring from the heat. Catherine seemed mesmerized as she stared at the mixture of gravel and reddish-brown dirt pathway leading to the house. Slowly, the smell of smoke reached them and part of the ruins became visible. In the distance, they saw a couple of small figures. The cart came to a halt, and Catherine got down, recognizing little Ana Dolores holding on to Braulia's hand. The older woman seemed to be in a daze, tightly holding on to the toddler. Realizing the situation struck Catherine. With sobbing cries, she hugged the old woman and child.

After embracing his wife in a comforting gesture, Dr. Moore said, "Wait for us here while Father and I go check things out." The beautiful Spanish-style stucco building was now charred ruins with beams still smoldering. The family members were all dead, shot trying to escape the fire. Five guards' corpses were lying around the grounds including the bodies of the hacienda's administrators, Don Rodolfo, and Don Rodrigo. Some laborers who had come to help were rummaging around the ruins while others were trying to gather what was left of the corpses for burial.

Anthony and Fray Francisco went back to Catherine and told her it was best not to go into the hacienda ruins. Her friend, Maria Luisa, was deceased as well as the rest of her family. The stench was unbearable. Even two beautiful horses of Iberian ancestry were burned. This was most odd because Indians usually valued good horses and took them with them.

The only thing they could do was ride back to Santo Tomás and take care of Braulia and the child. The little girl kept stroking her great-grandmother's hand and kissing it in an attempt to calm her down. Catherine thought, *What a precious child. We should be comforting her*, and put her arm around the older woman. They rode back in silence, except for an occasional cry from Braulia, "Malditos diablos!" and Fray Francisco's prayers:

> Blessed are those who endure in peace
> for by You, Most High, they shall be crowned.
> Praised be You, my Lord,
> through our Sister Bodily Death,
> from whom no living man can escape.
> Woe to those who die in mortal sin.
> Blessed are those whom death will
> find in Your most holy will,
> for the second death shall do them no harm.

Praise and bless my Lord,
and give Him thanks
and serve Him with great humility.

As they approached their home, Catherine asked the monk, "Father, I tried to understand what Braulia was saying, but my Spanish is not that good. From what I could grasp, she heard someone tell her to hide by a tree with Ana Dolores, and it was not Indians who attacked the hacienda but devils. Could you talk to her?"

The Franciscan talked to Braulia and calmed her down. She grew quieter after he prayed in unison with her. The monk turned to explain to Catherine. "She is an *espiritista*. She communes with spirits. She and the child sleep in the same room. Her guardian angel told her last night to grab Ana Dolores and run and hide behind the big live oak a little ways from the mansion. Like in a trance, she followed directions and had no time to warn anybody else as she carried the toddler and left through the back door by the kitchen, hidden partly by the tall grass. Yes, she insists, *los diablos* or devils attacked the hacienda and not Indians."

"I don't understand. Who are these devils?" Catherine asked.

The Franciscan crossed himself and explained, "Well, you need to first understand that the hacendados have been saying for a while that the Anglos want to take their lands. Many have lost their properties as they are unable to pay the taxes because of misfortunes like this one. They blame the attacks on people coming from the north, not really Indians, but 'white Indians'; that is, Americanos."

"They call us devils?" Catherine asked.

The monk said, "That is not what I meant, Señora. In Mexico, the *diablos del norte* are Americanos coming from the north that attack them."

"I can understand why this apprehension exists with the history of this area. Unfortunately, the presidio's militia has been replaced by *alguaciles*. These sheriffs maintain law and order, but I must admit, many don't care for the Tejano ranchers."

Catherine asked the monk, "What can we do to appease Braulia? Will she be able to live in town with us? You know that the property where we reside and have the clinic was Don Rodolfo's village property that we rent and now belongs to little Ana Dolores. So it is most natural that both Ana Dolores and Braulia live there from now on."

Fray Francisco rubbed his chin. "I will talk with her. She puts her trust in her guardian angel and knows there is a reason for God to save her charge, little Ana Dolores. Her spiritual guidance is strong, and she is sure her mission is to take care of the child. Right now, it is in the child's best interest to remain under your care."

Early the day after the raid, Dr. Moore visited the alcaldia with Fray Francisco and Juan Rodríguez, the wounded peon from the hacienda, as witnesses to the tragedy. With the help of the alcaldia's *síndico procurador* and *estribano*s who were the appointed unaccredited lawyer and notary, Dr. and Mrs. Moore were able to obtain guardianship of Ana Dolores Peregrino until the age of eighteen or her marriage. As part of her guardianship, Anthony Moore became responsible for the child's properties as well. After a Mass was ordered for the deceased, the Moores took Abuela Brau and Ana Dolores to the hacienda to visit the family burial sites and take them flowers.

The following week, Anthony went back to the hacienda with Juan. They were able to meet with the vaqueros of hacienda González, and under Juan's supervision, they were reassured of their wages by the sale of livestock and the property. Within a month, the property was abandoned; and financially, not much remained from the sale of cattle. Some of the vaqueros, peones, and their families were hired at nearby ranches while others left the area or moved into the village of Santo Tomás, like Juan Pérez, a liberto, who was a blacksmith and soon found work at the town's stables. Dr. Moore was unable to sell the land, there being so much unrest because of the political situation in Texas, and he knew that the State would eventually take it over for taxes due. All he could do was try and keep the building in town where they resided for Ana Dolores's inheritance.

The Moores called her Ana Dee and became her new parents. Catherine wore her light-brown hair tied to the back in a bun very much like Doña Maria Dolores, and Braulia wore hers. She had an attractive candid countenance, which drew Ana Dolores to her.

Ana Dee and the Moores' little girl, Elizabeth, became best playmates and later studied together under Catherine's tutelage. The girls grew up as sisters in the town of Santo Tomás. As young as ten years of age, they knew the workings at the clinic and helped with the patients. Ana Dee especially liked to read Dr. Moore's books on different countries and cultures, whereas Elizabeth preferred poetry and novels, whether historical or fictional.

There was one big difference between the girls. As soon as Ana Dee started speaking and recognizing colors, she would call people by colors, such as "the purple and yellow lady." The family thought it was cute and fun, thinking it had to do with the person's clothing, and tried to teach her people's names. Then one day, when she was barely three, Dr. Moore brought her to the clinic with him because everyone was busy in the house and he had no patients. An older man walked in, and as soon as Ana Dee saw him, she said, "Papa, colors are going." Asking her to stay in the waiting area with her toys, Anthony took the patient into the examining room. The man had a very weak pulse and asked for water. Dr. Moore had him sit down and went for a glass of water. When he came back, the man tried to get up but could barely stand straight. Dr. Moore made him sit back down and went to get his "factitious airs," the apparatus for oxygen inhalation; but before he could put the tube into the patient's mouth, the man lost control of his facial muscles. He died from a massive stroke.

After closing the clinic, Anthony took Ana Dee to their library, where his large collection included a series of esoteric books, and showed her pictures of people with color emanations from their bodies. He asked, "Ana Dee, do you see people like this with colors around them?"

She looked confused. "People always have colors. Right?"

"Well, sweetheart"—he took a deep breath—"not everyone can see those colors like you."

In the evening, he talked to Catherine about their foster child. Now they understood why Ana Dee referred to people by color. They looked back at all the instances that had made no sense to them before. They understood why Papa was blue and Mama was rose, Fray Francisco was yellow, and Abuela Brau was *violeta* —she addressed Abuela Brau in Spanish—and Elizabeth was multicolor, etc., and why the patient who died was losing his colors. They also knew they had to protect the child and teach her to use people's names and not colors; and for this, they conferred with the rest of the family—Manuela, Pedro, and Abuela Brau.

Catherine and Anthony did not expect the other three adults to already have an understanding of Ana Dee's gifts, but they did. Abuela Brau had sometimes been able to see peoples' auras, especially when they were excited, but she did not share this information lest she be accused of witchery. For Manuela and Pedro, the light surrounding people and animals was accepted by indigenous peoples; and for this, they treasured the child's "gift."

Ana Dolores played the secret game with her family, and as she grew older, auras started fading until they only became occasionally visible. She also grew more aware of her inner guidance. What Abuela Brau identified as a spiritual guide Ana Dee called "Voice." Her foster parents understood it to be her Higher Self.

If the "Voice" helped her with understanding her lessons, Mama would say "Ah, you contacted your Higher Self, perhaps you can teach Elizabeth how to do it," while Papa would exclaim, "Alas, she can no more teach her 'gift' than she can understand it."

CHAPTER 6

The Ximénez Family

The Earth does not belong to us . . .
we belong to the Earth.
                              —Chief Seattle

One Sunday afternoon when the clinic was closed, Pedro sat on the ground by the courtyard's mesquite tree, the only place on the patio that offered some shade in the hot afternoon. He was working with some sticks and black, white, red, and yellow cords and leather bits—making what he called sun crosses. He explained to the girls that the symbol of the cross inside a circle was ancient and represented perfect balance and harmony in our world. His wife, Manuela, would take the sun crosses to the mercado, along with some pastries, to sell the next day.

The couple had been taking care of the González house in town since he had helped build it some twenty years earlier. They had raised two girls there, who both married vaqueros. Their oldest daughter, Eugenia, perished during a raid shortly after she and her groom moved to work at a nearby hacienda. Their younger daughter, Lupita, moved to New Mexico, where her husband worked at a large rancho. Although they never saw Lupita again, two or three times a year, the Ximénezes received letters from her and knew she was happy with her husband and four children.

Manuela and Pedro's life now revolved around serving their new employers, the Moores. Manuela did housework and cooking and even watched the girls when needed while Pedro assisted at the clinic, brought daily water from the public *pozo*, and took care of the two horses and cart sheltered in the backyard stables. The yard was big enough so that Manuela and Pedro Ximénez also cared for their two goats and a chicken pen with five pampered tenants.

Pedro's features denoted his indigenous heritage with high cheekbones and almond-shaped eyes. He wore his long hair tied in a back braid, and from the straight posture of a five-inch-five-feet man, he projected an air of pride softened by a wisdom that only closeness to nature could provide. Pedro and his wife were descendants of Spanish and indigenous Adai peoples. These families had inhabited the mission and Presidio Nuestra Señora del Pilar de Los Adaes, located northwest near the border with Louisiana, and had been the first capital of Tejas. The families were moved to San Antonio when the mission and presidio were closed, but later, some managed to go back to the border area where their ancestors were from. Pedro and Manuela were taken as children to the Methodist community in Fort Miro, Louisiana, where they learned English. After they married in their late teens, they left the Methodist community and traveled south to San Antonio where they thought they still had relatives. Once there, they decided to continue south, not wanting to be part of the mission. When they came through Santo Tomás, manual labor was in demand, as the hacendados were building the village. It turned out to be the perfect place for them to start a family.

That afternoon, Pedro had two small task helpers: Ana Dolores and Elizabeth. Close to six years of age, Elizabeth being older by six months, they were about the same height but totally different in looks. Elizabeth was a little chubbier, had straight light-auburn hair, rosy complexion, and blue eyes. Ana Dolores had light olive skin, wavy brown hair, and greenish hazel eyes.

Elizabeth complained, "Why does Ana Dee get to wrap the red sticks? I want to do those."

Ana Dee handed her the red cords and chose to wrap her sticks with the black cord. She was used to giving in to her foster sister who claimed she was the oldest and therefore knew better. She said, "That's okay. I like the Earth, and it is what the black is."

Pedro asked the girls, "Do you also remember what the other colors represent?"

Elizabeth contributed, "Yes, they are air, water, and fire."

Pedro congratulated her. "Very good. Also, remember the sun rises every day for all of us."

Ana Dee asked, "Why do people buy these, Tio Pedro?"

"People buy these little wheels and wear them as necklaces or belts or any kind of adornment to show they welcome the blessings of Mother Earth. It's like saying that you open yourself to receive the gifts of Spirit. You do not directly ask Spirit for specific things because Spirit already knows what is best for you. They also wear them to show their respect for the Creator."

Doña Braulia heard Pedro's last sentence as she came into the courtyard and said, "*Quieres decir Dios.*"

Pedro explained, "*Sí*, Abuela Brau. I mean God. We must always be grateful for our blessings. I rise every morning and thank Father Sun for the warmth it provides for Mother Earth, as my father did before me and his father before him."

The older woman let him know in Spanish, "Just be sure the girls don't confuse Father Sun with our Creator."

When Abuela Brau moved away from them, Ana Dee asked Pedro, "But, Tio Pedro, what about when I pray for things at church? Abuela says I need to ask for us all and for the return of our land."

Pedro petted her on the head and said, "You must look within your heart, *mi niña*, and ask for your own guidance. There is truth in all paths."

Doña Braulia walked across the patio to the slightly cooler living room where Father Francisco waited for her for their weekly visit. He had been her friend since the rescue and was the only person she enjoyed conversing with fully in Spanish. She did not approve of the anglicized form of Spanish that was becoming the norm.

Father Francisco had a knack for making others comfortable by his presence. He had somewhat of a mystical air about him; he appeared youthful with enthusiasm and hope when needed, was mature when knowledge was required, and looked even older when the experience of age was called for. He noticed her agitation and asked what was the matter. Doña Braulia confided to him her concern about the teachings Pedro shared with the children and told him about the so-called sun worshipping.

The monk decided to share with her a poem by St. Francis, his Catholic patron saint:

> *Be praised, my Lord, through all your creatures,*
> *especially through my lord Brother Sun,*
> *who brings the day; and you give light through him.*
> *And he is beautiful and radiant in all his splendour!*
> *Of you, Most High, he bears the likeness.*
> *Praised be You, my Lord, through Sister Moon and the*
> *stars.*

After their conversation, Doña Braulia felt better about Pedro's teachings. Respect for all of God's creatures was important to St. Francis, who was known as the saint who loved all of nature's creatures, similar to Pedro's teachings. After all, people had judged her evil because she had the spiritual gift of communicating with a guardian angel. She practiced *espiritismo* like her mother and her mother's mother had. So she should not judge Don Pedro for respecting his ancestors' beliefs, especially when those beliefs resembled the teachings of St. Francis. She didn't know how, but Fray Francisco had a way of allaying her fears and distrust of others.

CHAPTER 7

*Tolerance and respect are values
that should not be limited
by internal or external borders.*
—Martín Balarezo García

When the girls turned six years of age, Catherine decided it was time they started their formal education. As there was no school in Santo Tomás, she set up a schedule of morning classes that she and Anthony would teach, with Fray Francisco's help. They covered reading and writing in both English and Spanish, arithmetic, science, history, and geography. She wanted Elizabeth to be a nurse and possibly go to New York and live with her parents so she could train there. Catherine knew she needn't worry about Ana Dee, who already owned the property they lived in, had deep ties to the town her grandfather had helped found, and would never leave Abuela Brau as long as the older woman was alive.

In the afternoons, after siesta, the girls learned to do housework like cleaning, cooking, and sewing under Manuela's supervision as well as start to help around the clinic under Catherine's guidance. They collected the laundry on Thursdays for the *lavandera*, who took the family and clinic clothes and linens down to the river to wash and returned it pressed the following week. Fridays, Saturdays, and

Sundays, they often got to meet with other children and play around the gazebo in the town's plaza.

They grew up as Tejanas, accepting the diversity of races in their town as the norm. Their friends were the five children of the Mexican couple, Andrés and Lola Gutiérrez, from the *ferretería* and general store; the three children of the Lebanese couple, Sharif and Amina Youssef, who owned the fabrics and sewing materials store; the son and daughters of the liberto blacksmith and his mestizo wife, Juan and Alma Pérez; the daughter of the Anglo man married to the Mexican woman, Pete and Maria Anderson, who ran the *pensión*; and many other playmates of Spanish and Native Mexican descent.

At the plaza, the children particularly enjoyed the popular tug-of-war game as they sang, "La Vibora del Mar":

A la víbora, víbora	*The serpent*
de la mar, de la mar	*serpent of the sea*
por aquí pueden pasar.	*here it can pass by.*
Los de adelante corren mucho	*Those in front run fast*
y los de atrás se quedarán	*those in back will be left*
tras, tras, tras, tras.	*behind.*

On occasion, Elizabeth brought their little green and yellow parakeet from their courtyard to the plaza. Periquito, as he was called, would stay safely perched on her shoulder as his wings had been clipped so he could not fly too far or too high. He knew several words, like *Periquito galleta* when he wanted a cracker, or *Periquito urria* when someone came into the house courtyard, which was his territory. Most of all, he liked to whistle. Much to Manuela's disapproval, Pedro taught him the wolf whistle, the sound made when an attractive girl went by. The children would hide the parakeet behind the bushes and had him whistle when older girls crossed the plaza, causing the older girls to accuse nearby men of being disrespectful.

The girls' best friends were Nadia Youssef and Carmen Pérez, and they often visited each other's homes.

By six o'clock, Abuela Brau or Manuela—whoever was looking after the girls—would bring them back home because after six, the adults and families would start coming out to promenade around the plaza.

CHAPTER 8

You can't hold a man down without
staying down with him.
            —Booker T. Washington

One afternoon after playing at the plaza, Ana Dee came home and asked Dr. Moore, "Papa, why is Carmencita's family going back to Mexico?"

Dr. Moore asked her, "Who is Carmencita, love?"

Ana Dee explained, "You know, the daughter of Sr. Pérez."

Squinting his eyes, Anthony asked her, "Do you mean Pérez the blacksmith?"

When she answered yes, Anthony Moore got up and cursed, which was totally out of character for him, and scared the child. He added, "Tell your mother I have to run an errand," and walked out of the house.

The alarmed child ran to tell her mother that her papa had left the house really angry. Catherine knew something grievous was happening for Anthony to be so disgruntled. When Ana Dee related to Catherine the conversation with her papa, her mother's concern showed in her face. She exclaimed, "I feared it would come to this!"

Catherine looked down at Ana Dee. "Sweetheart, tell Manuela that your father and I won't be back for dinner. You and Elizabeth have dinner without us."

Hearing her mother, Elizabeth asked where she was going. Catherine hugged her daughters and told them not to worry; they would explain everything in the morning.

Catherine caught up with her husband as he was leaving the blacksmith's home with Juan Pérez and heading for the church. The priest, Padre Jacinto, met with the three parishioners who asked for his help in gathering its members for a town meeting. A serious issue had come to pass.

On February of 1840, the Texas Congress, under President Lamar, had ordered all free blacks and mulattoes, then living in the republic, to move out within two years or face enslavement. Sections 8 and 10 further enacted that unless they had permission from Congress, they had to be gone by the first of January of 1842.

The town of Santo Tomás rose to the occasion. A meeting with the alcalde and city *regidores*, the aldermen in charge of tax collections and inspections, was held and attended by half of the town's citizens.

They drafted a request for Congress to *"establish permanent residence in Santo Tomás, Texas, for the free Negro Don Juan Pérez and his family,"* stating that he was a productive and necessary member of the community.

The letter was hand delivered by Peter Anderson, member of the City Council of Santo Tomás. The town had raised funds for Pete's four-day trip, deeming of great importance the safe arrival of the missive to Congress.

By the summer of 1841, Juan Pérez was granted permission by the Texas Congress to legally reside in Texas. Nevertheless, Juan did not travel outside of Santo Tomás, fearing any repercussions from the enacted law.

Texas president Sam Houston postponed the unjust law upon his reelection in 1841. However, because of the law's aftereffects, many free blacks moved to northern states or south to Mexico.

Ana Dee, Elizabeth, and Nadia were happy when they learned their friend Carmencita and the Pérez family did not have to leave Santo Tomás. It wasn't long, though, before Carmencita, who was the oldest of the group, became Señora Carmen. Their friend had met a young vaquero while promenading with her mama and had gotten married before her quinceañera. Shortly thereafter, Carmen moved with her husband to live in one of the casitas across town and only visited with her friends during the holidays. Carmen's marriage made the girls more curious about boy-and-girl relationships and courting and promenading.

CHAPTER 9

Without clarity there is no voice of Wisdom.
—Sor Juana Inés de la Cruz

By 1841, Ana Dee and Elizabeth were old enough to promenade in the evenings with their parents; and they could not wait to do so, especially on Saturdays and Sundays. People would be dressed in their finest. Young men would stand on the corners hoping to catch a pretty girl's eye and introduce themselves. All very formal, albeit most people already knew or knew of each other in the small town.

At the age of thirteen and at their insistence, the girls accompanied the Moores on an occasional promenade. During town festivities, there were vendors of sweetmeats, homemade toys, and *aguas frescas* of different fruits set around the plaza.

It was not until they were fifteen, though, when Ana Dee and Elizabeth could become proper participants of the promenade with a chaperone. For girls, turning fifteen was becoming an adult and considered of marriageable age. It was often celebrated with a Mass and a quinceañera fiesta, a party in which the birthday girl was accompanied by her court—a group of maids and chamberlains.

Dr. Moore did not take to such a tradition and certainly did not believe the girls were old enough to be debutants. He was, by then, more concerned with the area's unrest.

Texas had already declared itself independent by the Tejanos and Anglos, something Mexico did not totally accept. Now there was talk of annexation of Texas to the United States. There had been a lot of military movement in the countryside.

Anthony had heard that German-Mexican military officer, Adrian Woll, second in command to General Antonio Lopez de Santa Anna, had actually camped his troops about thirty miles from Santo Tomás. Amazingly, the town had again escaped havoc.

Dr. Moore did not care for the annexation of Texas to the United States. To him, the so-called "Manifest Destiny" doctrine was an excuse to obtain land for the work of slaves to cultivate it. However, because Santo Tomás was farther southwest, its Anglo inhabitants were still few and tended to blend well with the locals. In its shrouded sanctuary aura, it remained a tranquil town. Except for the occasional scouting Texas Ranger passing through, not much seemed to change.

Anthony was content. A voracious reader, he liked to spend his spare time in his library. His medical practice was his calling, his books were his entertainment, and his family was his love. Although he felt that the human condition in the world needed improvement, he was determined to focus only on those close to him and those who came to him by making sure their needs were met to the best of his ability. Coming up in middle age, his adventurous and idealistic spirit had decided to stop chasing windmills after Elizabeth's birth and settle in his comfortable and relatively small world. This decision fit his introvertive nature. His loving wife, Catherine, the pragmatic one in the family, on occasion had to steer him away from his absentmindedness. Naively, neither expected outside forces to disrupt their tranquil life.

CHAPTER 10

*Trust in dreams for in them is
hidden the gate to eternity.*
—Khalil Gibran

Ana Dolores had gone to bed excited about the next day's promenade. She woke up that Sunday morning the first week of April 1943 from an intriguing dream and immediately went to consult with Abuela Brau. The older woman was fairly strong for her age and would get up daily at the crack of dawn, pick up her mother-of-pearl embossed missal and go to church before joining the family for breakfast.

This morning, Ana Dolores caught her before she left the house to tell her about her dream. Abuela Brau was great at helping her interpret her dreams that she believed to be messages from the spiritual worlds. The urgency in the child's voice kept her home, and they went back to the bedroom to discuss the dream.

Ana Dee explained she saw the ocean, and it was very real even though she had never been to the coast. In the dream, birds were flying above the water and catching fish then flying high again. A ship was in the distance, and her stepsister, Elizabeth, was on the beach holding a baby. The dream was so vivid, it seemed real, more like a vision.

Abuela Brau thought it sounded like a premonition dream. Thinking Elizabeth would move to a coastal town, Ana Dee thought it might be New York with her grandparents. Abuela Brau disagreed. She pointed out the bird's actions probably meant "rising above water." Somehow Elizabeth would be able to resolve a situation. The ship was probably someone she was waiting for, coming from overseas. Abuela Brau felt the presence of a baby could mean a new beginning in Elizabeth's life.

When Ana Dee said she would tell Elizabeth about the dream, Abuela Brau convinced her to wait and let events take their course. She explained if you share predictions, they can be wrong or they could be misinterpreted. This confused Ana Dee, and she asked what was the point of receiving this message from Spirit, God's Voice? Wasn't it so one could share the information and help others?

Abuela Brau realized Ana Dolores was becoming a young woman, almost fifteen years old. She herself was getting older and might not be there to guide her charge in the near future. She knew the time had come to clear the child's identity, her heritage, and the importance of knowing when to share their spiritual gifts.

She explained to Ana Dee, "*Mi niña, tu bisabuelo*, Joaquin de la Cruz, was the love of my life, but his family never would accept me because of my Indian blood. He married Isabel Margarita Puente in order to have legal heirs of Castilian blood. Your grandmother, Maria Dolores, was born from our love. Isabel Margarita also gave birth to a girl. That baby was stillborn. Your great-grandfather replaced Maria Dolores with her stillborn, making Margarita believe she gave birth to a healthy child. Not long after, Margarita also died. I was able to raise my child, your grandmother, and watch her grow up with the comforts her father's station in life had to offer. For a time, Joaquin and I were happy. Still, he needed a legal male heir and thus remarried. The point is, my love, you are really my great-granddaughter and this is why you have inherited the spiritual gifts of my female ancestors. These you must manage responsibly with wisdom and discretion."

With a lump in her throat, Ana Dee said, "*Ahora entiendo.*" She felt even closer to Abuela Brau and understood many things that had puzzled her before. She and Abuela Brau shared ancestors! Her spiritual gifts came from them. Spiritual messages were for her own growth and not necessarily meant to be revealed to others. She felt a sense of relief from a weight she hadn't been consciously aware of. Weeping, they embraced each other. They would have many more conversations about her gift later on.

It was now time to join the family for breakfast and talk about the evening's promenade.

Chapter 11

*In the end, the facts are not the important
ones, but the fantasy about the facts.*
—Marcela Serrano

The girls were both now fifteen years of age.

Dr. Moore and Catherine had been promenading Sunday afternoons with the girls for the last three months, and he was tired of having to dress up and leave his library those days. He much preferred to go for a horse ride or go out in their carriage for a family picnic if he had to leave his home.

So Abuela Brau was in charge of the girls that particular Sunday. April had arrived with a pleasant light breeze perfect for strolling around the plaza, which Anthony thought would be good for Abuela's health. Besides, from his point of view, the only young men who had approached their little family and strolled with them were the kids who used to play in the plaza when the girls were growing up, and he knew those boys were too young to have any serious romantic intentions. The more mature eighteen-plus years old, those who could provide for a wife, never approached them to his relief and the girls' consternation. He simply thought others could tell his girls were too young, and in his aloofness, he hadn't an inkling of his threatening presence.

Fully aware of the situation, Catherine suggested they stay home and let Abuela Brau, a less intimidating chaperone, accompany the girls. She knew their family was well known and respected by the townspeople, and it was high time the girls joined in the wholesome tradition of promenading to meet prospective beaus.

After crossing the street to the plaza, two of their childhood friends ran over to join them. Elizabeth raised her hand in a stop gesture and said they did not want children with them this time. The boys had experienced the same type of refusal before with other female playmates who reached the age of fifteen, so they weren't surprised—but rather disappointed—and walked away with stooped shoulders.

As they strolled around the plaza, a couple of young vaqueros tried to introduce themselves, but neither girl gave them the required encouragement. They bought a bag of toasted *cacahuates* and found a vacant bench on the other side of the plaza. Ana Dee went to the sweetmeats booth and got a *pan dulce* for her great-grandmother, who was addicted to Mexican pastries. A soft sweet bread was something she could enjoy more than the toasted peanuts because she was missing teeth. In the background, music could be heard coming from the gazebo, where different bands played every Saturday evening and Sunday afternoon.

They noticed a slight commotion by the vendor of aguas frescas. Standing in front of the stand of fruity water refreshments were a couple of young men in bell-bottom white pants and blue shirts trying to communicate with the vendor.

Elizabeth commented, "It looks like they don't speak Spanish."

Ana Dee said, "I'm sure that Don Pancho can figure it out."

Elizabeth commented, "One of them seems upset. I wonder what the uniform represents. I think I'll go and help Don Pancho." Before Abuela Brau could stop her, she was gone. Ana Dee and Abuela Brau watched as the little group appeared to calm down, but it was a good ten minutes before Elizabeth came back to them.

"Well," Elizabeth explained, "they were arguing about the glasses. I explained they had to buy them or bring their own. Then they could not decide which flavor of agua fresca they wanted. Can you believe they are Texas sailors?" Both Abuela Brau's and Ana Dee's eyes opened wide in surprise, not because they were sailors but because they saw the connection with Ana Dee's dream.

They strolled around the plaza one more time and then decided to cut across through the center to go home. When someone reached out for Elizabeth's hand, Ana Dolores turned to protect her sister, making somewhat of a commotion. Suddenly, a cowboy in blue attire from his hat to his boots and a gun hanging in its holster was between the sailor and the girls.

He said, "Please leave the ladies be."

The sailor explained, "I just wanted to thank her and get her name."

Abuela Brau grabbed her charges, and as she rushed them away, the girl yelled back, "My name is Elizabeth Moore."

They did not discuss the event that evening, not wanting their parents to know. Ana Dee noticed her abuela seemed worried, so she went into her room to comfort her. She found Abuela Brau pensive and distraught.

She finally understood why the older woman was scared of the man in blue. Abuela said the man had been with the group that burned the hacienda. Ana Dee knew it was impossible since it had been over thirteen years ago, and at that time, the man in blue could not have been old enough. He barely looked to be twenty, which would have made him about seven when the raid took place. It was an hour before things settled, Braulia fell asleep, and Ana Dee went to lie on her bed and wonder about the day's events.

The next evening, although it was a weeknight, Manuela and Pedro offered to take the girls promenading. Weeknights on the plaza were not as busy, which was the time the Ximénez couple preferred to take their stroll. Both of their daughters had met their husbands through this old tradition, and they were convinced it was the proper custom to follow.

Several young men approached them and were nicely greeted by the Ximénez couple, who then asked the girls if they wanted their company. The girls did not. Elizabeth seemed to be looking out for someone in particular, and Ana Dee was not interested.

Once they reached the other side of the court, a freckled redhead with a twinkle in his brown eyes, in jeans, and a white shirt approached them. He introduced himself as James O'Reilly and said he would like to accompany Señorita Elizabeth. Pedro turned to Elizabeth for her approval, and once the blushing girl nodded, he allowed the couple to walk together in front of them while saying, "No touching."

Elizabeth asked the young man why he wasn't wearing his uniform. Standing tall, James said he preferred to blend in with the locals. Elizabeth tilted her head in amusement and hid a giggle, thinking, *As if he could!* while staring at his tall stature and red curls. He offered to buy the group sweetmeats and found a bench for the ladies.

James bought a bag full of candies and passed them out. He was on the lookout for a bench so he could sit alone with Elizabeth. Some young boys were sitting on a bench across from them. James crossed over and offered the boys sweetmeats in exchange for the bench. They agreed, and he invited Elizabeth to join him there. Before Tio Pedro could stop her, she agreed. Pedro gave James a smirky smile and sat down with Manuela and Ana Dee across from them.

In the background, they could hear the conjunto musicians playing a romantic ranchera. James commented he wished they could dance to it.

She asked, "Oh, you like to dance to that music?"

He answered, "Not really, I would just like to hold you."

This made her blush, but she was a daring soul and responded, "I would like it too."

They exchanged life stories. After losing both parents, James had come with his older brother to New Orleans from Ireland seeking a better life. His brother got a land grant in Texas, but they could not compete with other farmers who had slaves to do the work. To make ends meet, Sean went to work at a tavern and learned the business, leaving James running the farm, which turned out to be disastrous. Before he turned seventeen, James joined the Texas Navy and Sean sold the land and was able to eventually buy the tavern in the quiet town of Santo Tomás, which he named Cantina O'Reilly.

Manuela told Pedro it was time to go home. He said, "Well, Ana Dolores has not made any acquaintances, but we made some progress with Elizabeth."

Manuela reminded him, "You know, Dr. Moore does not really want the girls to be courting yet. You should not be so pleased with yourself."

"Nonsense," said Pedro. "Look what a nice couple Elizabeth and her young man make."

"Really, Pedro," she replied, "we know nothing about that young man. He is obviously not a local."

Pedro responded, "There you are wrong. I happen to know he is Sean O'Reilly's brother, and I met him at the tavern this afternoon when I took Sean some of your baked goods."

All she said was, "Aha! So you arranged all this."

Pedro smiled. "Well, when James asked me if I knew Elizabeth Moore this afternoon, I knew it was meant to be."

To Manuela's consternation, Ana Dee could not believe what she was hearing and started to laugh.

After half an hour, Pedro decided it was time to return home with the girls. They all got up, and as he shook James's hand, he commented, "We were lucky tonight that was a band playing. That is usually only on weekends. They must be new. As a rule, during the week, only amateurs come and play a solo guitar or harp for donations. But these musicians were pretty good. Don't you think so, James?"

The ladies never saw him wink at James who answered, "Yes, sir, very lucky." The young man walked with the party across the park to see them enter their home.

Neither the girls nor the Ximénez couple told the Moores about James. However, Ana Dee and Elizabeth spent a good hour giggling and talking about Elizabeth's conversation with James.

CHAPTER 12

Music. Melancholic food for those of us who live on love.
                                        —Julio Cortázar

Around midnight, Catherine and Anthony woke up to music. They opened the window shutters in their bedroom, the only room in the house facing the street. Through the decorative wrought iron bars, they faced a group of musicians serenading.

> *Noche de luna, para quererte.*
> *Noche de luna, hay para amarte.*
> *Noche de luna, para quererte.*
> *Noche de luna, hay para amarte . . .*
> *Moonlit night, to love you*
> *Moonlit night, to adore you*
> *Moonlit night, to love you*
> *Moonlit night, to adore you.*

Half asleep, Dr. Moore went to wake up the girls. "There is a serenade going on by my window. I doubt that it's for your mother."

Elizabeth's face became flushed as she rushed to her parents' bedroom while Ana Dee explained, "I am sure it's for Elizabeth, Papa. Someone she met this evening."

The whole family leaned on the windowsill to enjoy the serenade. When it was over and the musicians parted, James approached the window and introduced himself.

Dr. Moore said, "Thank you, young man . . . er . . . James. That was lovely. You may speak with Elizabeth for ten minutes." He then turned around and removed himself from the room, taking along his wife and other daughter.

James then asked Elizabeth if they could meet the next afternoon. First, she said she didn't know if she could; then she said she would get away around one o'clock during siesta time. Before they could discuss it any more, Dr. Moore was back, bidding James good night and closing the shutters. Elizabeth rushed back to her room before her papa could ask any questions. She knew she would be drilled in the morning during breakfast.

"So James seemed like a nice young man," Catherine commented as she buttered her *bolillo*.

This was followed by Anthony's first inquiries: "How did you meet him?" and "Who is his family? I don't recall seeing him in town before."

After Elizabeth's short explanations, Manuela came in with fresh coffee. As she was pouring the drink into Anthony's cup, he asked her, "What do you think of the young man Elizabeth met yesterday?"

She asked him, "The *marinero*?"

Dr. Moore exclaimed, "Ah, that explains it—a sailor! Well, he won't be in town much longer."

To Elizabeth's sigh of relief, the topic of conversation was dropped, which didn't go unnoticed by her mother. Later in the morning, Elizabeth asked Abuela Brau if she would take them to the plaza in the evening. Abuela Brau said she would consult with Catherine and let her know.

As she did her chores that morning, Elizabeth was reserved and pensive. This was usual behavior for Elizabeth, and Ana Dee suspected her sister was up to something. After lunch, everyone went to their respective rooms for the siesta. When Elizabeth quietly left the house fifteen minutes later, unbeknownst to her, Ana Dee watched from one of the clinic's windows.

Elizabeth crossed the plaza and heard a whistle coming from behind the gazebo. She backtracked her steps and, seeing James, rushed to meet him. "I only have about half an hour, plus I have to pick up some ribbons at the fabric store in case they ask where I was when I get back home."

James had taken her hands in his and kissed them. As she pulled back, he asked, "So we are meeting in secret? Are you scared?"

"It's not that I am scared," she said. "It's just that I'm not used to this, you know."

He asked, "You mean, your parents would not approve of our meeting?"

Lowering her gaze, she answered, "No. Not without a chaperone."

James turned her chin up to look at him and declared, "Señorita Elly, I would like to court you with your parents' permission."

"They'll think we are moving rather fast," she said as she removed his hand from her face.

"Is that how you feel, Elly? Because I feel like we've known each other for a long time. I can't get you out of my mind, or your beautiful eyes, or your tempting lips. Let's go talk to them right now."

Wanting to avoid the issue, she said, "What if they say no? I have to go, James. I will try to come to the promenade this evening, and we can talk then."

"I will be waiting for you, Elly, my Elly."

As she turned to go to the store, Elizabeth said her goodbye. "I like that you call me Elly. No one has ever called me that before."

Ana Dee greeted her sister when she tried to quietly enter the house. "I saw you going to the plaza. Did you meet James?"

Nonplussed, Elizabeth answered, "Well, if you were watching, you already know."

"I actually lost sight of you when you turned toward the gazebo. It's okay, I won't tell anyone. Do you really like him? I mean . . . like . . . enough to kiss him?"

Elizabeth responded, "For your information, we have not kissed. I am thinking that we might tonight if they let us go."

Catherine and Abuela Brau decided the girls could go out that evening again, as long as they came home early. Ana Dolores wasn't interested in going but acceded to go after her sister begged her. Privately, Elizabeth explained to Ana that she wanted to sit on a bench alone with James, not with James and Abuela. If Ana Dee went, they could occupy two separate benches. She could also distract Abuela so she and James might try a kiss.

Ana Dee knew in her heart that the sailor would take her sister away, just as her dream prophesied. This saddened her, but Abuela told her it was destiny and they must accept it and to just love, protect, and support Elizabeth.

They went to the plaza early, around 6:30 p.m. It was still daylight outside, but being a weeknight, they were supposed to be back by 8:00 p.m.

Elizabeth felt her heart beat faster when she saw James already across the street in the plaza waiting for her, with a small bouquet of flowers. He offered the flowers to Abuela Brau, who seemed to appreciate the gesture and said he was a gentleman, *"Que Galante!"*

As they strolled around the plaza, Elizabeth took James's arm while Ana Dee and Abuela Brau followed them until they came to two benches across from each other. The plaza was far from crowded at that time. The weeknight vendors weren't even there yet.

The young sweethearts conversed in whispers that neither Abuela Brau nor Ana Dee could understand what they were saying. "I think you are right, Abuela Brau— they seem to be falling in love." Ana saw the sweetmeats vendor setting up and told Abuela Brau to wait on the bench while she went to get her a pan dulce.

Halfway there, Ana Dee was intercepted by the man in blue. He held out a pan dulce for her. *"Este es para su abuelita.* Please tell her she needn't fear me."

Mesmerized by his steel-blue eyes, she held out her hand. He looked even younger than she had thought, possibly as young as James, less than twenty. She lowered her eyelids with the flustered action of her long eyelashes as she took the bread and thanked him. His hand touched hers, and a strong, gentle electrifying current tingled up her arm and then a feeling of warmth enveloped her. He looked transfixed, staring at her. Confused, she pulled away, and he slowly turned around and walked toward the gazebo. She noticed he carried a type of elongated leather suitcase.

Ana Dee gave the pan dulce to her great-grandmother and related to her the experience, emphatically adding he was too young to have been in the raid and Abuela needn't fear him. She wondered, though, how the young man had perceived Abuela's fear. The older woman caressed her great-granddaughter's face, feeling the comforting warmth Ana Dee was experiencing; and in her heart, she knew her child's future had changed.

While Abuela and Ana Dee were in deep conversation, Elizabeth sat closer to James, and they shared a kiss. After this, she had no doubt in her mind about the shared tender feelings for each other. She sadly told him, "I won't be coming back to the plaza again until Friday." This was only two evenings away, but it seemed an eternity to both of them.

The strum of a flamenco guitar could be heard in the background. People started gathering around the gazebo. Ana Dee could barely hear the melody and, wanting to better enjoy it, asked Abuela if she could leave her to chaperone her sister alone for a little while so she could get close to the gazebo. After Abuela Brau resignedly gave her consent, Ana Dee was able to find a spot close enough to see the guitar player.

The man in blue was playing with such fire that the enthusiastic crowd started tapping and clapping along with the beat of the music. The performance was stirring. When he stopped, the audience asked for more. An attractive señorita went up to the guitarist and gave him a big kiss. Everyone applauded. Ana Dolores wanted to run away and did not understand why. She didn't stay for the next performance.

Abuela Brau asked her if she liked the music. Turning her head away from Abuela, Ana Dee answered in a low-key voice that it had been nice. The older woman signaled to the couple across the bench that it was time to leave. Elizabeth signaled back for five more minutes.

James told her, "You know, Elly, that I am leaving next week. I want to spend every hour I can with you before then. Please let me talk to your parents so I can visit with you at your house before Friday."

"James, I am so scared that Papa won't let me see you again, precisely because you will be leaving so soon. Never mind that you will be involved in a war. He hates the war."

"What do you want me to do? I can't leave the navy now. My intent was to make a career out of it, but that's no longer important. I will quit when my term is over if that is what you want me to do."

"Perhaps we are moving too fast. I have to think about this. I feel confused. I will have an answer by Friday, if you still want to meet me then."

They all walked back to the house. The three young ones did not look like they had enjoyed the outing. Even Abuela Brau did not seem content, carrying her bread to give to Periquito.

The next day, Elizabeth went around self-absorbed, moping. Only Ana Dee knew how involved her sister was with James; but Catherine, as her mother, suspected something was going on.

Ana Dee advised her sister, "Mother is worried about you, Elizabeth. If anyone can help you in this situation, it is she. Please talk to her."

Resolved to confide in Catherine first thing the next morning, Elizabeth went to bed teary-eyed.

Early Thursday morning, Catherine entered her daughter's bedroom. Sitting on the bed, she petted Elizabeth's head and said,

"Darling girl, tell me what is troubling you. Are you falling for unrequited love?"

Elizabeth sat up in bed. Looking down at her hands, she whispered, "Yes and no. He loves me too, I think."

Catherine embraced the sobbing girl and asked, "Well, what is the problem?"

Elizabeth could not contain herself any longer and between uncontrollable whimpers explained James was a sailor. He would soon be leaving. She was also worried about her father's reaction. Catherine remembered her husband's comment when Manuela mentioned the young man was a sailor. He had been dismissive of the whole affair because he did not consider it serious. The fact that James would have to leave town soon seemed a plus to him. She herself deemed her daughter rather fickle and did not expect her feelings to be as deep as Elizabeth claimed. She consoled her daughter while hoping Elizabeth would get over her infatuation soon. "You can write to each other, and he can visit on his next leave."

Across town, James was arguing with his brother. "I didn't get up because I am not leaving town with George. I can wait till Monday and still have a month to get to New Orleans and catch my ship on time. George left because he did not enjoy the local atmosphere."

Sean asked, "What do you mean . . . atmosphere?"

"He thinks you should only allow white people in the bar."

Shaking his head, Sean said, "Ha! I would go broke. This is a Mexican town. The population is quite mixed. He didn't mind flirting with the bar señoritas, which I am surprised you pay no attention to. You've been moping since yesterday. What's going on?"

James felt he had to come clean with his brother. "I'm in love, Sean. I know it's bad timing because I am being shipped out. I'm afraid that when I leave, I will lose Elizabeth forever. I tried to make our engagement official, but she is afraid her family will not approve."

"Does she love you back? Are you sure this isn't a passing infatuation on your part?"

Flustered, James flopped down on the bed. "Yes, I am sure we are truly in love. I have never been more sure. I would marry her right now, if possible."

Rubbing his chin, Sean said, "Well then, get married. After all, you are going to war! Tell her you might die in action. That should convince her to marry and love you before you leave. If that doesn't do the trick, she doesn't love you enough."

James decided he was not going to wait another day, so around 8:00 p.m., he went to knock on the Moores' front door. When Manuela opened the door, he asked if he could see Elizabeth. She did not let him in but asked him to wait and she would get her niña.

When Elizabeth slipped outside, she wanted to run into his arms but instead said, "We aren't supposed to meet until tomorrow night."

He was able to take her hand in his. "I could not wait for an answer any longer, Elly." He kissed her hand and continued, "Tell me that you love me and meet me in the gazebo tomorrow morning, so we can make plans for our future."

Elly lifted her finger to his lips. "Just stop talking," she said and leaned to kiss him. Then she turned to go back inside, and just before closing the door, she whispered, "I'll be there around ten in the morning."

James left with a new feeling of hope. He intended to talk to Father Murphy in the morning after the 6:00 a.m. Mass.

As far as Elizabeth was concerned, she had made up her mind. She had thought things through for two whole days and was over crying and worrying. Her passionate and determined character was back. James truly loved her, and she was not going to let him go without a serious proposal. It is safe to say both lovebirds slept better that evening.

CHAPTER 13

To fall in love is to create a religion whose God is fallible.
—Jorge Luis Borges

Friday morning, Elizabeth talked Ana Dolores into going to the market with her for some fruits she said she had a craving for. It was not uncommon on occasion for the girls to go to the street market by themselves. But Ana did not buy it. She asked her sister what she was up to as soon as they stepped outside.

"I knew I could not fool you," Elizabeth said. "I need you to cover for me. Please go to the market and buy whatever fruit you can find that we are out of at home. And take about half an hour before you come back. I'm meeting James at the gazebo."

Ana Dee pulled at her. "Please don't do anything crazy, Elizabeth."

When they walked far enough into the plaza, they saw James waiting, and Elizabeth gave her sister a small push. "I promise, all right?" As soon as Ana Dee was out of sight, Elizabeth ran into his arms. Leaning against the gazebo, they kissed with more daring and passion than before. The two days apart only served to provoke more desire for each other.

Elizabeth caught her breath and said, "I missed you so much."

He embraced her more tightly and whispered in her ear, "We need to get married before I leave."

She wasn't sure she heard right, but it was music to her ears. She asked, "How?"

James pulled her away, just enough to see her face, and explained, "I talked to Father Murphy. He is willing to marry us in the morning, without having to wait, because I will be leaving Monday and going to war."

"Don't I need my parents' permission?" Elizabeth asked.

He said, "Elly, you are fifteen, of marriageable age, and I am almost nineteen, definitely an independent man."

Looking puzzled, she said, "I am not sure, James. Are you telling me the truth? Does Father Murphy know who I am?"

"He knows we are both Catholic," James said.

Not fully convinced, Elizabeth said, "I think I better go talk to him."

"That means you'll consider it? Okay, we'll go right now," James replied.

They walked into the church and found Father Murphy talking with a parishioner. The priest was a burly affable character who left Connecticut because of the community's intolerance of the Catholic church and traveled to Texas where the church needed English-speaking clergy. As luck would have it, he ended up in a Spanish-speaking community. Instead of seeing this turn of events as a mischance, he accepted it as a preordained duty to help Americanize Santo Tomás. To his advantage, being fluent in Latin certainly helped him understand Spanish.

"Ah, the blessed couple!" he said, walking toward James and Elizabeth.

Convinced James had already spoken to the priest, Elly asked, "When would you be able to marry us?"

The priest replied, "As soon as you are available. I am glad you are taking this holy step. It is the right thing to do once you are compromised. Is tomorrow morning at seven thirty a good time for both of you?"

James turned red and would not look at Elly, but he managed to agree to the appointed time and thank the priest. Father Murphy blessed them with the sign of the cross and said his goodbyes.

Elizabeth was too excited to ask the priest anything else. She followed her now fiancé who had her hand and was almost pulling her out of the church. They could see Ana Dee crossing the plaza over to the gazebo and hurried to meet her. Elizabeth called to her sister, "Ana Dee, let me say goodbye to my fiancé, and I will be right with you." She turned to James. "I will see you tonight for our stroll, and we can discuss our plans." She gave him a peck on his cheek and took off with her sister.

Ana Dee asked, "What were you doing in the church?"

Elizabeth explained, "The priest agreed to bless our *compromiso*, you know, 'engagement,' tomorrow morning."

Ana Dee questioned the word *compromiso* since Father Murphy's Spanish was not great.

Elizabeth laughed. "Well, it actually sounded like compromise, but you know he is trying. I want you to go with me in the morning, but don't tell anyone. I love you, and you'll be my only family there."

They hugged each other and went into their home. Each was excited about the evening's promenade.

In the afternoon, James went to a jeweler Sean had sent him to and bought a couple of thin gold bands with his brother's credit. It was Sean's gift to the bride and groom.

By 7:00 p.m., James was waiting in the plaza across from the Moores' residence. Fifteen minutes later, he saw the ladies coming out with Catherine, who had decided to accompany the girls. She wanted to have a chat with James and learn more about him. Elizabeth was nervous at the turn of events, but she was glad her papa had not wanted to come as well. Besides, she knew James could easily charm her mother.

As soon as they crossed over to the plaza, James greeted them and introduced himself to Catherine, offering his arm for her to stroll with him. She welcomed the unexpected gesture and took it as a chance to converse with him. By the time they had strolled around the plaza once, she figured she knew more about him than her daughter. Catherine got to the point: "Why do you want to court my daughter when you are leaving in a couple of days?"

James had practiced an answer all afternoon, knowing it was bound to come up. "Yes, I will soon be shipping out to war. I carry Elly in my heart and will be back to her as soon as it's possible. I will be able to leave the navy in about a year when my turn is over, if that is what she wants me to do. I love my military service, but if Elly does not want to make our home a port town, I have no qualms about finding another trade."

Catherine was impressed by his ardor and knew she could not discourage her impetuous daughter from seeing him. "I believe your intentions are honorable. Your love for each other remains to be tested by time. In the meantime, go ahead and stroll with Elly, as you call her." She handed his arm to her daughter.

The couple walked behind Catherine and Ana Dee this time. They hardly spoke except for James whispering, "Seven thirty tomorrow morning." Elizabeth was happy to hear about her mother's approval, which made her more at ease with their secret marriage plans. James was convinced he had expressed his true feelings and intentions to Catherine, so he buried the guilt of keeping their secret marriage plans. They would prove to everyone their love was "till death do us part."

Ana Dee watched the whole event that evening with love and happiness for her sister, but also with trepidation.

CHAPTER 14

Love is not thought, it is felt or not felt.
—Laura Esquivel

On Saturday morning, the girls got up at the crack of dawn to bathe Elizabeth in the big old wooden tub before she got dressed. She wore a peasant all-white embroidered blouse, a plain white skirt, white cloth sandals, and a white mantilla held to her loose hair with a brooch hairpin. Ana Dee wore the same ensemble but in pink. They waited to leave the house until Doña Braulia got home from church and went into her room. Sneaking out, they arrived at the church five minutes late.

A sexton shut the church doors after them, meaning a private ceremony was taking place. As the girls advanced to the altar, they heard the soft melody of a strumming guitar. Ana Dee followed its sound to see the man in blue. He stopped playing when the girls reached the altar. Their eyes met, and as he left the church, he winked at her.

Father Murphy waited at the altar with James in his sailor uniform and his proud brother Sean, who was holding a small velvet sack containing the wedding bands. Before Ana Dee realized it, it was a marriage ceremony, not an engagement one, and rings and "I dos" were exchanged. The bride and groom fervently kissed each other, and everyone hugged them.

Sean came up to Ana Dee. "Well, lassie, we must give the young couple some privacy. Will you join me for some breakfast at Guadalupe's Cafe, little sister?"

Elizabeth gave Ana a hug and explained, "I'll meet you at the gazebo at noon. Don't worry, nothing has changed, except that we are married. I am not going away with James if that's what you think. Please go with Sean for now."

The church doors were quietly opened by a hooded monk to let the group out and the town parishioners back in for confessions. Trusting her sister, Ana Dee took Sean's arm, and they walked to the cafe next to the alcaldia for her favorite breakfast tacos, still half in a daze and in need of a strong cup of java.

In the meantime, Elizabeth and James walked hand in hand to the pensión, where James had reserved the best room for the occasion if, as he told her, it was okay with her. The room rental had also been a wedding gift from his brother. He explained they need not do anything but talk if that's what she wanted. Elizabeth had immediately agreed to go with him, thinking she did not want to wait another year to become his real wife and lover. They had a light breakfast at the pensión and then went to their room. After he closed the door to their temporary private space, he started to talk about their future. She told him to be quiet and proceeded to unbutton his shirt while eagerly kissing him.

True to her word, Elizabeth met Ana Dee at midday at the plaza. As she took her wedding band off and put it in her pocket, she said, "I will have to wear it in a chain and under my blouse, but I am still a married woman, Ana Dee."

As they walked back home, Ana Dee asked, "I guess you intend to keep this a secret from the family. I figured out why Father Murphy agreed to marry you without talking to Papa. He really thought you were compromised, and he did not mean compromiso or engagement. James misled him."

Amused and laughing, Elizabeth said, "You are right! What a trickster! That's my man. He'll do anything for our love. Please, Ana Dee, don't tell Mom and Dad. I could not let him go without a commitment, but I know Papa was not going to agree. Now that we are legally married, James said if something were to happen to him at war, I would be entitled to his pension. See, he is already looking out after me."

Ana Dee shook her head. "Really, Elizabeth, I hate to lie, especially about something of such importance. But I will keep your secret from Mama and Papa, as I am already a conspirator. I hope we don't come to regret this." She never promised to lie to Abuela Brau because she knew the old woman could see the truth just by looking at Elizabeth, whose aura had changed.

That afternoon, Catherine noticed her daughter's happiness and figured it was because they had agreed to the courtship. The girls looked so pretty in their festive outfits. They had put their mantillas away and added colorful sun-crossed waistbands to their ensembles. It was rather early in the day to dress up, but Catherine thought they must be excited for the evening. She wondered if Ana Dee also had a romantic interest but was not sharing it with the family. The girl had an air of secrecy.

CHAPTER 15

Our hours in love have wings; in absence, crutches.
—Miguel de Cervantes

Saturday night promenades were pretty congested, not Anthony and Catherine's preference. It was Manuela and Pedro's usual day to stroll and visit with the plaza vendors, and it was taken for granted the couple would chaperone the girls. Thinking Pedro was rather strict, Catherine let him know James and Elizabeth were courting and it was okay for them to hold hands.

It was a happy night for the secretive newlyweds.

Several young men approached Ana Dee, and she eventually agreed to stroll with the brother of one of her old playmates whom she had met before. He was about six inches taller than Ana Dee, of dark complexion and straight black hair. His aquiline nose denoted his Indian heritage. His name was Ricardo Guzmán, better known as Ricky.

Walking behind the two young couples reminded Manuela and Pedro of the days when they promenaded with their own daughters. "They both make nice couples, don't they, Pedro? I could bet you anything we have a wedding within the year," Manuela commented.

Pedro's observation was different. "Possibly, if James comes back within a year. They are serious about each other. But Ana Dee is not really interested in Ricky, except as a friend. Besides, he's just a flirt. No chance of a marriage there."

On Sunday morning, James came to the house to pick up Elizabeth and take her to Mass. Ana Dee and Catherine went with them. Upon their return, James was invited to have lunch with them and spend the afternoon visiting with Elizabeth in the parlor. They had some privacy for most of the afternoon and declared their affection for each with words and stolen kisses, sweet or in desperation thinking of James's approaching departure. Elizabeth reminded him to put on his wedding band as soon as he left Santo Tomás and to never take it off.

At 6:00 p.m., James was invited to dinner but declined, saying he had yet to pack for his trip as he was catching the early stagecoach. He shook everyone's hands on his way out and, after opening the front door, told Elizabeth, "I will write to you as soon as I arrive in New Orleans." He then kissed her goodbye in front of the whole family and left. Elizabeth ran to her room crying her heart out. Catherine wanted to follow and comfort her, but Anthony held her back. "She needs to be alone, love."

With tears in her eyes, Ana Dee turned to hug her abuela. Doña Braulia petted her great-grandchild and told her in a whisper, "Love can hurt, but it is what life is about. She will be fine, you'll see. Remember your dream." It was a quiet dinner.

A month went by before Elizabeth received her first letter. She ran to her room to read it while the rest of her family waited for her to come out and share the news. They were praying the news would make her happy again. She had been in a sad mood since James left. They could not interest her in taking part in any of the entertainments she had previously enjoyed. There had been no outings to the market or any of the stores, no horseback riding, and definitely no promenading. Elizabeth simply did her daily house chores and helped at the clinic. Sometimes she sat in the courtyard and talked to Periquito who learned some new words: *Jamie, sad, miss him.*

When she came out of her room, she found everyone waiting in suspense. Her eyes were puffy, but her voice sounded almost joyful. "He is fine. By now, he must be sailing. He misses me and Santo Tomás and can't wait to come back." When everyone kept waiting for more, she blushed and added, "That's all I am going to share with you." There were several sighs of relief from her loved ones, as the family dispersed to continue with whatever task they were doing.

Elizabeth slowly regained her usual temperament and joy of life. James had not forgotten her. She sent Tio Pedro to let Sean know she had received the letter. Sean sent her thanks back with Pedro, adding his brother must truly love her because he was actually a very lazy writer.

Since her sister had lost all interest in going out, Ana Dee didn't care to go out on her own. She only went promenading with Manuela and Pedro one more time that summer and saw Ricky strolling with another señorita. Pedro gave Manuela a look as if to say, *I told you so.* Even though Ana Dee had only been interested in Ricky as a friend, it had been enough to discourage her from doing the evening stroll again.

So Ana Dee's free time was spent playing board games with the family and reading history books recommended by Dr. Moore. She loved world history, and the current situation in the Americas interested her. She wanted to learn all about liberators such as Simon Bolívar and San Martín and then discuss it with her papa. They often argued about politics, but in the end, they made peace with each other.

In June, Elizabeth received two letters from James. They had different dates, so apparently, James had to wait to mail them together. The letters covered at length the battle of Campeche: how his ship, the Texas navy flagship sloop of war *Austin*, under Commodore Edwin Ward Moore, along with another small Texas ship, had fought and won against two large Mexican ships. When they arrived in Galveston, its citizens acclaimed the commodore and his men as heroes; however, President Houston had declared Commodore Moore a pirate for failing to follow orders and had him court-martialed. It would take another year for the officer to be cleared of the charges.

A third letter arrived a few days later, saying James's regiment had been dismissed. He was coming home before reassignment, if any. Elizabeth jumped for joy.

The news could not have come at a better time. She had missed her regular menstruation and confided her concern to Ana Dee. She was beginning to feel nauseous and had thrown up a couple of times.

Ana Dee calculated her sister was going on two months of pregnancy, and it would soon be obvious. She told Elizabeth, "You need to tell our parents the truth now!"

"I would rather have James beside me when I do," she said.

Ana Dee urged her, "Well, talk to Abuela. She could help with your nausea. It's not like she doesn't already know."

"Oh my God! Why didn't she say anything to me?" cried Elizabeth.

"Abuela Brau says that we should respect another's space and that you would come to her when you were ready. Anyway, she knew since the day you and James got married."

Abuela Brau was praying when Elizabeth knocked on her bedroom door. As soon as she saw her, she extended her arms and embraced the girl. With comforting words, she let Elizabeth know everything would be fine. James adored her and would soon be back to stand by her. It was meant to be. She left Elizabeth reclined on her bed and went to get her a cup of herbal tea.

Chapter 16

Too much sanity may be madness and the maddest of all,
to see life as it is and not as it should be.
—Miguel Cervantes

It was an uncomfortably hot summer day. Elizabeth felt sicker than ever. She had been losing weight instead of gaining it, mostly because of stress, first worrying about James being involved in the war and then with the unexpected pregnancy.

Except for Abuela Brau and Manuela, who were in the kitchen, everyone was busy at the clinic. Elizabeth heard a knock at the front door. Her heart jumped a beat as she rushed to open it. Before the door was completely opened, they fell into each other's arms, stumbling into the foyer and clumsily landing on the settee.

James's uniform was disheveled, and he had unkempt bandages around his left arm and leg. When Elizabeth was able to catch her breath, she said, "Let's take you to the clinic to fix that bandage and have Papa check you out." She tried to get him to follow her.

Instead, James pulled her back to him. "Elly, my love, I am fine. I just need a bath and a change of clothes."

She responded, "Well, you are not leaving to do that. I'll get Manuela to help me fix the tub for you to take a relaxing bath, and you can borrow some of Papa's clothes." She picked up his left hand to feel the wedding band. "It's time I wear mine as well," she said and took out the neck chain from under her blouse.

Manuela got Dr. Moore from the clinic to come and see James's wounds. Anthony was shocked to see his daughter in the tub room helping a naked James take a bath.

She glanced up as her father walked in and said, "It's okay, Papa. Remember, I am a nurse, and furthermore, this is my husband." She lifted her hand with the wedding ring.

A somber papa said, "Elizabeth, please leave the room and get Pedro over here to assist me." Once his daughter left the room and Pedro helped dry James up, a pensive Dr. Moore proceeded to quietly work on James's wounds. When he was satisfied James's arm and leg would heal well, he asked, "When were you and Elizabeth married?"

After James nervously related as much of the story as he dared to his father-in-law, he expected some kind of reprimand. Instead, Anthony asked Pedro to help the young man get dressed and walked out back to the clinic.

James's arrival happened to be an evening when Fray Francisco was invited to dinner. The monk no longer taught the girls Spanish grammar or literature, but occasionally held a *tertulia* with them and discussed classic literature such as *El Cid* or *Don Quixote de la Mancha*. He often visited Doña Braulia, who considered him her best friend. Last but not least, he and Anthony met a couple of times a month to discuss theology. Anthony was supposed to be a Catholic, as per his conditions for settling in Texas; but although his family practiced the religion, he did not. They covered spiritual topics such as world prophets, philosophers, different religious paths, and reincarnation. Anthony admired Fray Francisco's open-mindedness and respected his opinions. Fray Francisco was certainly not your usual Catholic cleric, and Anthony often questioned the monk's true faith.

At dinner, Fray Francisco welcomed James back to town and expressed his gratitude to Spirit for having kept the young man safe. "I know what a relief it is for our Elizabeth to have you back."

As he looked around the dinner table, he noticed the young couple. In spite of their preoccupation with each other, they were not oblivious to the family's myriad emotions: from Anthony's confusion and anger, to Catherine's resentment for being kept in the dark, to the Ximénezes' guilt as conspirators, to concern by Ana Dee, and resignation by Abuela Brau. Instead of this making him feel like an outsider, he felt he was there to try to smooth things out and speak of the wonderful love uniting this family.

Fray Francisco stood up, catching everyone's attention. "I would like to say a few words before we partake of this wonderful meal, which is always so good because when Doña Catherine, Doña Manuela, and Doña Braulia cook, they always use the indispensable main ingredient of love. Please bear with me. After I have spoken, I ask you to seriously dwell on my words while we share bread."

Catherine was about to say something, but Anthony touched her hand as if to stop her and they turned their attention back to the monk, who continued. "I know that Dr. Moore cannot understand why his daughter did not come to him about her marriage, before or after. I also know that Elizabeth was absolutely sure her father would have impeded the wedding. Catherine feels disappointed and resentful that Elizabeth did not confide in her all this time. Whereas Elizabeth knew that telling her mother was as good as telling her papa because those two keep no secrets from each other—just as she hopes her own marriage will be. James, for his part, will do anything his wife asks.

"As for the rest of us, I might add that although some of us suspected or even knew of the situation, it was not our place to interfere. If you truly reflect on the situation and deal with the present, because the past cannot be undone, the storm will pass. One important note to add: put yourselves in each other's shoes." He repeated, "Put yourselves in each other's shoes. Now, forgive my boldness. I just wanted to give you some food for thought while we share some food for nourishment."

While some ate and others stared at the meal, no one seemed to want to break the silence during or after dinner.

Eventually, Anthony, still wearing a frown, went to his library accompanied by Fray Francisco. The rest of the family sat quietly in the living room.

James could not help his occasional yawning until Abuela Brau commented in Spanish that he must be tired from his long trip and should go to bed. Catherine turned to James and said, "Yes, you should go home to rest now."

With amazing dexterity for her age, Abuela got up and stood between the young couple and Catherine. "*No, Aquí.* His place is with his wife. Or would you prefer that Elizabeth move with him into one of the rooms at the cantina? That is not an appropriate place, especially for a pregnant woman."

Comprehending the full state of affairs, Catherine nodded her head, letting the couple go to Elizabeth's room, wondering how she could possibly have missed her daughter's pregnancy. She kept wringing her hands. Oddly enough, in her muddled state, it occurred to her how fortunate it was that all the bedrooms had double beds!

Ana Dee witnessed her mama's discomfiture and gave her an understanding embrace.

In the meantime, in the library, Fray Francisco and Anthony were having their own discourse on the day's events.

"So you are wondering why Elizabeth didn't tell you about her marriage."

"No, you explained that quite clearly. I am wondering why she is afraid of me."

"She isn't afraid of you. She was afraid of you prohibiting the marriage."

"What's the difference?"

"The difference is that she absolutely knew you would not have approved the wedding and she would have to obey you."

"So she does not trust my judgment?"

"I dare say, as impulsive as your daughter is, she always obeyed you before. I rather think that she does trust your judgment. No? The explanation is more profound than that. When you do your daily meditations, do you not seek to surrender to spiritual guidance? You've confided to me that you've even been entranced by what you call a universal music."

"How does that relate to my daughter's behavior?"

"When you surrender to your inner experience, you are seeking and trusting God's love. You are able to reach a higher love. Human love is a step toward God's love, which in the end is what we are living for. We cannot learn to receive God's love unless we love someone else more than ourselves unconditionally. You already love Catherine and your girls that way."

"So you can't know God's love because you haven't known love for a wife or children?"

"Please, Anthony, you really don't know whom I have loved or, as you believe, might have loved in a past life. I have been blessed by God's divine light during contemplation."

"Fine, so where are we going with this?"

"Total surrender, my dear sir. Elizabeth was not willing to let James leave without their knowing total emotional and physical surrender for each other. She worried that he would be killed in battle. Face it, she could have been intimate with James without marrying him, but she respected you too much to do that."

"Thank you for your enlightenment, Father Saint. I must admit some of my perplexity is gone, but not so much my annoyance."

When Fray Francisco left, Anthony found that everyone had retired to their respective bedrooms. He wanted to talk with Catherine and hoped she wasn't asleep. She was lying down, but awake and waiting for him. She leaned on his chest when he joined her in bed.

Anthony stroked his wife's hair and said, "I just had a talk with our friend, Saint Monk. He gave me a discourse on the spirituality of carnal love. Can you believe that, a celibate man professing to know more about the meaning of physical love than those with experience in it?"

They found themselves laughing at the irony of it all. He added, "It is funny. Oddly enough, some of it made sense. Do you remember how your parents were upset thinking that we had deceived them when we didn't confide in them our plans to move south before we got married?"

Catherine responded, "That's true! But we were older, at least you were. I suppose the kids have proved that theirs was not a passing infatuation. The time they were apart from each other seemed to reinforce their love."

Anthony kissed his wife and whispered in a hoarse voice, "Time has only strengthened our love." He slipped off her camisole.

CHAPTER 17

Don't speak unless you can improve on the silence.
—Jorge Luis Borges

Dr. Moore's impassive approach to the new family arrangement baffled James. Having an impulsive and emotional personality himself, he expected his father-in-law to confront him in anger. Elizabeth understood that the years of contemplative training had molded her dad's temperament to an inscrutable appearance, with stoic control of his emotions. She explained her dad's emotional reticence to James and said he just needed time to get acquainted with his new son-in-law to know what a sweet and loyal person he was.

The fact that she had disillusioned Dr. Moore did not escape Elizabeth's understanding. She set out to regain Anthony's trust by catering to his every need at the clinic and at home. Slowly, after some heartfelt excuses on her part, father and daughter made peace.

Gradually, their lives' routines became part of the general acceptance of the new family member and father of the expected and welcomed new grandbaby.

James tried to help with whatever chores he was allowed to do. After he visited his brother, he told Elizabeth he could work as a bartender at the cantina until his military status was resolved. He got news from his old friend, George, who was joining the United States Navy, where they were accepting the Texian navy veterans in their ranks. Elizabeth knew James really wanted a navy career, but because of his love and sense of responsibility for her, however, he would not leave. His resigned attitude endeared him more to her.

James went to work with Sean from 3:00 p.m. until midnight on weekdays and even later on Fridays and Saturdays. The money he made was mostly saved since the Moores would not take any payment for rent.

In the meantime, Elizabeth was thinking that once their child was born, she would consider her husband joining the navy again, even if it meant they would have to move to a port town. James had confided to her he wanted to join the United States Navy whenever Texas was annexed, which he felt would be soon. Loving him as she did, she knew they would eventually move to a port town.

On December 17 of 1843, a little redheaded boy came into this world. He brought joy and laughter to the household. Little Billy had barely turned six months old when Elizabeth announced a second pregnancy. Her first pregnancy had been difficult and left her so weak she stopped breastfeeding her baby after three months. The second pregnancy didn't seem to be any better. She and James considered moving to another house on their own, but with her poor health, she was better off staying where her family could help.

CHAPTER 18

Because between us there is no distance, or time, or space,
our love will be eternal.
—Marco Antonio Solis

Life revolved around the young O'Reilly family at the Moores' household. This was possibly why Anthony was able to hide his illness as long as he did. He was very reticent about his pains. His only complaint was about light headaches. These were somewhat relieved with the tea Pedro prepared for him from willow bark.

Ana Dee noticed that her papa's memory was failing him and he had started taking copious notes to remind himself. She kept constant watch on him at the clinic, covering up for his forgetfulness. He told her he did not want to worry Catherine about his health thinking she already had her hands full with Elizabeth's care. Ana Dee knew it would not be long before her mother noticed his weakness, though.

A week had passed since she and Robert visited the circle of stones, Tlazolia Occepa. Ana Dee's mind kept reliving those cherished moments and wondered if Spirit would keep the Ranger safe and bring him back to her. Since their first encounter, she and Robert had a strong unexplainable connection. She knew she was emotionally attracted to him and remembered how uncomfortable she had been when the girl at the gazebo had kissed him after his guitar performance, recognizing her reaction had obviously been one of jealousy.

Her thoughts were interrupted by a loud banging noise coming from the examining room. She ran to check it out and found her stepfather on the floor. "Papa, what happened?"

Dr. Moore said, "I'm fine, child, just tripped."

Ana Dee tried to help him up, but he could not move his left leg. "Get Pedro to help me up."

With Pedro's help, they brought him into the house and closed the clinic for the rest of the day. By the next day, Dr. Moore had recovered the use of his leg, but had no explanation as to what had caused the temporary paralysis. He was also having trouble using his left arm. At that point, Catherine began to worry. She begged him to travel to New York to a good hospital. Instead, he insisted he just needed some rest and started the search for a doctor to join him at the clinic.

There were a few doctors moving to Texas at the time, and after interviewing two candidates, he chose a young German immigrant who stayed current on progressive medical treatment and research. Hermann Meyer was a blond young man, about five feet eight, slightly overweight, and of a convivial disposition. He had decided to move to a warmer climate from Chicago, where the cold windy weather reminded him of one of the reasons he left home. When he arrived in San Antonio, he found out about the job opening in Santo Tomás and decided to check it out. He was instantly attracted to its friendly inhabitants, the pretty señoritas, and the peaceful atmosphere of the town. Once he had a job agreement with Dr. Moore, he extended his stay at Andersons' pensión to a monthly rent.

As he worked along with Dr. Moore, Dr. Meyer slowly gained the trust of the townsfolk. Ana Dee did her best to assist him knowing her father required more daily rest. Within a couple of months, Dr. Meyer and Ana Dee were running the clinic by themselves. By then, Dr. Moore had completely lost the use of his left arm as well as his left leg and was slurring his words.

After consulting with Dr. Meyer, Catherine's fears were confirmed. It was apparent Dr. Moore had a brain tumor so large it was affecting his motor skills. The prognosis was not good. The damage was increasing rapidly. They could not know how much longer Dr. Moore would live until he became bedridden and started hallucinating.

Abuela Brau was at his bedside when Anthony started talking to his deceased mother. She knew then Dr. Moore would not live through the night and told Catherine and the girls to say their goodbyes to him.

Fray Francisco came in the evening as he had been doing for the past two weeks, sat with his friend, and read to him quotes by Saint Francis: *"All the darkness in the world cannot extinguish the light of a single candle."*

The midnight church bells rang when Anthony Moore left his body to join his Creator. He was surrounded by his loving family and closest friends. It seemed the whole town of Santo Tomás attended Dr. Moore's funeral mass. For nine consecutive days after the memorial service, people visited the family to offer their condolences, bringing food and white candles and praying the *novena* for nine days led by Abuela Braulia. She, Manuela, and Pedro took care of the preparations of the evening events, sheltering Catherine and the girls from all the traditional bustle.

Ana Dee and her mother and sister knew Papa considered all those ceremonial activities unnecessary, but they also knew his respect for others' beliefs. Catherine preferred to immerse herself in quiet contemplation in Anthony's favorite room, his library, where she could silently cry while reading Rumi's poetry. Elizabeth had James to console her and share her papa's memories with. Ana Dee and Abuela Brau spent hours recalling what an important role he had played in their lives.

Ana Dee also sought her *padrino*'s company to discuss more esoteric topics like she used to do with her papa and listen to the monk's reassurance of man's spiritual journey. To them, Dr. Anthony Moore was a spiritually advanced soul.

Although they missed Anthony a lot and remembered all his endearing qualities, the family slowly adjusted to his absence. The new toddler kept the family distracted, and their daily routine fell back to its normal tempo.

During her second pregnancy, Elizabeth's health remained poor, hardly able to keep anything in her stomach despite Dr. Meyer's medical recommendations, or Catherine's ministrations, or Pedro's teas. James was so concerned he actually sent her love notes throughout the day: "Remember I love you," "*mo chuisle*," "I will bring you some sweets tonight," etc., which at least made her laugh.

Catherine was busy with her little grandson, Billy, who kept her on her toes as he was starting to walk and trying to reach Periquito from his perch.

Also concerned for Elizabeth, Abuela Brau prayed a lot.

Fray Francisco stayed in close contact with the family, keeping his biweekly visits and dinners and thus filling in for the strong calming presence of his departed friend. Abuela Brau took Anthony's place in the evening tertulias with him, and Ana Dee joined them on occasion.

CHAPTER 19

El hombre propone y Dios dispone.

After Dr. Moore's death, Hermann Meyer knew he had big shoes to fill. Every day he felt closer to Ana Dee and appreciated her efficiency and professionalism. She was able to help Dr. Moore's patients come to trust him. He admired how she cared for others and applied the "golden rule" in her life. Although he was a Lutheran, he accompanied the family to the Catholic church, as it was the only Christian congregation in town.

He couldn't help but discuss the differences of their beliefs with Ana Dee, and she reminded him, "God loves us all the same. Where you worship is not important. Papa hardly ever went to church, but everyone knew he was a God-loving man." He noted she never said "God-fearing" although Father Murphy used those words rather often.

Ana Dee was unaware of the growing feelings Hermann had for her. She just knew they were becoming good friends and coworkers. Besides, Elizabeth's tribulations were hers as well. Those days concern for her sister's health and child kept Ana Dee's attention.

Abuela Brau had told Catherine they should hire a wet nurse for the expected baby because she did not think Elizabeth would be up to nursing her infant. She was right.

The day frail little Cassandra came to the world after an exhausting ten-hour labor and postpartum hemorrhaging, Elizabeth was left weak and exhausted. She lost too much blood. Dr. Meyer immediately suggested someone else care for the baby. Father Murphy had already recommended a strong healthy wet nurse from the congregation to Abuela Brau. Manuela brought the woman over to nurse Cassandra. The baby grew healthier and stronger and in six months was drinking Manuela's goat's milk instead.

Elizabeth recuperated as well, but slowly. Even James went to church to pray for her. His brother gave him a couple of days off weekly knowing Elizabeth wanted her husband by her side. Thanks to the care and love of everyone in the household, the young mother survived.

By the time of Texas's annexation to the United States, December 29, 1845, Cassie was nine months of age, and Elizabeth was in better health. She was ready to talk to James about joining the United States Navy. He told her he wanted to go back on duty. She acquiesced but wanted them both to consult with her mother and sister before taking the necessary steps.

Catherine and Ana Dee were not happy with Elizabeth's decision to move away with her young family. After giving it much thought, Catherine gathered the family to discuss what she thought would be a reasonable resolution. She wanted to accompany Elizabeth and family on their new venture. She felt Elizabeth was not strong enough to cope with a new life away from any needed family support. Naval service would require James to be at sea most of the time and away from home. However, she could not ask Ana Dee to move with them. Her roots were in Santo Tomás with Abuela Brau, who was getting too old to make the change. The property, house, and clinic belonged to Ana Dee, who was doing well as the assisting nurse at the clinic and was under Catherine's guardianship until she turned eighteen years of age in nine months. She proposed that they wait another nine months and then Catherine could move away with her other daughter.

Although Elizabeth wasn't sure James would agree, he accepted the compromise. He had yet to apply to enlist and possibly travel to different naval bases for training. He had been a midshipman in training for officers when he left the Texian navy and did not know what would be required or what he needed to do to continue his training in the United States Navy. It would all take time and most likely traveling before they could pick out a home base. There was no need, nor was it practical for his family to be following him around before they could actually settle in a place.

This seemed the best solution, and they all agreed. To Ana Dee's chagrin, there was no argument she could make. She exchanged looks with Abuela Brau who nodded as if to tell her, "Remember your dream."

Catherine turned to her stepdaughter and told her she had some things to go over with her. They moved to Ana Dee's bedroom. Catherine hugged her stepdaughter and said, "Much can still happen in a year. In the meantime, we need to get you ready to run this household and be in charge of the clinic as a business. You know Papa had been setting aside rent money for you on a monthly basis. The funds are kept in two strongboxes for safety reasons. The weekly allowances, funds that come in and go out, are in the cast iron trunk in my bedroom. Once a month, rent is deposited in the strongbox hidden in the library. Your share has grown nicely for the past fourteen years. So when I leave, you won't be financially helpless. You will also have Abuela, Manuela, and Pedro at your side. Perhaps you will even consider marrying Hermann. I believe he is enamored of you."

Teary-eyed, Ana Dee said, "I don't think so. I don't like him that way."

Catherine caressed her and said, "You should give him a chance, my love."

Their conversation was cut short when they heard Billy's cries and went to check. Manuela was trying to console the child who had just found Periquito lifeless on the ground, having fallen from his patio perch. Billy kept blaming his little sister for screaming at the bird while Pedro tried to explain to him the bird was almost ten years old and his demise was to be expected. The event was a distraction for the adults to stop talking about James and Elizabeth's plans and instead concentrate on a small funeral in the backyard.

Two weeks later, having received a letter from his friend George, James left for Houston, Texas, to make his first inquiries. He promised to write and keep them informed every step of the way. Elizabeth had been clinging to him like a child the whole previous week and would have left with him if it hadn't been because she knew it would not be fair to travel with the children under such uncertainty.

Ana Dee, on the other hand, was relieved that she got to spend more time with her adoring niece and nephew. Every afternoon after her work at the clinic was over, she would play with the children, take them to the park, read to them, or feed them. She knew it would break her heart when they left and seriously considered courting Hermann if it meant she could eventually have a child of her own.

Come March, she invited Dr. Hermann Meyer to promenade with her. One Friday afternoon after work and dinner with the family, he accompanied Ana Dee to the stroll around the plaza.

This time, there was no chaperone. Her friends were pleasantly caught off guard seeing her again. Some stopped to converse and be introduced if they hadn't met the doctor yet.

Hermann was learning Spanish, out of necessity, so he didn't totally understand all they were saying. He enjoyed the señoritas' attention and bought everyone aguas frescas and sweetmeats.

The next morning at work, Hermann asked Ana Dee if they could promenade in the evening again. She acceded, thinking she should put more effort into their companionship. They closed the clinic at 1:00 p.m., the usual time for a Saturday.

At 7:30 p.m. promptly, he knocked on the door. Ana Dee was surprised to see Hermann wearing a bright sarape and a cowboy hat. He smiled and explained, "I went to *mercado*." She smiled and told him it was perfect. They found out they could enjoy each other's company more by being more relaxed.

CHAPTER 20

We are here to transcend, not just to breathe.
—Martín Balarezo García

On a quiet Wednesday evening, Elizabeth and Catherine decided to promenade with the children. Abuela Brau and Fray Francisco were headed to the library for their spiritual tertulia. Ana Dee was invited to join them, and she did.

"Tonight I will be reading Dr. Moore's manuscript of the *Tao Te Ching*. Do you know anything about this path, Ana Dee?" asked Fray Francisco.

"Papa did talk to me about the Tao. He said he had obtained his notes from a patient in New York. The man was a Protestant missionary who had come back from China. He gave Papa his precious translations in his dying bed."

"Interesting story. I never asked Dr. Moore how he had obtained this priceless document. So what do you make of it?"

"It is about the right way to live life. Papa always said one must meditate on each verse to really reach an understanding of the Tao or Way."

Abuela Brau then commented, "*Me parece que* it contradicts itself a lot."

"That is why, like Ana says, we should contemplate on the verses or look within ourselves for its spiritual message. We are not going in the order in which the verses are annotated. I would rather read one today that describes the path. It seems, like you say, Abuela Brau, to contradict itself. But try and look deeper for its meaning."

> *Verse 41*
> *When the aware student learns of the Tao, he practices it*
> *with great care,*
> *When the average student hears of the Tao, he is hesitant*
> *in its practice.*
> *When the unaware student hears about the Tao, he laughs*
> *out loud.*
> *If he did not laugh, it would not be the Tao.*
> *Thus it is said:*
> *The way that is lit, seems dark;*
> *Forward movement, seems like regress;*
> *The way that is easy, seems austere;*
> *The highest virtue, seems meaningless;*
> *The most pure, seems dirty;*
> *Much virtue, seems lacking;*
> *Strong virtue, seems weak;*
> *True virtue, seems fictitious;*
> *An actual square has no corners;*
> *Knowingness takes time;*
> *The real sound is hard to hear;*
> *The greatest reflection has no shape.*
> *The Tao is veiled without a name.*
> *The Tao alone bestows fulfillment.*

Abuela Brau shook her head. "*Ves*, what I mean. It contradicts itself."

"It's clear as a bell, Abuela," Ana Dee said, laughing.

"If I may, I think it is telling us that truth is hard to comprehend. How often do we not dismiss it when it is right in front of us? How often do we fail to follow our inner nudges and thus make the wrong decision? Those inner nudges are often Spirit's messages."

"*¿Cómo se sabe la diferencia?*"

"Papa used to say to 'go within.' If you are unsure about any action you need to take, contemplate on it and learn to hear that inner nudge. You know, Abuela, like the messages you get with your dreams."

"*Bueno*, I really do hear a guardian angel's voice. But yes, sometimes I know what to do instinctively."

"I think you are already blessed, sister Braulia. Therefore you are practicing the Tao, or Spiritual Way."

"You know, Abuela, that those who dismiss your warnings or think them foolish don't recognize the Tao in you. Just like we read about the students who are aware as opposed to those who laugh at it."

Sitting in silence absorbing the night's reading, they heard the excited children coming back from the promenade. Unable to resist the happy little voices, they went to join them.

CHAPTER 21

Death leaves a heartache no one can heal,
love leaves a memory no one can steal.

The little children were the center of family life. Catherine enjoyed being with them all the time. When she needed to go to the market, she took little Cassie with her to give Elizabeth some quiet time. Later in the week, she noticed the toddler was fidgeting and had a fever. She took her to Dr. Meyer, who noticed that the child's eyes were yellowish. He immediately said, "We need to isolate her, *ja, sicher*. It might be contagious. Where has she been today?"

Catherine said the last time Cassie went out of the house had been a couple of days before, when she took her to the market and bought some vegetables and fruits that had arrived from Galveston. Dr. Meyer suspected it was the "malignant fever" although uncommon this far inland. But when she mentioned Galveston, it confirmed his suspicions. At the time, they thought yellow fever was contagious. Catherine fixed the extra examining room for the toddler and would not leave her sight. Elizabeth and the rest of the family weren't allowed into the clinic. Concerned with the spread of the disease, Dr. Meyer closed it up.

Pleading with her mother, Elizabeth tried to get past Catherine to see to her child.

Catherine's knuckles turned white, grabbing her daughter by the shoulders. "No, Elizabeth. Think of little Billy. You must take care that neither of you catches the fever. I will take care of Cassie."

Ana Dee helped hold her sister and kept a vigilant eye on her for the next couple of days. Food and liquids were left at the door for Catherine and her granddaughter. Only Hermann ministered to their needs.

The toddler's fever would not come down no matter what Dr. Meyer and Catherine did. The child couldn't keep any food down, vomiting everything, becoming dehydrated. For three days, they constantly patted the child's forehead and body with wet towels. Whenever Ana Dee could leave her distraught sister's side, she would knock on the clinic's door and ask her mother how her niece was doing and tell her, "Everyone is praying for our baby, Mama."

By the third day, it was clear they could not save the child's life.

"We are losing her," Catherine told Ana Dee, wringing her hands. "I know you want to help me with her, but please stay away. Hermann says that it is contagious."

Through the half-opened door, Ana Dee caught a glimpse of her mother. It was hard to see her in wrinkled clothes and hair in disarray, she who had always insisted on neatness. But now her full dedication and attention went to the care of little Cassie. Wiping her tears, Ana Dee left the clinic and went to the library to do a contemplation for guidance. Before she finished her twenty minutes of meditation, she saw Papa Moore on her mental screen. Instinctively, she reached out for his medical writings.

Ana Dee checked some of her papa's notes on "malignant fever" and found out he did not believe the disease to be contagious, but rather caused by a mosquito bite. She sneaked into the clinic at a moment when Catherine went to relieve herself. Once in the child's room, she checked her for any bite sign. Her niece was so frail and exhausted, no longer conscious. Ana Dee found a blistering mosquito bite in the child's right leg. Trusting her papa's notes, she believed the toddler was not contagious.

Ana Dee went to see her sister who was so distressed she looked as emaciated as her daughter. Elizabeth begged her, "Please, Ana Dee, tell me I can see my baby. I need to hold her and comfort her. Please tell Mama." Seeing Ana Dee's trembling lips, she started whimpering, "Oh God, no no!"

Abuela Brau came to her and held her in an embrace, whispering the old prayer, "Ave Maria, gratia plena, Dominus tecum . . ."

Reading Papa's notes, Ana Dee knew it had been Spirit's message, and she should convince Catherine and Dr. Meyer to allow Elizabeth to hold her child before she passed away. She went back to the clinic and entered the room where the child lay sick. Catherine tried to stop her, but she said, "Mama, please listen to me." She explained what she had discovered in her papa's papers and hadn't followed through because it was not common where they resided.

Ana Dee continued, "I suspect some mosquitoes' larvae were inside the bags of vegetables at the market from Galveston that hatched."

Catherine was shaking uncontrollably and didn't respond. Hermann felt such a tightness in his throat he could not argue against Ana Dee's reasoning. He cupped his hand on Catherine's shoulder in a comforting gesture.

Ana Dee continued with determination in her voice. "I'm going to take little Cassie to her mother so she can hold her and say her goodbyes. We know the baby won't make it past this day." She picked up the child and, rushing out of the clinic, took the little girl to Elizabeth. The young mother wrapped her arms around the little bony figure and started to rock and moan. Catherine walked into Elizabeth's room and fell to the floor crying with her children.

While everyone was gathered in the room, praying in between sobs, from behind Manuela's skirts, little Billy observed the frightening sight of his usually rambunctious baby sister lying so very quietly in his mama's arms.

When the hush of prayers died down and turned into somber quietude, Hermann approached Elizabeth. It was time. *How hard was it to gently pry a lifeless child from its mother's cuddling arms?* Elizabeth wouldn't let go of her precious bundle.

Ana Dee hugged her sister. "Look, darling, Papa is here to take Cassie to their new home." Trusting her sister's words, Elizabeth loosened her grip on her child. Ana Dee added, "Cassie is taking his hand and waving bye to us."

Elizabeth released the small body to Hermann who thought Ana Dee was just humoring her sister. He was the only one there who didn't believe Anthony Moore's presence.

Chapter 22

Alas! all music jars when the soul's out of tune.
—Miguel de Cervantes

On Friday evening after Cassie's funeral, Ana Dee didn't want to go promenading, but Hermann said it would do her good. Catherine assured her that she and Elizabeth would be fine because Pedro and Manuela were overwhelmingly attentive to their needs.

As they crossed the street to the plaza, many of her friends approached them to offer their sympathies, and Hermann put his protective arms around Ana Dee as she started to cry. They approached a bench, and the couple sitting in it, whom they knew, got up and invited them to use it. As if to himself, Hermann said, "Little Cassie is an angel now."

Ana asked him, "Why do you think her life was so short?"

"No reason. God just wanted her to be an angel, *da bin ich mir sicher!*"

"You don't believe she had a purpose in our lives?"

He said, "I think that God took Cassie away before she could sin so she could be an angel. You and I have to work at it. We need to accept Christ as our Savior before we can enter heaven. I know you like to say that one must be a God-loving person, but one must also be a God-fearing person."

If Ana Dee was going to consider marrying Hermann, she felt she needed to be up front with him as to her beliefs. She said, "I don't agree with that premise, Hermann. Saint Teresa de Ávila said, 'I am quite sure I am more afraid of people who are themselves terrified of the devil than I am of the devil himself.'" She noticed Hermann's questioning stare and continued, "I believe in a loving God. Most of humanity has not ever known of Christ, so according to your premise, most people haven't got a chance to enter heaven."

After a little cough, Hermann tapped his chin with two fingers. "I thought Catholics believed in Christ as the World Savior, too. You are Catholic, *nicht wahr?*"

Ana Dee answered, "Papa used to say that people interpret their religion as it suits them, meaning that their interpretation or understanding of their religion is simply their opinion and is therefore a reflection of themselves. I don't agree with everything the Catholic priests teach. Not all representatives of the Catholic teachings agree on everything either. Let's just say that I agree on Jesus's message of love. You know, the golden rule of loving thy neighbor and doing to others what you would have them do unto you."

Hermann understood her to be somewhat annoyed and changed the subject by asking if she wanted an agua fresca.

With both her papa and her little niece gone, Ana Dee realized the emptiness that would take place when the rest of her family left to follow James. She tried to console her sister who sought Abuela Brau's company, hoping to communicate with her daughter's soul. Elizabeth missed her little girl so much that she rubbed her arms and whimpered, "They hurt." Ana Dee understood that her sister's yearning for her daughter had turned into physical pain that only time could relieve.

One thing Ana Dee was learning: basing security in what we know is an illusion. We come to this life to learn, and lessons come with change.

Their life was being altered.

CHAPTER 23

Living consists of building future memories.
—Ernesto Sabato

Once Texas was annexed to the United States, more and more Anglo families came into the area. The properties the old Mexican hacendados lost were divided and sold to the new migrants. Surveyors did well in the area. English was becoming the standard language. The Anglos coming in expected the locals to speak it and saw no need to learn Spanish. The newcomers made their own communities.

As time went by, Ana Dee saw the need for a school to teach English to the original Spanish-speaking inhabitants of Santo Tomás. Catherine totally agreed with her and suggested they start giving English classes in the evenings for the adults and day classes for the children. Within a week, they had ten students in the evening, mostly the neighbors around the plaza and their children during the day. With Elizabeth's help, Catherine took care of the children during the day and in the evenings Ana Dee and Catherine taught the adults.

Ana Dee had a busy and fulfilling life. She was contributing to the town she loved. In the back of her mind, though, the prospect of losing the three people she most loved filled her with anxiety. The inevitability of it was daunting. All she could do was enjoy her family while they were with her.

94

From the time he left, letters had been arriving from James, but he had yet to send an address where Elizabeth could correspond, so he was unaware of the loss of his baby girl. It was July when Elizabeth received a letter with an address in New Jersey where she could write to her husband. He told her he would be joining the Revenue Cutters Service Engineering Corps—the equivalent of today's Coast Guard Service—after he specialized in steam engine technology. It would take a good three months before he knew where his base location would be. To have an address to write to was a relief for Elizabeth although she hated to send him the news of Cassie's death.

Catherine was excited and gave Elizabeth her parents' address to send to James in case he had a chance to go to New York.

Whereas time seemed slow for Elizabeth, it felt definitely fast for Catherine and Ana Dee. September arrived with Ana Dee's eighteenth birthday. Her family would soon be leaving.

Come October, Catherine, Elizabeth, and little Billy were in a stagecoach heading north all the way to New York. They promised to write often and hoped Ana Dee would come and visit them in the not-too-far future.

Catherine still had hopes of her stepdaughter marrying Dr. Meyer, but Ana Dee felt nothing more than friendship for Hermann and refused to settle for that.

With Catherine's departure, the children's English classes had to be suspended, but with Fray Francisco's help, Ana Dee continued giving evening adult classes. She was glad to keep busy and not think of her family so far away. Every Wednesday before class, Fray Francisco joined Abuela Brau and Ana Dee for dinner, and Hermann started joining them as well. They had no time for the tertulias during the week so they were changed to Sunday afternoons.

By the winter of 1846, the Mexican-American War was waging. The United States Navy had occupied the town of Tampico in Tamaulipas, Mexico. When Elizabeth wrote, James was taking part in the action overseas; Ana Dee worried again for her sister. It seemed Elizabeth had a heavy cross to bear in this life.

When Ana Dee shared the news with Fray Francisco, she also thought of the blue Ranger, and her heart sank. He was probably as involved in the fight, or more than James. The monk looked at her as if he knew her thoughts and said, "James will be fine, and so will our friend."

It's been said that eventful happenings come in threes. Abuela Brau caught pneumonia in winter and was bedridden for two months. With the arrival of spring, Ana Dee thought her great-grandmother would be recuperating. Dr. Meyer did his best for her. Fray Francisco came to see her almost every day. Manuela and Pedro catered to her every whim. Ana Dee checked on her throughout the day.

One Sunday, Father Murphy came to see his parishioner, who had not been to the 6:00 a.m. Mass in over a month. Upon seeing Abuela Brau's fragile state, he said, "I knew you had to be very sick to miss our daily Mass."

In her broken English, she told him he should be prepared to give her the last rites soon. He dismissed her words by a wave of his hand.

Ana Dee heard the conversation and went back to the clinic teary-eyed. When Hermann saw her, he tried to console her. As she leaned against his chest, he said, "Ana Dee, your great-grandmother has had a long life, *doch*? She has been very lucky to have you to care for. She has seen what a beautiful person you have grown into. She has been surrounded by love, like you believe we should live our lives. Now she is tired, and you must be prepared to let her go."

Ana Dee wiped her tears. "I know, Hermann. Thank you for caring, but I don't know what I'll do without her."

He stared into her eyes. "I'm still here, *meine Liebe*."

Ana Dee felt an immense emptiness and knew Hermann could not fill the void. She canceled classes and sat by Abuela Brau bedside for a week, wanting to spend as much time as she could with her.

One evening, Abuela Brau asked her to come closer because she was running out of breath and could hardly talk. *"Mija,* I couldn't salvage your parents' inheritance for you, and I am sorry for that. But you inherited my spiritual gift, and you must cultivate it and care for it so that it may serve you in the future. For that, trust only Fray Francisco. My last gift to you came in a dream: I saw you with lots of children and the man you love very much."

Ana Dee told Abuela she had been her strength all along. Abuela Brau had saved her life and protected her for which Ana Dee owed her everything. She lay down next to Abuela until they both fell asleep.

The following day Doña Braulia asked for Father Murphy to come and give her the last confession and communion, which he did. She was in a good mood after he left, almost as if she had recuperated from her illness. But when Ana Dee went to sit with her after she closed the clinic, she found that precious soul, Abuela Brau, had departed.

They had an intimate and small Mass service for Doña Braulia, but the love in the church was palpable. After the funeral, Ana Dee went home and locked herself in her papa's library with her thoughts. Abuela Brau's dream filled her with hope. She knew the man in the dream was not Hermann. Abuela said it was someone she loved very much, and she only liked Hermann as a friend. She had to break their courtship. It had gone on too long, and it was unfair to Hermann.

CHAPTER 24

Agua que no has de beber déjala correr.

Hermann was deeply hurt when Ana Dee did not turn to him in her hour of need. Pedro saw the young doctor sitting alone in the living room and went to talk with him. Hermann looked at Pedro with a sad expression. "Why won't she want to be with me? I can comfort her."

Pursing his lips, Pedro explained, "Ana Dee needs to be alone right now. Would you like to go to the cantina with me? You know Sean, he was at the funeral. He's a friend of the family, actually, James's brother. Anyway, he owns the cantina and will treat us right. *Vámonos.*"

Pedro took Hermann to the bar after telling Manuela where they were going and to keep an eye on Ana Dee. Manuela thought it was an odd thing for Pedro to do because just one glass of *pulque* usually was enough to put him to sleep. Pedro had his reasons, though. He knew Hermann thought Ana Dee would eventually marry him, and he also knew she did not feel the same way about him. It was time someone made Hermann see the reality of the situation.

When they entered the O'Reilly's cantina, Hermann was astounded. It wasn't a noisy, dirty bar, perhaps because it was a weeknight. Only three tables were occupied: one with four vaqueros playing cards, one with an old man silently drinking himself to oblivion, and one with a vaquero and a señorita in a seriously intimate conversation.

They walked up to the bar, and after exchanging greetings with Sean, Pedro said, "Can you have your girlfriend, Paula, bring us some *tostadas* with hot salsa and a couple of beers?"

Sean handed him the corn chips and whispered, "Shhhh, I left Paula over six months ago. Margarita is my girlfriend now."

Pedro shook his head and walked to a table with Hermann. "I hope a beer is okay. I don't think you would like a tequila. What do you usually drink?"

"*Eigentlich*, I prefer wine. Usually with my meal."

Pedro ignored him, thinking to himself, *Good luck with that here.* Instead, he said, "I think you should forget about Ana Dee."

"Pedro, why do you say that? We have been courting for a while. *Ja!*"

Margarita brought the chips and beers to the table, and Pedro paid her. After he dipped a chip into the salsa and took a sip of his beer, he said, "Drink your beer, it will make you feel better. I think I should order you a *pulque*. You might need something stronger for what I have to tell you." He called the waitress back.

"The beer is enough, Pedro, danke. For me, ten beers are like ten glasses of water." He took a sip from his bottle.

"Dr. Meyer, Ana Dee loves someone else."

"What are you talking about? *Nein!* Who?" Hermann asked, thinking he had not met anyone Ana Dee seemed attracted to. "I am with her every day. *Ja!* There is no one else that she is with."

"I am sorry to say that the young man in question is right now fighting for our country who left Santo Tomás before you came."

"I think she would have told me or Mrs. Moore would have said something. *Oder?*" Pedro shook his head in the negative. He said, "I will have that other drink." He waved for the waitress's attention then went on. "What is his name? I need to hear this from her. Why hasn't she told me this before?" he asked the girl for the stronger drink.

Pedro told Margarita, "He means a double tequila. If you don't have it, a *pulque* will do."

The waitress raised her eyebrows and, with a sideways glance at Hermann, said, "*Cómo usted diga.*"

"It is a complicated situation. They never even courted. But Doña Braulia knew him and told me all about it. The point is Ana Dee has been pining for him all this time. She won't let go unless she finds out if he died in action."

Hermann got his tequila and gulped it down.

Pedro had been drinking his beer very slowly, watching Hermann order one drink after another until he fell over the table. Sean had to help Pedro carry the young doctor to one of his upstairs bedrooms.

"Don't worry, Sean. He's good for the money," Pedro said after they left Hermann fast asleep in the room.

Sean asked, "What's eating the lad, Pedro? He can't be that upset about Doña Braulia's death. Must be an affair of the heart. I heard that he was courting Ana Dee. Did she give him the boot?"

"Yes and no," said Pedro. "It is about Ana Dee. She didn't break up with him, but I had to let the poor man know that Ana Dee would never marry him."

"Man, is that any of your business? Why didn't you let her tell him?" asked Sean.

Pedro indignantly pointed a finger at Sean and, as he left the bar, said, "I am doing both of them a favor or they will never move on with their lives."

Friday morning, Sean sent some breakfast tacos and a strong coffee to Hermann on the house. Because of his splitting headache, Hermann did not come out of the room until way past noon. Confused as to where he was, he sat up and scratched his head. He was trying to figure out if he was still in the cantina when Margarita brought his breakfast. After thanking Sean profusely and paying his bill, Hermann went directly to his room at the Andersons' boardinghouse to bathe and rest for the afternoon. Fortunately, the clinic was closed due to mourning and he wasn't expected at work.

The next day, a Saturday, Ana Dee and Hermann worked their usual half day. They were busy and did not communicate except for medical matters and glad the following day, Sunday, they would have a break from each other.

Hermann went to Sunday Mass, but Ana Dee didn't. Two of her friends sat next to him at Mass, which he found unexpectedly pleasant.

CHAPTER 25

The bond that links your true family is not one of blood,
but of respect and joy in each other's life.

—Richard Bach

Ana Dee sat in their house courtyard watching Pedro work on one of his crafty projects. He picked up a leather strip and threaded it through three colorful beads. Then he picked up a feather from a group of floating feathers, which curiously remained in the same spot, and pulled its quill side through the beads as well. Ana Dee watched, amazed that the feathers didn't get blown away. She waited silently while he repeated the process with another leather strip. She decided to talk to him before he began threading the next strip.

"Tio," she started to say, and instantly, the floating feathers dropped into a pile on the ground when Pedro looked up at her. She continued. "I'm sorry to interrupt your 'feather dance,' but I have been wondering what you mean when you talk about being a spiritual descendant of the ancients."

"Let me ask you a question first," he responded. "What do you do when you are really worried or upset? Don't answer right away. Go within and seek your answer."

Ana Dee sat quietly contemplating on what she had done after the recent deaths of three beloved people in her life. As if by habit, she started humming. The realization hit her, and she said, "I hum to myself!" She was more surprised by her answer than Pedro was.

Pedro asked her, "Good, but why do you do that?"

"Because it calms me down."

"And who taught you to do that?"

With a puzzled look, she answered, "I don't know. I just know."

Pedro then explained, "You know because Spirit has shown you that repeating that particular inner sound soothes you. Nobody had to teach you. If you can find your own spiritual answers, you are communicating with Spirit. That makes you a spiritual descendant of the ancients. There is a spiritual connection between God's creatures. Now that you discovered yourself, go contemplate on this truth and more will be revealed as you are ready."

How Ana Dee wished Papa Anthony was with her! She could discuss things with him at length. With Tio Pedro, she had to seek answers on her own.

As she was going to the library, Pedro added, "By the way, I think Dr. Meyer got the message that waiting for you to love him is futile."

Ana Dee blushed and didn't respond to his assertion, not wanting to know how he was involved. Tio was often two steps ahead of her.

Monday was a busy day at the clinic. Ana Dee and Dr. Meyer's conversation was strictly in reference to the patients. It took a couple of days for them to feel comfortable with each other again. They did not approach the subject of their attitude change toward each other. They didn't need to. They both knew their courting days—almost a year had gone by—were over, but their relationship remained amicable.

On Friday evening, Ana Dee didn't expect to go promenading with Hermann, so she was surprised when he asked her to accompany him for the usual stroll. She was even more stunned when he said, "I would like your friend Nadia to accompany us when we meet." Ana

Dee was delighted at the prospect of finding Hermann a sweetheart and cheerfully agreed.

For her part, Nadia was very agreeable when she understood Dr. Meyer was interested in courting her with her friend's approval. Her parents had tried to get her engaged to a Lebanese man from Mexico without luck because he would not come to live in Texas now that it was Anglicized territory.

Nadia, being a free-spirited young woman of the frontier, refused to move to Mexico. Her older brother had been more traditional and brought a Lebanese wife from Mexico to their parents' satisfaction.

Amina and Sharif Youssef resigned themselves to their daughter's courtship with Dr. Hermann Meyer. They immediately assumed it meant their daughter was engaged and gave their permission to her promenading with Hermann as long as Ana Dee accompanied them.

CHAPTER 26

To give pleasure to a single heart by a single act
is better than a thousand heads bowing in prayer.
—Mahatma Gandhi

On one of the strolls with Nadia and Hermann, a child of about seven years old came up to Ana Dee and begged her for some of her peanuts. She bent down to his level and asked him where his parents were. He said they had been killed during an Indian raid and he escaped with some laborers, but they dropped him off in town to seek help on his own. Seeing how ragged he was and knowing how hungry he had to be, Ana Dee told Hermann to excuse her because she had to take the boy to her house and feed him. Hermann and Nadia were so involved with each other they barely acknowledged what she was saying.

She found out the boy's name was David Martínez who had no relatives in the area. She couldn't help but admire the brave little fellow who was too young to be fending for himself. When she and the little boy arrived at the house, she called Manuela to help find something for him to wear so he could wash up and change while they made him some tacos. They could not find any pants that fit, so they gave him a grown man's shirt, which covered him down past his knees.

After he washed up and had eaten, Ana Dee insisted he go to bed in her old room, as she had moved to the larger master bedroom with the street window. Manuela was a little concerned with them taking a stranger into the house, but Pedro and David immediately became friends; he assured his wife it would be safe and the right thing to do. Ana Dee promised to talk to the priest in the morning. The church would surely know how to house refugees and help them find relatives.

Saturday morning after working at the clinic, Ana Dee went to the store to get some clothes for little David. Then she went back home and got him dressed up to meet Father Murphy.

The priest was saddened to hear about David's case and explained that several children had already been brought to him that month after a series of Indian raids on the area ranches. The Comanche Indians often took the children as captives, at times adopting them to the Native's way of life, whereas surviving children left behind were orphaned and often left homeless.

Father Murphy had been able to find accommodations for other abandoned children among the church parishioners. He reminded Ana Dee she had herself been taken into a home after her parents were killed. It was the usual procedure as the town did not have an orphanage. He asked Ana Dee if she would be willing to do the same for little David. Ana Dee, who had not thought about that particular solution since she was single, was excited to hear it was possible. Father Murphy volunteered to go to the *alcaldia* that still handled courthouse duties and recommend her as guardian. He even said, "If you weren't so young, Ana Dee, they would think he is your child. He has your coloring." Thinking about Manuela's tasty food, Little David looked up at her with his big brown eyes and promised to behave if she would keep him.

It wasn't a problem for Ana Dee to gain informal guardianship of the child. The demand for families to take in orphans was high, and there was no trace of a living relative in David's case. Between the ensuing wars from 1835 all the way to 1848, Texas against Mexico, then the United States and Texas against Mexico, many minors in the area were left orphaned and homeless. Oftentimes, farmers took in the children and used them for hard labor in exchange for room and board. For a while, the Rangers had helped protect the children, but now they were too involved in the war zones to bother with the town's vicinity. The war, however, didn't disturb Santo Tomás itself because of the town's location.

At first, Manuela wasn't fond of the idea of taking care of another tenant. However, David's pleasing disposition soon won her over. She and Pedro eventually thought of David as a grandchild. Ana Dee got busy teaching him to read, write, and do arithmetic. Like when she was growing up with the Moores, David was assigned household chores under Pedro's supervision.

Ana Dee kept taking time off from the clinic to teach the adult English classes, as well as tend to David's needs. Although the clinic was not that busy, Hermann was at a loss without his assistant. Things were disorganized under his care. Ana Dee realized he could not handle the office work and accounts on his own. The idea that Nadia could help them with the office duties at the clinic came to her on a nudge. After all, Nadia had been helping her parents at the fabrics store since she was a child. Ana Dee suggested it to Hermann. He didn't appear too convinced, but in reality was hiding his pleasure at the prospect of spending more time with Nadia and getting to know her better. Nadia was allowed to work at the clinic, and it turned out to be beneficial for all parties involved. She not only helped with the office work and keeping things organized, but also started learning nursing under Ana Dee's instructions. Hermann could hardly contain his pride for his fiancée.

One morning, Fray Francisco stopped by to check on Ana Dee and David. "I see that little David is coming along well. I also understand that Nadia has become an excellent pupil of yours. You are a good teacher. I think you have found your vocation."

"I have to admit, I enjoy teaching, especially children."

"I could help you with David's studies. You know, possibly history and Spanish literature."

"That would be wonderful, Father. He really is a good student."

"I actually came this morning to drop this off for you." The monk handed her a letter. "I can come back this evening, and we can make plans for David's studies."

Ana Dee took the letter but contained her curiosity and desire to open the envelope. Instead she continued, "I can probably leave the clinic early this afternoon. Why don't you come for dinner and get to know David better? Then we can have a tertulia in Papa's library. I really miss discussing his spiritual manuscripts and books."

CHAPTER 27

Give me your hand and we will dance; give me
your hand and you will love me. Like a single
flower we will be, like a flower and nothing else.
—Gabriela Mistral

After the monk left, Ana Dee went to her room to be alone and read the letter. Something told her it was special. The only mail she received those days was from Elizabeth and Catherine, and she would pick those up at the Andersons' pensión where the mail stagecoach dropped them off. So this letter could not be from them. She felt a lump in her throat upon reading the greeting:

My Dear Anita,

> *I was sad to hear about the death of your loved ones from our Spiritual Master.*
> *I wished I had been there to give you my shoulder to lean on at such times. The war has taken me all over Texas and Mexico except for Santo Tomás, which has been distanced from it all, and that is good. On the other hand, not good in the sense that I have not been able to see you. I carry with me the memory of your sweet smile, which gives me strength to survive through the furious skirmishes that our platoon faces. My mission now is to*

protect and prevent injuries to the innocents in our path. I wish to become part of Santo Tomás' constabulary and settle there when this war is over. Hopefully, that should happen sometime next year.

Please take care of yourself, little sister.

Robert
2nd of April of 1847

It had been so long since she had seen or heard from him! Ana Dee was enraptured by the loving words Robert Hughes had written until she read the farewell sentence. Did he think of her as a friend—a sister—and not a sweetheart? Was it a love letter or a friendly note? She didn't know whether to be happy or disappointed. Her feelings toward him had always been of a romantic nature.

Although she had only come across the Ranger four times, she knew there was a strong connection between them. Also, who was their spiritual master? Fray Francisco? They knew each other! She put the letter in her skirt pocket and thought Fray Francisco had a lot to answer for.

As usual, Fray Francisco was there promptly for the 6:00 p.m. dinner. Manuela and Pedro sat at the dinner table with Fray Francisco, Ana, and David. Since Abuela's death, Ana had insisted on the couple joining her for the meals. She considered them family, and their company was a comfort to her.

Fray Francisco revealed his plans for teaching literature and history to David who commented, "As long as it does not interfere with my morning chores." They all laughed with mirth at his pronouncement.

Fray Francisco said, "What a responsible child!"

Pedro clarified, "He means that it won't interrupt his care of Lumen. He brushes and feeds the old horse daily. The two have bonded. Poor Lumen has been lonely since our other horse died."

After dinner, while David went to his room to do homework, Ana Dee and Fray Francisco retired to the library to plan for the classes and have a spiritual discussion.

Fray Francisco said, "I think it is best that I teach David from 2:00 to 4:00 p.m. That way, you can teach him from 1:00 to 2:00 p.m. after his lunch and siesta and also from 4:00 to 5:00 p.m."

"That sounds perfect since I work at the clinic in the morning and only need to help a couple of hours in the afternoon. With Nadia's help, I can leave the clinic at 4:00 p.m."

"Now that we've taken care of the schedule, I sense you want to address something else before we go on with a spiritual discussion."

"You are correct. I'm somewhat puzzled by the letter you gave me earlier today. I have several questions that you might be able to answer."

"Of course, *mija*. First, I want to clarify that Robert is under my spiritual tutelage."

"I think I can safely assume you knew that Mr. Hughes and I knew each other."

"Yes, I did."

"So you are his spiritual master?"

"I am one of many spiritual teachers."

"How did you know where to contact him to keep him informed of my misfortunes? What does he mean by 'our spiritual teacher'?"

"I am afraid he assumes you know more than you do since you are my godchild. I am sure he believes you are under my spiritual tutelage as well since you were my pupil when you were growing up. That is my fault, or rather faulty communication."

"I am still confused. How did you communicate?"

"Let us backtrack a bit. I am a member of an ancient order of spiritual masters—guides, if you will. Robert is one of my pupils, and I communicate with him through inner channels."

"You mean like Abuela Brau's guardian angels? But you are a living person!"

"I am not a guardian angel. I am simply someone who can transcend the physical barriers, when Spirit allows it, and use inner channels to contact other members of our teachings."

"So you contacted Robert in your mind to tell him about me?"

"Not exactly through my mind. We are all really Souls, and I can contact one another through Spirit."

"I know I am a Soul, but I can't do that."

"Well, it takes practice. Often I visit with Robert through dreams, which is how I let him know about your situation. He told me he wanted to see you and I was his contact with you. The problem is oftentimes, when we bring back the dream experience to this physical plane, it is not complete."

"That's what Abuela Brau used to say." She blushed as she said, "I wish I could see Robert in my dreams."

"Don't be embarrassed, mija. You and Robert have been students of Spirit together in past lives. Love is God's gift to all creatures, and it comes to us in many forms, over and over again. It often brings kindred souls back together in their new lives, Tlazolia Occepa. That's why you feel like you know each other even though you haven't met but a couple of times in this lifetime."

"I know you believe in reincarnation like Papa did. I understand why you two were such good friends. Will you teach me your path?"

"You know, there are many spiritual paths. They all seek to understand God's love. You were born a spiritual seeker. Your foster parents already knew this. So did your Abuela and so does Pedro. They followed different paths but with the same goal. They were the reason your life changed at such an early age. These people could be near you as you grew up, protect you, and foster your spiritual gifts. Thus, when called upon, you are able to serve others with love and spiritual guidance. I will be honored to be your spiritual guide from now on. Let's start with understanding your dreams. Will that suit you?"

She nodded enthusiastically.

Ana Dee kept thinking she hadn't asked everything she wanted to know, but for now, the information was overwhelming and she thought it best to slow down and maybe her answers would come when she was more able to absorb them.

Therein ensued her first official spiritual lesson by learning to remember and understand her dream world.

CHAPTER 28

The future of children is always today.
Tomorrow will be too late.
—Gabriela Mistral

Ana Dee's nineteenth birthday was coming up. Mama Catherine had sent her a sapphire brooch, which she wrote symbolized spiritual enlightenment. Ana Dee had written to her about the discourses with Fray Francisco. She also wrote about Hermann and Nadia's engagement, disappointing Catherine who was worried her stepdaughter was lonely without someone close to her age to share her life.

Ana Dee was admiring her new brooch and considering buying some pretty fabric to make herself a dress to wear it with when there was a knock at the front door. She put the brooch safely away and went to open the door. To her surprise, there stood Mayor Stanley. The old alcalde, Juan Acevedo, had retired around the time of Papa Moore's demise. She invited the six-feet-four man in, who had to stoop down as he crossed the threshold into the foyer. They walked through the courtyard to seat themselves in the living room. As customary, she offered him an agua fresca, which he graciously accepted. After Manuela brought the drinks and they were comfortably enjoying them, the mayor started the conversation.

"Ms. Moore," he said and then corrected himself. "Sorry, Ms. Peregrino. I was wondering if you would be interested in becoming the teacher for Santo Tomás's first public school. We are entitled to some funds assigned to education by the state of Texas in 1845 and are ready to start our first public school. We haven't received the funds yet, but the community is wanting to finance our endeavors rather than wait for politics to settle upon their disposition. Many of our prominent citizens have recommended you for the position."

"This is wonderful news, Mayor Stanley." Ana Dee asked, "When will the position be taking place?"

Mayor Stanley continued, "The council has approved the program to start in a month's time, around the middle of September. We should have about twenty children of various ages, from six to fourteen, able to attend."

"I do have one important question. I hope you are not offended. Will it be open for children of all races and backgrounds?" Ana Dee asked. "I realized we are now in the United States and that the public schools for the Anglo children do not accept Tejano students, that is, students of races other than Anglos, which although it means English speaking, they understand as 'white.' I will only teach in a school that accepts all the children."

"I am not offended, Ms. Peregrino." Mayor Stanley went on to say, "The bulk of the population in the town of Santo Tomás is of Mexican descent. The bulk of the taxes paid in this town is from them. Frankly, I happen to be the only Anglo, or should I say Texian, on the city council and my wife is Tejana. You can be assured that the school will be mostly of Tejano children, but the few Anglos in town will be accepted as well."

They shared a quick chuckle at his last comment, and he proceeded to add, "We, that is, the city aldermen, would like to invite you to join our meeting this coming Friday at the alcaldia at 3:00 p.m. to discuss the plan and your salary."

He got up to leave, and Ana Dee thanked him and assured him she would be there.

Ana Dee could not wait to share the news with the rest of the household. She told Hermann she knew Nadia was prepared to take over her job full-time. She was also giving him full responsibility for the clinic's administration and only expected to receive the monthly rent. Hermann was grateful and pleasantly surprised she was not considering charging him for taking over the medical practice.

He gave her a big hug and said, "*Schön*, I can ask Nadia to marry me now."

Ana Dee replied, "I am glad you aren't going to wait a year," and they shared a friendly laugh together.

CHAPTER 29

*And so I loved you daily, without
a law, without a schedule.*
—Reyli Barba

For her Friday appointment with the town council, Ana Dee wore her hair in a chignon, thinking it made her look more mature. When she arrived at the alcaldia, the council was already in session. A man, probably in his early twenties and dressed too formally with a vested suit to be a local, was presenting the case for a little girl who was scared and holding on to his leg.

Mayor Stanley was saying, ". . . and so we cannot do much in such cases. Our sheriff is too busy to get involved in a wild-goose chase, but we will inform him to keep on the lookout for any information. In the meantime, we recommend that you visit with Father Murphy who can get the town's congregation involved as they have always done. Case dismissed." He gaveled the young man's audition to an end.

The young man appeared confused as he walked past Ana Dee, carrying the child.

Ana Dee's interview was short. The alcalde and three regidores explained that the available classroom would be in the corner room of the alcaldia, which opened to a fenced yard they intended to fix as a playground. They informed her of her proposed salary, to which she agreed, going over the numbers in her head. The salary was sufficient to replace the income from her nursing and clinic administration jobs.

As she left the meeting, Ana Dee decided to go to the church and find out what the situation was with the nicely dressed young man and the small blonde girl.

She found Father Murphy in deep conversation with the gentleman. Upon seeing her in the church, Father Murphy waved a hand as if to ask her to come forward. He said, "Ana Dee, come and meet Monsieur André Fournier." The priest continued, "André, this is Ana Dolores Peregrino."

Ana Dee approached and nodded. "You must be related to the Fournier brothers from the apothecary."

The young man responded, "*Mais oui*, I am André, their nephew. *Enchantée, mademoiselle.*"

Father Murphy added, "This is a situation of a lost, or perhaps abandoned, child. She is too young to explain what happened. About four years in age, don't you think, Ana Dee? Anyway, André found her alone crying in the plaza's gazebo. The plaza was practically empty at the time, but André went around with the child asking if she belonged to anyone."

André explained, "She didn't recognize anyone either. A man told me about the council meeting this afternoon, thinking they could help. So I took the little one to eat at Guadalupe's Cafe and waited for the meeting. Here we are. I don't know what to do with the little one."

The child with the golden curls pulled on André and said, "We go home, Père."

Ana Dee looked at André Fournier and asked, "She calls you father?"

André laughed. "I kept asking where her father was, in English and French. She thought I was saying my name." He turned toward the child and said, "Just a minute, *ma chérie*. I don't know where your home is."

Father Murphy interjected, "Well, she needs to stay somewhere until this is resolved. It's obvious that André, being a single man, can't keep her although she looks like him, blond and all. I was actually going to suggest that you, Ana Dee, see to the child until we find her parents. She is well kept, look at her pretty dress. I am sure her parents will be looking for her."

Ana Dee bent down to the child's eye level and asked, "What is your name?"

The little girl stared back at her and said, "Mary." She then hid behind André.

"I see she has taken a liking to you, Monsieur Fournier," Ana Dee said, straightening back up and addressing André. "I'm not sure she'll want to go with me."

Eagerly, André answered, "If you will do us this favor, I can come with you now and stay until she gets used to you."

"Well, that's great," Father Murphy commented as he walked them out of the church. "I'll be sure to spread the word through our parishioners."

André picked up the child and walked across the plaza with Ana Dee.

When they walked into the residence, David came running. "We are late for my class, Ana Dee . . ." He then stopped in his tracks as he saw the two strangers with his guardian.

Ana Dee said, "David, I want you to meet Mr. Fournier and little Mary. She will be staying with us for a while."

Mary got down from André's arms and went up to the other child. She took his hand and asked, "Play?"

David looked up at Ana Dee and asked, "Is it okay to skip class today?"

Ana Dee answered, "Just this once because we want to welcome Mary to our home." As the children went into the courtyard, Ana Dee turned to André, smiling. "I think we'll be able to manage." She invited him for some tea.

André kept saying how grateful he was for her help, thinking what a generous person she was. Ana Dee was thinking how caring André was while shyly staring at his baby-blue eyes. They reminded her of Elizabeth's and Papa Moore's.

A week passed with no news about Mary's identity. André came over to check on Mary every day and saw Ana Dee with her hair combed in her usual braids, looking a lot younger than when he met her wearing her hair in a chignon. His first thoughts were "a child taking care of a child," but promptly changed his mind as he watched her run the household. He got to know her more and soon made good friends with the entire family.

André had gone to the market and bought some needed clothes for little Mary, whom he considered to be his charge. This act endeared him to Manuela and Pedro considerably. He even personally delivered some of the medicinal compounds from the apothecary to Dr. Meyer, who truly appreciated the gesture.

André had come from France to visit his uncles via New Orleans. After attending the University of Montpellier, he wanted to open his own apothecary in the United States, like his uncles. The best way to learn the business was to stay with his uncles as an intern in their business before he opened his own establishment, which he hoped to do in New Orleans. He confided his plans to Ana Dee. She told him her papa, Dr. Moore, had attended the University of Montpellier in his youth.

"Dr. Anthony Moore, a student from Montpellier, was your father? I thought you were Peregrino."

Ana shared with him the story of her past and how Catherine and Anthony Moore had raised her.

"So he was the doctor before Dr. Meyer! *Intéressant!* Did you know that I had to study a research paper of his, who was named Dr. Muir at the time, when I was a student at Montpellier? They still used his dissertation as an example of proper investigatory techniques. The man was a genius." He thought then that theirs was not a coincidental meeting and had a strange feeling they already knew each other.

Ana Dee was very happy and proud to hear such effusive admiration of her papa and wrote to Catherine telling her all about it. She also wrote to Catherine how nice André was and that she recognized him as a kindred soul.

André and Ana Dee became good friends. That whole week, they visited continuously. They were concerned about little Mary's care and what would happen to the child if no one claimed her. Ana Dee would be starting to teach soon and didn't think it would be fair to have Manuela and Pedro take care of the child, especially since David would be attending school and could not stay to help with Mary.

Manuela and Pedro had taken a liking to the little girl, as it was in their nature to love children. After Dr. Moore's passing, however, they no longer received regular wages. Catherine had left them a nice amount of funds so they could stay with her foster daughter as companions, thinking it should cover wages until Ana Dee got married. For their part, the Ximénez couple loved Ana Dee as their own and thought the roof over their heads and the meals they shared were enough compensation. To ease Ana Dee's concern, Pedro told her not to worry because they could handle the care of the child until the parents were found; and besides, André was there to help as well and could take care of Mary part of the day.

After the first week of knowing each other and having found out about Friday's promenades, André asked Ana Dee to take a stroll with him and the children, of course. David and Mary were excited at the prospect and begged Ana Dee to agree. The couple and two children were the picture of a regular family taking a stroll. Ana Dee and André both enjoyed it so much that they continued to do the Friday promenades with the children.

A church fiesta for the Virgin Mary's birth date was going on the first full week in September. The plaza was brightly decorated, and entire families joined the festivities with great bands playing in the gazebo. André enjoyed the children's screams of delight at the goodies the vendors had to offer. He bought Mary a corn-husk doll dressed in a bright Mexican dress and David a small wooden toy horse. Watching him with the children warmed Ana Dee's heart. For his part, André couldn't help but admire how well the kids took to Ana Dee. Albeit her young appearance, she was a great mother.

They came across Hermann and Nadia, who were talking about wedding plans. They also ran into Fray Francisco, who already knew

André from the apothecary. The monk took the opportunity to confirm the next monthly spiritual discussion meeting with Ana Dee for the following Monday. Intrigued, André asked if he could join them. Ana Dee turned to the monk questioningly.

"I suppose we could have a sort of introductory class and you could lead it, Ana Dee. It would be a good experience for you," suggested Fray Francisco.

Ana Dee was thinking André might not be ready for their esoteric lessons, but trusted her spiritual teacher's instincts, and so it was settled.

Since the fiesta celebration was continuing for the rest of the week, André asked Ana Dee if they could go back Saturday night. Of course, the children were delighted by the suggestion, and she said it would be okay for one more time.

When André dropped them by their house as usual, he gave little Mary a peck on her cheek, and she gave him a big hug. He then shook David's hand and kissed Ana Dee's hands good night.

The next night, the little pretend family enjoyed their time strolling and munching goodies. When André took them to their home, he asked Ana Dee if she would like to go promenading on Sunday without the children. He reminded her of a little boy who had not had enough candy. He added that once the children were in bed, she could take a deserved break. Thinking she did need some adult companionship and conversation, Ana Dee agreed.

On his way to open the door for André Sunday evening, Pedro passed Ana, who was putting the children to bed, and whispered to her, "I like this young man, Ana Dee. I am just sorry you are going to break his heart and I'll have to pick up the pieces again."

Ana Dee could not believe what she heard. She gave Pedro an indignant stare and commented, "We are just friends."

"Aha," was all Pedro muttered as he went to the front door. Of course, Pedro wasn't entirely wrong. André was beginning to have romantic feelings for Ana Dee. He brought her some flowers, which she sheepishly handed to Pedro to put in water as she left.

André was so attentive all evening that Ana Dee started feeling guilty. She asked, "When are you planning to move to New Orleans?"

"I'm not sure yet. Perhaps I won't," he answered hesitantly.

The answer set off alarm bells in Ana Dee's head, who decided to change the subject. "I'm still puzzled as to what to do about Mary. We should talk to Father Murphy and see if he has any options for her care."

"Perhaps they will allow me to be her guardian."

Ana Dee thought he wasn't serious and told him so. He stopped walking and, holding on to her arm, turned her to face him. "Perhaps if we do it together they won't oppose it."

She looked at him inquisitively and said, "How would that work? We are not related or married to care for a child together."

"We are kind of doing it now. Besides, it would solve the problem. While you are at work, she could stay with me at the apothecary shop. My uncles won't mind."

"Frankly, André, I don't think the church or town council would allow a little girl to live with three grown men, unless they are related to her, of course."

"Well, do you think they would let me adopt her?"

She shook her head. "As it is, her parents or a relative might still show up."

They continued strolling, greeting friends as they walked by, and stopped for sweet bread and aguas frescas.

Ana Dee wondered if André's plans to move to New Orleans had changed because of Mary or perhaps because of her, as Pedro had warned her. If that was the case, maybe she could try to reciprocate his feelings. They certainly got along well, and she did like him. He was definitely someone she could relate to. After all, she had not heard again from Robert, and for all she knew, he wasn't even romantically interested in her. *His sister indeed!* She needed to clear her head and review the situation thoroughly. The best person to help her would be Fray Francisco, whom she would see the following day. Then she thought, *But wait, André is planning to join us on that occasion!* By the time André walked her home, she had developed a headache. André noticed her discomfiture and attributed it to her headache, so he gave her a sweet peck on her cheek.

"I hope you feel better soon. Have a good night's sleep. That always helps, ma chérie."

Ana Dee didn't respond but opened the door and hurried inside, waving André good night.

Chapter 30

How beautiful and strange a man who listens can be!
—Marcela Serrano

Since dinner with Fray Francisco was at 6:00 p.m. and André was not due to arrive for the class until 7:00 p.m., Ana Dee entreated Manuela to take care of the children's bedtime and rushed through the meal, asking Fray Francisco to join her in the library. The poor man had barely eaten half his plate, but sensing her urgency, grabbed his coffee and followed her. Ana Dee closed the library door behind them.

She asked, "I am so embarrassed, Padrino, but I have to ask you, do you believe that Robert loves me romantically or as a sister?"

"Well, I think so."

Vexed, she paced the room. "What do you mean? I have been waiting for a sign to know his feelings and if he is coming back to court me. But I haven't seen him in my dreams, like you said we could communicate." By then, she and Fray Francisco had been having the spiritual classes for six months.

"Ana Dee, these things take time. You are so young. What is the hurry?"

"I am not young! Both of my mothers were married by the time they were my age. And don't even mention my sister's age when she married. You have to know something. Please tell me. I have asked my Voice to no avail. Yes, I am considering a relationship with André, but not if Robert and I are meant to be."

There was a knock on the library door, and Ana Dee jumped up. "He's here already! I am still at a loss."

"Let's converse with André tonight, and you might get some answers to your questions." Fray Francisco called out, "Please come in, André."

After the expected greetings, André said, "Thank you for allowing me to join your class. I am not a religious person, but I am open to others' opinions. My intention is not to offend you, but I must clarify: I agree with Voltaire and am what you call a 'theist.' My belief in God is of my own personal following. I dislike organized religion and am for keeping the separation of church and state."

"Well, it looks like you will fit right in with our group," said the monk.

"Forgive my presumption, but I thought you served the Catholic church."

"I serve where I am needed. If I have to wear this habit to do so, so be it. The Catholic church has provided me a way to serve Spirit. Many orders within the church have differences in beliefs, just like the Protestant branches of belief. I do prefer to follow my own path, as you do. In this class, we have one important premise. Would you like to address it, Ana Dee?"

"Yes, of course. God is the same for all humans. We are all a spark of God, and God is Divine Love."

"How do you explain all the horrors of this world if God cares so much for us?"

"We certainly have gotten into a good discussion right away. Do you care to answer him, Ana Dee?"

"André, I am of the belief, like my papa and Fray Francisco here, that we are responsible for our own mishaps, not God. The way I have come to understand that is through reincarnation and the law of cause and effect."

"I have never studied reincarnation. It is an interesting concept. Do you discuss it in more depth in this class?"

"We can prepare some information for our next class if you like. Right now, suffice it to say that through reincarnation, we are working toward becoming more spiritual and enlightened with each lifetime. The foundation that we are building comes from love. Of course, we grow spiritually with what we are ready to learn in each life. For example, if you row upstream, you move forward, but as soon as you stop, you automatically move backward. There is no staying still. Each life is a lesson, a needed experience. What you do now determines what you get in the future."

"That's an old concept. So basically 'ye reap what ye sow.'"

She added, "Yes. You will reap what ye sow but possibly not in this lifetime."

"We've agreed to discuss reincarnation further next time. So until our next monthly gathering, let's put reincarnation aside. I think you had prepared some topics to cover, Ana Dee. Would you like to proceed?"

"Surely. I was thinking that for a presentation to a new fellow participant"—she pointed at André—"I would like to have a short overview of the principles of this class. First, I want to touch upon the ancient order of spiritual teachers."

She looked at Fray Francisco for approval and help. He nodded, encouraging her to go on. "Although we practice our own personal path and spiritual growth, we have help from spiritual guides. Their mission is not to mandate but to support. We may call them masters in the sense that they have reached a higher spiritual consciousness. They might teach us techniques to become more spiritually aware when needed. As we progress, though, we discover these teachings ourselves. It looks like you have a question, André. Please feel free to ask anything."

"Merci, Ana Dee. So you and Fray Francisco are in a special order or religion?"

Ana Dee nodded but added, "We study with a special order of spiritual masters and we each follow our own spiritual path, but we are not a religion."

"I must clarify here that many of our students are practitioners of different religions."

"About these spiritual guides, are they in the flesh, or are they visions?"

"They are physical as well as spiritual beings. Fray Francisco is my spiritual guide because he has had a lot more experience in his path than I have. But yes, we may also see an inner guide, especially when we dream. Or we hear an inner guide as we go about our daily life. You know, like when you have a nudge to do one thing instead of something else."

"Ana Dee and I each study our own particular spiritual path. We follow the path to higher awareness, but individually." He nodded toward Ana Dee and added, "Those of us on this journey call each other brothers or sisters. We have traveled together in past lives and often recognize each other when we meet again in a new life."

Ana Dee stared back at the monk, thinking, *That's why Robert called me sister!* "We learn daily if we listen. Sometimes inner messages can be confusing, and we need to contemplate on them."

Fray Francisco explained, "That is another point we should include in a beginners' introduction. The daily contemplation of the teachings. What I mean is that we set aside some time during the day, from twenty to thirty minutes, to sit quietly and listen to the spiritual sound. We must learn to quiet the mind so we, Soul, can become aware of Spirit's presence. There are many techniques to make this easier. If you wish, we can show you a very simple one."

André half closed his eyes and sighed. "I wouldn't mind trying it. It sounds *détendre*, you know, to ease the mind if nothing else."

Ana Dee said, "One simple way is to repeat God's ancient name quietly to yourself. Pronounced 'hue' like so: Huuuuuu, Huuuuuu, and so on."

"I had never heard that name for God before."

"It is an ancient name for God still used in some parts of the world. In this exercise, you are simply clearing your mind of any material influence and allowing your love for God to rise above the mundane. It is our daily prayer, a gift of love. Using this simple technique during your contemplation will lead you to self-recognition." There was a moment of silence and then he continued. "When Ana Dee was small, she discovered it on her own or possibly remembered it from a past life. She would make a humming sound and rock herself when upset. It had a calming effect on her."

She added, "Also, when you contemplate, you might see a master who can guide you then through inner planes. Those are places that exist besides this physical plane."

"That is a little beyond my conception."

Ana Dee volunteered, "Not so much. You have probably traveled there in your dreams."

"Yes. Everyone has dreams. That is why masters often use the students' dreams to teach them about Spirit. Of course, it is all with the students' permission. We would never come into anyone's space unless invited."

"Through dreams, you can also remember a past life if it brings a pertinent message to your present one."

"I am curious. Do you think I have met either one of you in a past life? Sometimes I feel like I have known you before." He looked at Ana Dee.

Fray Francisco tilted his head, smiling. "That is possible. Why don't you try the daily contemplation and see if you get an answer to that question? You might want to share it with us next time."

"Speaking of next time, we need to adjourn. But before we leave, I would like to invite you both to Wednesday's *merienda*. I turn nineteen, and Manuela is baking a cake to serve with our afternoon tea to celebrate my birthday. Hermann and Nadia will also be coming."

The monk winked at her and said, "Count me in, my dear sister."

"*Oh là là, ça c'est bon! J'en suis content!* We will have a *grande* party. May I take you promenading that evening to celebrate as well, Ana Dee?"

"I would love to go to the plaza with you on my birthday, André."

CHAPTER 31

I love you not for who you are but for
who I am when I am with you.
—Gabriel García Márquez

On Wednesday, they celebrated Ana Dee's birthday with tacos of melted goat cheese and *pico de gallo*, followed by tea and cake at 2:00 p.m. Afterward, they all sat in the living room watching Ana Dee open her presents.

The children had made her beaded necklaces and bracelets they crafted under Pedro's instructions.

Fray Francisco brought her a historic romantic novella he had obtained from Mexico—*Atala* by Chateaubriand.

André gave her a box of French bonbons he had brought from New Orleans (probably originally meant for his uncles) and a bouquet of flowers.

Manuela had made her a beautiful colorful skirt.

Hermann and Nadia brought her a translucent fabric with gold and silver threads she could turn into a rebozo or sew into a dress. Ana Dee appreciated the clothing materials because although she did not wear tight corsets, crinoline petticoats, or gigot sleeves, all fashionable at the time, she did like pretty fabrics that made her unpretentious *china poblana*–style clothes more charming.

They visited until 5:00 p.m. when the guests went home.

Ana Dee went to get ready for the evening's promenade. It was a special night for the town festivities, the celebration of the Virgin Mary's birth. She decided to wear a pretty white peasant blouse to show off her new sapphire brooch and the skirt Manuela had made her. She tied her hair with a sapphire color ribbon, letting her curls hang in a cascade down to her waist. Manuela had her put a little rouge on her cheeks and just a touch on her lips, which she wiped almost all off before she came out of her room to open the front door for André.

"Ma chérie, you look beautiful," he said admiringly as he took her hands and kissed them. He wore the vested suit she had first seen him in and must have combed his blond hair back with gel.

"I prefer your hair looking more *naturale*, André."

"Whatever you say, mademoiselle." He took a comb out of his pocket and, passing it over his head, shook his bushy blond curls back in disarray. They both laughed and went across to the plaza and joined the promenade.

"I really enjoyed my bonbons, André. I had to hide them because the children could not stop eating them. I can't believe you were able to hold on to them since you left New Orleans. It's almost impossible to find those here. I had only had them once before when Mama Catherine got some from her parents in New York."

"How would you like to someday visit New Orleans or, closer yet, Galveston with me?"

"Wouldn't that be wonderful! I don't see how, though. Too many responsibilities in Santo Tomás, besides the war, that make it impossible."

"Someday. Not now of course. I don't want to leave Santo Tomás now." He took Ana Dee's right hand and placed it on his chest. "You are right in here, ma chérie."

"Are you wanting to court me, André?" she dared ask.

"Most, most definitely, *je t'aime.*"

"You hardly know me." She drew back her hand.

"I know enough about you to love you. I wasn't sure that you wanted my attention after last Sunday. Then Monday evening and today, you seemed to be sending me different signals. Please tell me I have not imagined it."

"No, you haven't. I am just so confused, André. I don't want to lead you on if I am not ready. The last thing I want to do is hurt you because I like you so much."

"Now you are confusing me. I am sure about my feelings for you. You say you like me. That is a good beginning. Give us a chance. I'll woo you into loving me."

"I'll tell you what. Let's just have fun tonight. Give me a week to think about it. We mustn't see each other for a few days. It will give me a chance to think clearly."

"That is a terrible idea. I am lonely already. I will be pining for you when I could be convincing you of our love."

"You should try meeting some of the other señoritas in town."

"You are not serious. I have met many a woman in my life and travels to know when I am truly smitten."

She rolled her eyes and said in a sarcastic tone, "Aah! I am speaking to a man of experience, an older mature man of, what, twenty-two years of age?"

"Twenty-five, for your information. Fine, I will wait for you to realize I am your future. In the meantime, I will be contemplating and reaching you with my inner communication skills," he said jokingly.

"That's not really funny. You should not try to control or influence others that way," she said, smiling and holding a finger across his lips.

André kept his promise and stayed away for a couple of days, concentrating on his apothecary internship and planning on how to approach his uncles about letting him take charge of the business.

They were getting up in age and should consider retiring in the near future anyway.

Ana Dee talked to Manuela and Pedro about little Mary's situation. She wondered if they could possibly find some young girl to help watch Mary while she taught at the new school. She would not be able to pay very much, but she knew André would not mind taking Mary for a couple of hours each day. Manuela told her not to worry; they would figure out a practical schedule for all involved.

Manuela was right. André was already in the habit of picking up little Mary every day after lunch and bringing her back by six in the afternoon.

CHAPTER 32

Love is, above all, the gift of oneself.
—Jean Anouilh

Ana Dee spent the weekend preparing her lesson plans for reading, writing, math, and history to be ready for school the following Monday. She had no idea what reading levels she would be dealing with until she could meet and evaluate her students. She remembered how Mama Catherine had worked with Elizabeth and her and how she prepared different lessons for each of them. That seemed to be the best method for learning in this case with such a diverse group in age and cognition. Once she met the children, eighteen in all, including her David, she divided the class into four groups, and by the end of the week, it all started working out. She found she not only enjoyed her job but she was also good at it.

Before the week was over, she had agreed to meet with André. Having been so busy with her new job, she had failed to take time and consider his proposal as she had promised.

On Thursday morning, he was waiting outside her door when she and David came out to walk to the school. They greeted each other almost in a whisper. She could see the longing for her approval in his eyes and felt guilty, though she was not sure why. He walked with them.

Before she entered the schoolyard, she turned to him and said, "We'll talk tonight. Please wait till then."

He answered, "I'll be over to see you at 7:00 p.m." He walked away.

All day, Ana Dee kept thinking about her answer to André's proposal. The children noticed her distraction when they had to ask her the same question twice. On her lunch break, she and David grabbed a couple of tacos from Guadalupe's Cafe and sweet rice milk *horchata* drinks. When David asked her if something was wrong, she realized she had been aloof all morning and decided to make an effort to concentrate back on school.

When school let out at 4:00 p.m., she went home and closed herself in the library. She started a contemplation and immediately saw Robert in her mind's eye. She almost jumped from her chair. His image was so clear, but it left just as fast. She was certain she had a spiritual connection with Robert, but he was physically gone from her life now. She sang the soothing sound of HU to herself until she felt at peace. The knowingness of what to do came in an instant. She was to follow her heart at that moment and not worry about the future. Her heart was with André right then. She saw herself and André in an embrace. His baby-blue eyes were brilliant and mesmerizing, and she knew they had been together before.

When he arrived, Ana Dee's smile told André all would be well. They sat in the living room drinking tea. The children were in bed, and to Ana Dee's surprise, Manuela and Pedro left them alone. For the most part, they managed to discuss the day's events; but before he left, they agreed they were courting. When he took her in his arms and kissed her good night, it was no longer a peck on the cheek.

As Ana Dee got ready for bed, she remembered Abuela Brau's last dream about her. She was with a man she loved and children around her. It was not what she herself had pictured. When Abuela related it to her, she thought the man was Robert and the kids were theirs, not her students as it turned out. Though Abuela did not describe the man in her dream, Ana Dee now believed it had to be André. The fact that all those kids were not her own, but probably students, was a relief! Abuela had warned her about misinterpreting dream messages.

André came to visit her every evening, and either Manuela or Pedro joined them or were within sight. On Fridays, they went promenading with the children and on Saturdays by themselves. Ana Dee hadn't felt this happy since before her papa's death. The young couple found similar likes and dislikes in spite of their different backgrounds.

They often strolled along with Nadia and Hermann. The girls would walk together in front of their beaus sharing intimate confidences.

The men walked behind them talking about weather, the news on the war, and the political state of their new nation and of their nations of origin. The men formed a camaraderie, both being recent arrivals from the Old World and because of their shared interest in healing.

The girls met with other childhood girlfriends and would catch up on the town's gossip. On those occasions, Ana Dee would look back at André to make sure he was still there and smiled at him. André would smile back as if to reassure her he was.

It had occurred to him why Ana Dee had been hesitant to accept his courtship. She was afraid he would eventually tire of her and leave. André thought it understandable considering the most important people in her life had died or left her at such a young age. His heart melted thinking of her insecurity in spite of the hard shell she wore. He felt he could not leave her any more than he would want to stop breathing. As soon as he told his uncles about his courtship with Ana Dee, they were so glad to hear the news that they offered him the apothecary as their heir, to his satisfaction.

By September 1847, the young couple were so involved with their romantic courtship that the nation's war affairs took a secondary place in their minds. The news that American soldiers and Rangers had descended on Mexico City and attacked the Chapultepec Castle had not reached them.

CHAPTER 33

War is to distract us from the good.
　　　　　　　　　　—Gabriela Mistral

After crossing the vacant deserts, cacti's domain, Tinto nickered at the sight of conifers and oak trees. Robert understood his loyal steed's happiness; he too craved some shade. They rode into the higher grounds of the Sierra Madre Oriental of Mexico.

Robert had been involved in the Mexican-American War (1846–1848), better known as President Polk's War, since its beginning. Exhausted, the Ranger wished he could go back home. But this time, the colonel had sent for him because of his scouting abilities and knowledge of the Mexican countryside. As a Ranger Scout, he was privy to a freedom that others in his platoon envied but not even his superiors understood.

The conquering army preferred other routes to reach the capital. But having grown up in these mountains, Robert knew the terrain well. He replenished their supplies in the hilly town of Rio Verde, where he had friends, and got a decent night's sleep.

"Time to go," he said to Tinto and saddled him up that morning. Tinto put his nose close to his master's face and grunted. Robert patted the black muscular neck and said, "I have a feeling that the Voice will contact us in Mexico City."

Almost a week later, they were looking down the valley surrounded by the emerald peaks of the Sierras. It used to be Lake Texcoco but was now the Basin of Mexico. Robert pulled back his Stetson and got out the binoculars from his satchel. His steel-blue eyes focused through the lens at Chapultepec Hill, situated toward the west side of a city of over 120,000 inhabitants. He steered Tinto in that direction. "Our mission is approaching, my friend." The stallion neighed, lightly pawing with his front hooves, ready to gallop toward Chapultepec's military academy.

They entered the city at the crack of dawn, a reddish morning light illuminating the way. The soft gentle breeze of Frangipani felt incongruous with the ongoing cries and flight of *Mejicanos* running from the *Americanos del Norte*. Robert wondered if he should stop and help some of the victims, but the Voice kept Tinto going until they turned into a lonely alley. A woman lay bent over with her bloodied shawl around her. Tinto's ears pinned back; he flanked her body with his.

"What? You want me to get down and help her? She is definitely dead." Then he heard it, a muffled cry. Hurriedly, he unmounted and turned the body over. Wrapped in the shawl was an infant. Robert pried it away from the rigid arms.

For the first time that night, he heard the Voice: *Tap on the door three times.*

"What door?" he asked. "I see no door."

Tinto snorted, his nostrils fluttering as he trotted down the alley and stopped in front of a passageway. Robert followed. He slipped behind a dilapidated stairway and saw the hidden door. He knocked three times.

"Mama, you are back. We were so sca—" The young girl who opened the door stood shaking, her eyes wide. Robert held out an arm to the door before she could slam it shut on his face. He told her in Spanish that he was bringing her the baby whose mother had died. She let out a strangling sob and put out her arms for the child.

Tinto groaned and Robert knew they had to leave. "One life saved today," he said. He straddled his horse. "I wonder what awaits us at Chapultepec."

That morning, September 13, 1847, the American troops took over Chapultepec Castle, Mexico City's military academy. The Voice kept guiding him toward the school of cadets. Robert knew that's where he was supposed to go. Whether he found the colonel or not was irrelevant. The military orders were mere subterfuge to the real mission that the spiritual travelers had sent him on. Leaning forward on his saddle, Robert led Tinto trotting uphill, miraculously avoiding the ongoing fight between the armies.

He had to laugh when Tinto drew a big audible sigh through his mouth and nostrils upon cresting the climb. It was Tinto's way of saying, "Fait accompli, now it's your turn."

Robert dismounted and went inside the castle. The body of a young cadet lay limp by the entrance with several bullet wounds. Inside the plaza, Robert did not immediately see any cadets or Mexican soldiers, just American troops and Rangers yelling and running about. Suddenly, a small body wrapped in the Mexican flag was seen jumping from the high tower into the dark abyss. For a second, no one moved—just for a second.

Another youth came running toward the *Americanos*. He yelled, "Por la Patria," and shot one of the invaders.

In vain, Robert shouted, "Stop, he is only a child!" The cadet couldn't be more than fourteen years of age. But it was too late; he was immediately killed by several men.

In his head, Robert heard the Voice: *Find him.* He grabbed one of the men, shaking him by the shoulders. "They are only children."

Shrugging, as if to explain, the soldier yelled back, "We ain't taking any prisoners."

There was another cry, "The tower! Another jumper."

Soldiers started running into the tower. Robert chased after them. No one would listen to his cries. "Stop, they are children! This is insane!"

Inside the tower, they found a quivering child cadet, hunkered against the wall, covering his face. He was instantly shot to death by the unruly men. Robert ran up the stairs wanting to protect any other cadets before his men found them. One soldier had already started to climb the steps in pursuit of another cadet. They reached the last floor as the child tried to hide behind some old mattresses. The soldier took aim and fired.

Robert pushed the crazed soldier aside and picked up the injured child. "Get out!" he yelled.

The soldier's rapid blinking bloodshot eyes recognized the Ranger Scout. He spat at Robert's boots and turned around. After a short scuffle, he and the rest of the men who had followed them went back downstairs.

Robert lay the grievously wounded child on a table. He had seen enough battle casualties to know the cadet would not live much longer. Unable to stop the bleeding, he covered the boy with an old sheet he found to keep him from shivering and held his hand. The Voice was pounding in his head again: *Find him.*

He scratched his temple and asked, "Who?"

His patient struggled to say something. Robert bent his head down to hear the cadet whisper, "Ayúdalo," as his eyes closed forever.

Robert looked over at the wall of mattresses. He could see a strange halo coming from that direction and knew it was a spiritual traveler's presence. He grabbed a mattress and pushed it over. When he had pulled two more out of the way, a little boy, not in cadet uniform, stood with legs planted wide and a wooden sword pointed at him. "Surrender," he said in Spanish.

Taken aback, Robert raised his arms. His lips held tight, holding a chuckle, he answered in Spanish, "I am your prisoner, sir."

A soldier walked into the room. "Captain, I heard you were up here. Uh, who do we have here?"

As Robert turned to see the soldier, the boy hit him on the leg with his wooden weapon.

"Ouch! Stop that before you hurt someone," Robert said, taking away the sword and restraining the young one. Addressing the soldier, he said, "My God, William, it appears the troops have gone berserk killing children! Where is the colonel?"

"Yes, Captain. I am sorry to say there was no one to control them. After General Bravo retreated from the hill with his troops, only six brave young cadets stayed behind to guard the castle. We have found five, all dead now. Is this child the sixth one?"

"I believe the one on the table is the last one," Robert said, pointing at the dead cadet while struggling to keep his prisoner still. "What happened to our colonel?"

"The colonel is arranging some quarters for our soldiers. The Rodríguez family has no respect for their corrupt government and is assisting us."

"Please tell him that I am going to be scouting the surroundings of the city and will be back in a couple of days."

"What do you intend to do with your little catch?"

"I suppose I should take him back to his family."

"You'll have to get him out of here unobserved first. How about wrapping him up with a sheet? You know, make it look like a sack of potatoes."

The kid had finally settled down and was sitting in a corner, his arms crossed and lips pushed forward. Robert had thrown his wooden sword out the window.

"You are not my prisoner, but I am not yours either. We need to take you to your home. What's your name?"

The child stood up and with his hands on his hips proudly explained, "I am Pablo Alvarez. This is my home. I am the school's mascot. My parents are dead."

Robert translated the conversation to William, who asked where he would take the child.

"I know where to take him," he answered. The Voice was clearly telling him, *Bring him home.*

William helped bundle Pablo inside a sheet and place him on Robert's shoulder.

No one stopped them as they crossed the plaza of the now American troops' garrison. They almost tripped over two dead

American soldiers. Robert's inner voice nudged him to take their caps with the Lone Star insignia.

Robert and William parted ways at the gate. He whistled for Tinto.

The stallion came out of the bushes whinnying and tossing his head. Robert unwrapped Pablo and sat behind him as they mounted the horse, who swiftly cantered downhill from the east side of the castle to avoid most of the fighting that had taken place on the west side. After witnessing the killing of the *niños* heroes, Robert Hughes left the Chapultepec Castle guilt-ridden.

Little Pablo asked him, "Where are you taking me, sir?"

"To my old home where you will be safe. To your new school in Kulkanzin, where the spiritual travelers await you."

Racing down the hill, Robert spotted what seemed like two American soldiers fighting each other. Robert unmounted Tinto and asked Pablo to stay put.

One called the other a traitor. He was hit by a rifle butt and fell to the ground.

"What's going on, soldiers?" Robert asked in a threatening tone, holding his Colt against a man's head. "Have we killed enough Mexicans that now we have to kill one another?"

The soldier with the gun said, "We are not traitors, sir. Our battalion, St. Patrick's, is against this war, though."

Robert remarked, "I can't say I disagree with you on that. What is your name, soldier?"

"I am Liam, and he's Brady, sir," the soldier answered.

Robert put his gun down and handed the military caps to the two men. "I admire your courage. There is no need for more blood to be spilled. Ride away as fast as you can." As the two men disappeared into the night, Robert mounted Tinto, and they were on their way again.

The bloodied sun shed its crimson for amber lights, sending golden rays across the gray and cobalt sky, as the lithesome trio disappeared into the deep forest of the Sierra Madre.

CHAPTER 34

There is the immense joy of living and of being fair,
but above all there is the immense joy of serving.
—Gabriela Mistral

It was the first week in October, and the evenings were cooler in Santo Tomás. The weekly theological discussion meeting with Fray Francisco was coming up. Ana Dee remembered they were to go over reincarnation and wrote some notes with points to cover for André's information. She thought about how his desire to share her spiritual beliefs made her happy. She remembered what her blue Ranger had said, "Your path likens my path," and finally understood what he had meant; it struck her so simple. She also thought about how she could ever explain to André what Robert meant to her, a brother in faith. She knew she and André would get married; they did love each other. But if Robert came back, how would she introduce him to André? Before any of that happened, she needed to tell André about Robert. Could he understand that Robert was her spiritual brother?

While Ana Dee was preparing for their class, André stopped by the clinic to see Hermann. Nadia let him in and pointed to the second examination room where Hermann was studying some pamphlets he had received on the latest research on cholera. As André walked into the room, Hermann greeted him and had him sit down on the one chair in the room while he sat on the bed. "Frenchie! How are you?"

"Fine, *merci*. How about you old *Würstli*?"

"*Gut, ja, danke*. What brings you here?"

"I understand that you know how to get ahold of the town's jeweler."

"Aah. You wish to buy a present for Ana Dee. Did you run out of bonbons?"

"Unfortunately! *Mais non*, I want to get wedding bands."

"So soon? Are you sure she reciprocates your feelings?"

"That's a strange question. We are in love. Why wait?"

"*Bitte, entschuldige*. Well, because . . . I think you should ask her before you invest in the rings."

"That would ruin the surprise. I am sure. So will you help me? Where do I contact the jeweler?"

"He comes to the market occasionally. But if you are in a hurry, we can go to his home in the outskirts of town. Gut?"

"Très bien."

"I suppose we can close the clinic early tomorrow. We'll check the market, and if he is not there, we'll hire a couple of horses at the public stable and ride to his house. *Du reitest doch, nicht wahr?*"

"But of course, I can go horseback riding! So I will be here around four o'clock in the afternoon."

Their plans made, André took his leave and went to Ana Dee's house. Fray Francisco was also there. They went in for dinner, after which the children retired to their rooms with Manuela and Pedro's help.

Fray Francisco and André followed Ana Dee into the library.

"Well, the topic tonight is reincarnation. I would like to know, André, what your understanding on this subject is."

"I think it means that you die and then you are born again. Your actions in one life determine what will happen in your next life. I do have some questions: One, why don't we remember past lives? Two, how can we make any spiritual progress if we don't know what we need to learn in the new life? Three, how many times are we usually reborn? And four, do we come back with the same families?"

Both Fray Francisco and Ana Dee laughed at the number of questions André posed.

The monk turned to Ana. "Did you write down all his questions?"

"Yes, Padre, I wrote all four."

"Good. Let's take one at a time, and some will be answered by the material you have already prepared. Please read the first question."

"Why don't we remember a past life? My answer is you don't need to remember because if you learn a past lesson, you won't have to repeat it; and if you didn't learn it, you will experience it again until you get it right. Besides, because we live so many lives—some teachings say millions—it would be overwhelming for our little brains to deal with. As Soul, you do remember, though. I believe I've answered three of your questions: why we don't remember, if we need to remember past lives, and how many times we are reborn. The last question was about being born within the same family. I would say yes and no. Once the necessary experience is completed with a particular person or Soul, we will probably move on to someone else in the next life." She let out a big sigh.

Fray Francisco patted her on the shoulder and addressed André. "If anything could help you understand family karmic ties, think of little Mary. That little girl and you have ties from a past life. I dare say they are good family ties. Why don't we proceed to discuss more general information on reincarnation? But before we do, I have a question for you."

"Oui?"

"Did you have any experiences from your daily contemplations or answers to your questions? I guess I should first ask if you did the contemplation."

"I did the meditation technique repeating HU. I asked to know if we had met in a past life but didn't get any answers. I heard no special message except for sometimes a weird ringing in my ears."

Ana Dee and Fray Francisco looked at each other and smiled knowingly.

"I am so jealous, André! You were in contact with the inner sound on your first try! That ringing was part of experiencing God's voice."

"Are you sure?"

"Oh yes. Did you see any light with your inner vision?"

"Not really, just images of my daily life, which I kept trying to avoid and would go back to repeating HU."

"Well, the spiritual sound you kept hearing might be an inner master trying to make contact with you. Don't you think so, Fray Francisco?"

"I can't answer that for you. You need to check it out yourself, André. If you wish to invite a guide into your inner vision, you must ask, though."

"Well, should we continue with the topic of reincarnation?"

"Oui, I am ready to hear more about reincarnation."

"Okay. So Soul comes to our planet for the sole purpose of evolving life after life until it is polished enough and doesn't have to return to the physical plane or world. At the risk of getting ahead in our discourse, I might add that the advanced Soul then may serve in the capacity of God's helper."

"Ah, we are training to be God's helpers? In what capacity?"

"Yes, that's the actual purpose of our purification. But like Ana Dee said, we are getting ahead of ourselves. To understand in what capacity, let's first better understand the progression through reincarnation. Please continue, Ana Dee."

"When I was studying with my papa, he read a poem to me that explains reincarnation very simply. As you know, Papa traveled extensively in his youth and collected many esoteric books and manuscripts, some so rare that the translations are handwritten copies."

"I think I know which one you are referring to. Is it from the Sufi master Rumi?"

"It's from Rumi's *Masnavi* collection from his *Spiritual Couplets*."

"Please share it with us."

I have again and again grown like grass,

I have experienced seven hundred and seventy moulds.
I have died a mineral and become a plant,
I died a plant and rose to animal,
I died as animal and I was a man.
Why should I fear? When was I less by dying?
Next time I shall die bringing forth
Wings and feathers like angels;
After that soaring higher than angels.
What you cannot imagine, I shall be that.
                    By Jalal din Rumi (Sufi 1207–1273)

After some quiet contemplation on the poem, André said, "I can see why you chose that poem. It explains the process of reincarnation in its progression. So we have been minerals and animals before being human?"

Fray Francisco answered, "With the understanding that we, meaning Soul, have occupied many physical covers, yes. Soul needs all kinds of experiences in this world. Each experience is an opportunity to move on toward its purification and know divine love."

"How do you accomplish that?"

"Putting it in its simplest form, reincarnating from mineral to human is just a progression of higher levels of awareness. When Soul is reborn in the human form, it has the chance by its actions and their consequences to rise in fortune in its next life or not. This action and reaction is called karma."

"In other words, we gain spiritual unfoldment because of our good deeds and are born to a better life?"

"Basically yes, but it is not so easy. The physical world is meant to constantly bring grief. That is the way it is designed. It is a testing ground for Soul to learn. You might have good karma, but the strife in the world around you will bring you more lessons to surpass. Until you have totally liberated yourself from karma, good or bad, you cannot gain total spiritual liberation."

"How, then, can we accomplish that?"

"You purify yourself faster by doing your contemplations and really listening to your inner guidance. Only your inner guide can help you with that."

"I really don't like the idea of placing my full trust in a guide I don't know. Perhaps he isn't a good spirit."

Ana explained, "You would really be surrendering to the guidance of Spirit through someone who has achieved God realization. You would know if the guide isn't God's messenger. It would not feel right."

"Once you have achieved the level of enlightenment that a spiritual master has, you can begin to serve and help others in their spiritual path. You may serve again in this world in the capacity of a teacher to guide other souls, or you might serve in other planes of existence. There are myriad capacities by which you might serve God. Next time, we can discuss those virtues we need to acquire in order to climb the proverbial ladder." Fray Francisco then stood up and said, "By the way, I am afraid I am busy next month so we can't meet until Monday the twenty-second of November. That will be all for tonight. I have to rise early tomorrow."

"If you have any more questions on reincarnation and karma, you and I can talk anytime, André," Ana Dee added.

"Merci, Ana Dee. I'll keep doing my contemplations and possibly get my own answers so I won't need to ask you."

They all laughed.

"You certainly are a fast learner, André!"

CHAPTER 35

*We choose our joys and sorrows long
before we experience them.*
—Khalil Gibran

As they walked out of the library and Fray Francisco left, André asked Ana Dee if they could discuss a different matter. He followed her to the living room. He had been thinking maybe Hermann had a point and he should get Ana Dee's opinion and not assume she agreed with him.

They sat in the living room and she said, "I am glad you want to talk because I need to tell you something as well."

"Would you like to go first?"

"I think I prefer to hear you first."

"Très bien." André got down on one knee. "Will you marry me, ma chérie?"

Ana Dee let out a little sigh. "Before I give you an answer, please sit back up next to me." She nervously took his hands in hers.

"Whatever it is, I won't change my mind, mon amour."

"André, I know that you have loved or courted others before me."

"I can't deny that. They meant nothing. You are my one true love."

"Perhaps you think I haven't loved before."

"Ma chérie, what happened before us is of no importance."

149

"Well, it might be. Please let me explain. Over three years ago, I thought I was in love with a very special person. We never courted because he left to fight in the war."

"So he died in battle?"

"No . . . well . . . I don't think so. He only wrote to me once this whole time. The point is that he might still come back—I mean, to Santo Tomás."

"Do you still love him?"

"No, of course not, André. I would not have agreed to our relationship if I thought so. That is what I want to explain, I do love you now. I want you to know that if he, that person, comes back, I will not betray you with him."

"Ma chérie, I don't think you had to tell me about your previous love, if ever it was that. But thank you for trusting me with your secret. I don't even want to know who that 'special person' is or was. If he comes back and you don't introduce us, I will be more than happy not knowing him. I will admit it might make me jealous if I did know him. However, I trust you with all my heart. So now, will you say you will marry me?"

"Yes, I will marry you, mon chérie."

André left, excited. He couldn't wait to buy the rings.

The next day, André asked Pedro and Manuela if they could watch little Mary in the afternoon and confided to them the reason for his request. Manuela was happy to hear the news of the engagement, but Pedro questioned him, "Just to be sure, she has agreed to your holy union?"

"You are the second person to ask that. Isn't the fact that we have been courting over a month now enough?"

"Precisely. That's not long at all. After she and Dr. Meyer courted for almost a year, she broke his heart. Oops, so sorry. I've said too much."

"Aha, that's why Hermann also asked if I was sure. I am sure. She never loved Hermann because at the time, she loved another."

"So you know about the Ranger? Well, I guess she is over him if she told you about it."

André left Mary with the couple and went to meet Hermann. He was thinking about what he had learned. *A Texas Ranger, no less! I can't believe my sweet Ana Dee would love a rough person like that. It had to be a childhood crush.*

On the way to the jeweler, who was not to be found at the market, André could not help but ask Hermann, "So you courted Ana Dee before Nadia?"

Hermann gave him a smirk. "Ja. But we are really only friends now. I love my Nadia. We have so much in common. We plan to marry by the Christmas holidays."

"Bien, that's nice! We can have a double wedding. I know you think it's too soon for Ana Dee and me to marry. But you know, we Frenchmen know the art of romance. She could not resist my charm. We are ready, as they say, to tie the knot."

"I hope you are right, Frenchie. I guess I better start calling you André instead. I don't want Ana Dee to be upset with me. We must behave like serious married men, ja?" he said solemnly.

While promenading Saturday night, André asked Ana Dee if they should try to obtain Mary's guardianship since they were now engaged. After due diligence on their part, the following week, the city granted them Mary's temporary guardianship. That pronouncement made them feel like a family already. Little Mary started calling Ana Dee Mama, and David, not wanting to be left behind, did as well. They were both already calling André Père.

CHAPTER 36

The purpose of our lives is to be happy.
—Dalai Lama

On their next Saturday promenade date, André asked Ana Dee if they could go home early for a private conversation. Once they were alone in the living room, he held her hands and took out the bands from his pocket. He slipped the smaller one on her left-hand ring finger. "With this ring, I promise to be yours forever."

He handed her the other band. "Will you like to make a promise to me?"

Ana Dee could not help but giggle shyly, accepting the band and placing it on his finger. "With this ring, I promise to love and disobey you."

André cracked up, laughing. He picked up his fiancé in an embrace.

"I would not have it any other way. I know who the boss is. We are now engaged! By the way, Hermann and Nadia are getting married this December before Christmas," he said as he put her down. "Do you want to make it a double wedding?"

"That would be too soon. Tio Pedro and Tia Manuela are going to be shocked. Besides, Hermann and Nadia are having a huge event, mostly her parents' idea. I would not want to crash their celebration. I prefer a more intimate ceremony like what Elizabeth and James had."

"Tell me about that wedding. We have never talked about your sister and her love story."

"Well, they courted for a short time. Actually, just a week. Sean, James's brother, and I were the only ones present besides the priest." She thought about Robert playing his guitar in the background, but decided not to mention it. "I just got a letter from her. Would you like to hear it?"

"Mais oui. I want to know all about your family."

Ana Dee got the letter from her room and, unfolding it, read it aloud:

Dearest Sister,

> *Happy Birthday! I hope all is well with you.*
>
> *Mama, Billy and I are doing well.*
>
> *We were very sad to hear about dear Abuela Brau. I am sure you received Mama's letter about Abuela's passing this past Summer. I miss Abuela a lot.*
>
> *We were sorry it didn't work out with Hermann. He is a wonderful person.*
>
> *I hope that you will find your James soon.*
>
> *I have some sad news from Mama. That is why Mama asked me to write to you instead. She is too distressed right now. Both my grandparents passed away within a month of each other.*
>
> *We are thinking of selling our home, which is north of New Jersey, and renting a home close to Long Beach Island, which is near the Tuckerton Seaport Lighthouse, since James lands near there when he comes home on furlough. He has been to see us twice now, but our house is a day's land trip for him. As soon as the war is over, he will be able to be home more often since they schedule their shifts on a weekly basis. As you can imagine, I can't wait to have him home.*

Little Billy is almost four years old and getting so big. Young David is very lucky to have you. He sounds like a very precocious child. Please write us more about him.

We miss you very much and hope that someday you can come visit. Hugs and kisses from Mama and Billy.

With love,

Elly
2nd of September of 1847

"I am sorry about your mother's parents. I guess you never met them. So you haven't told your mother and sister about us?"

"Yes, I have. I wrote about you and our little Mary. This letter is from September before I wrote to them. We've really had a short courtship. I can't believe we are engaged already."

"You just said your sister's courtship was shorter yet. When you know it's real love, why wait?"

"They were different circumstances. James was going to be shipped out."

"Why do you think we should wait longer?"

"Why do you think we should marry right away?"

"Isn't it obvious? I don't want to be with you just a few hours a day. Ma chérie, I want us to build a life together. I want to come home to you and whisper loving words in the privacy of our bedroom."

"Will you whisper them in French?" With a flirtatious glance, she added, "It sounds more romantic."

"I knew you preferred it to German!"

She ignored his comment. "You really need to go home now, André. I promise to think about the best time for our wedding and make a decision by next week."

"By tomorrow, you mean. I miss you, *tous les soirs.*"

After a prolonged good night kiss, Ana Dee walked a resisting André to the door with the excuse that it was getting late and she had to work the next day.

CHAPTER 37

*A true friend is the one who holds your
hand and touches your heart.*
—Gabriel García Márquez

Toward the end of October, Ana Dee went to see Nadia at the clinic during a lunch break. She thought they could go over the wedding plans. She and André had been chosen to be the *lazo padrinos*. This was an old tradition whereby the sponsors of the wedding tie a garland of orange blossoms in the shape of an eight and place it on the bride and groom's shoulders as a symbol of their tie or union. Manuela and Pedro had already said they would make the white-and-cherry-colored garland, but Ana Dee wanted to know if there was anything else Nadia needed help with, as the big day was rapidly approaching, only a month and a half away.

She found Nadia alone in the front office. After greeting each other, Ana Dee noticed her friend was not as enthusiastic about the wedding plans as she expected. "Is something wrong?"

"I might as well tell you. I need to confide in someone or go crazy."

"Don't tell me you've changed your mind about marrying Hermann?"

"No, quite the opposite. I wish we could marry tomorrow."

"I am afraid your parents would be very, very disappointed after all the preparations they have been making."

"I know. I am afraid my mother will be very upset when she finds out that the wedding dress is going to be too small by the time of the ceremony."

"Are you planning to eat for two?" Ana Dee raised her eyebrows, realizing what she just said might be true. She shook her head in disbelief as she noticed her friend's guilty expression. "Are you sure?"

"Pretty sure. I missed my courses. This week, I have been very nauseous."

"How long have you been in . . . ?"

"My condition? Pregnant, Ana Dee, you can say it. Well, Hermann and I were intimate on the day of your birthday so that would be about six to seven weeks."

"But where? I mean, you are never alone."

"Well, we came into the clinic after having a couple of drinks at your party. You know that I am really not used to drinking. Since we were already engaged and it was so quiet and private here . . ."

"You are not serious! Never mind. What is done is done. You will just have to starve yourself until December and hope your belly does not show until later."

"You think that will work?"

"I've seen many women in your condition who hardly show at all the first three months. Elizabeth's second pregnancy was that way. She could hardly keep any food in her stomach, though. Let's hope you won't show either. Just make sure you don't eat much *fecula*. No tortillas or rice either."

"What am I supposed to eat?"

"You know, vegetables, chicken, and milk. 'You'll need milk,' my papa used to tell women in your condition, especially milch ass. You can always tell your mother that you want to look good for the wedding and are dieting."

"It's a good thing she always thought I was overweight. I will be miserable until my wedding day."

"So that's that. I can get some tea for nausea from Manuela. I guess I can tell her you asked for a patient. Please, you and your German Casanova behave until you are officially married. Especially here in the clinic."

"You know that since I am already pregnant it does not matter, so why not enjoy it?"

"Shame on you, Nadia!"

"Oh, don't worry. It's not like I feel like doing anything except throw up these days."

"I better get you some of that tea."

Ana Dee went to talk to Manuela who told her the apothecary had a tea that combined the herbs chamomile and ginger for pregnancy nausea. Then she asked, "But Dr. Meyer knows that, why doesn't he get it from them?"

Thinking fast, Ana Dee said, "Yes, well, the patient is there now and Nadia wants to give her something to feel better now. So could you please take a cup to Nadia? I have to get back to school. Thank you, Tia."

CHAPTER 38

Preservation of one's own culture does not require
Contempt or disrespect for other cultures.
—Cesar Chavez

Ana Dee went back to the clinic on her way to school to tell Nadia what she had said to Manuela. Poor Nadia was a distressing sight, and as she left, Ana Dee thought, *Manuela was no fool and will figure it all out.*

Back at school, the children were excitedly waiting for her. She asked them to calm down and explain what was going on. The oldest girl in the class, Teresita, asked her if they could participate as a group in the Christmas *Las Posadas* in December. This was a Catholic tradition of a reenactment of the pregnant Virgin Mary and her husband Joseph's pilgrimage from Nazareth to Bethlehem. This procession involved singing, musical instruments, and dressing up as the different pilgrim personages as well as the participation of some animals, including a donkey the Virgin Mary would ride. It was celebrated between December 16 and December 24, nine nights symbolizing the nine months of pregnancy.

Ana Dee was delighted the kids wanted to take part in the town's tradition and told them she would talk with Father Murphy. She reminded them the school would be closed at the time, and they needed to learn their parts and the litanies before then. There was a lot of work to be done, and they had about a month and a half to prepare. She would just have to divide her attention between Virgin Mary's and Nadia's pregnancies.

She shared the school events with the family at dinnertime. Manuela commented that Teresita, the student who asked Ana Dee about participating in the town's Las Posadas, would make a nice Virgin Mary. Then she added, "Of course, if they want an adult, Nadia would be a good candidate."

Ana Dee shook her head, and Pedro commented, "Why her? There are a couple of young ladies expecting in town, who would be more realistic." Ana Dee almost choked on her food.

When André came over in the evening, David told him all about the plans for him and his schoolmates to participate in the Christmas festivities. He then mentioned Manuela's suggestion for Nadia to play the part of the Virgin Mary. André's only comment was, "Really?"

After the kids went to bed, he told Ana Dee, "I think it is strange that Manuela thinks Nadia should play the part of Virgin Mary. For one thing, she is too busy with planning her wedding, which will be the same week the festivities start."

She bit her lower lip. "Umm."

"Why would she suggest that? By the way, do you know that Manuela came over to the apothecary herself to pick up a tea for nausea? I prepared the mixture of herbs myself because she said it was for pregnancy nausea and I only had some compounds with licorice root ready, which is not advisable for pregnancies. I thought it odd that Manuela came over. These days, if anyone comes, it's Pedro, and not so much. I usually deliver the medicines to Dr. Hermann Meyer myself."

Her only comment was, "Umm."

"I guess we aren't communicating tonight. You haven't said much. Have you thought about our wedding date?"

"I did. Right now, though, I am awfully busy. How do you feel about spring?"

"So far away, ma chérie!" He gave a big sigh. "Do you really want to wait that long?"

"Well, January is bad luck for weddings, and February is too cold."

"How about between Christmas and New Year? That way, you'll be off for the holidays. You don't go back until after Epiphany day, January 6. I checked."

"Mon chérie, that's perfect. Why hadn't I thought about it before?"

"*Oh là là! Tu me rends très heureux!* I was beginning to think that we would have to wait a long time, like Hermann and Nadia, to make love."

Ana Dee could not hold her mirth. She laughed so hard that tears trickled down her cheeks. André smiled in puzzlement. She gave him a mischievous look and said, "Who do you think needed the tea?"

"*Non! Non?* That sly Würstli!"

"Please, please don't say anything. I don't want you embarrassing my friends. Goodness, what possessed me to tell you? Promise me, André."

"I won't. I promise."

"Besides, it wasn't all Hermann's doing. Nadia had a hand in it too. After all, Hermann and I courted for a year, and he was a perfect gentleman."

"*Sournois*, if you ask me. I think you just didn't give him a chance. I should know."

"André, I never loved him. You know that. He was . . . is . . . a good friend, and I won't have you disparaging him. I do think that Nadia and Hermann are truly in love, and like my sister, Elizabeth, they felt the need to show their affection for each other."

"You are such a naive person. I love you the more for it. I better go before I devour you. Not that I could with Tio Pedro in the next room waiting for me to leave."

Before he left, though, André did steal a kiss, all the while thinking he would not share the information publicly; but he certainly wasn't going to miss the chance to tease the good doctor.

On Saturday morning, Ana Dee joined Nadia at the clinic to go over wedding plans. She found her friend was tired of coping with the nausea, but in better spirits. Her parents' wedding gift was a house that they had been renting out on the street behind their fabric shop. It had only two bedrooms but with a large lot so they could expand the home. Hermann had been concerned about their prospective dwelling, thinking they would have to stay at the Anderson pensión or move in with the in-laws. The latter was not a choice Hermann would agree to. Nadia's brother, his wife, and two-month-old baby, were already residing with the Youssefs. As their tradition dictated, the wife was to join the husband's family. Of course, Hermann had no family in Santo Tomás, thus their dilemma.

Hermann was relieved and grateful to Nadia's parents and offered to make monthly payments to his in-laws. Sharif Youssef refused the offer, saying the young couple needed to save the money and enlarge the house to accommodate their future children. Hermann and Nadia thought with remorse her parents had no idea how true that was.

Nadia told Ana Dee how hard it was to keep from confiding in her mother. Ana Dee wondered what difference it would make. All they could do was make the couple get married, which they were already doing. She said as much to her friend, and Nadia responded, "Oh no! They would never trust me again. They already think I am too free-spirited. They think that my trustworthy husband has been a good influence on me. I like that they think Hermann is such a gentleman because he really is."

Ana Dee could not help thinking how similar the situation was to her sister's love story. Since she met André, she thought him to be the wildest of the bunch; that is, compared to James and Hermann. Truth be told, that was part of his charm. Yet here he was, the most sincere, genuine, and ethical person she knew. How could she not appreciate those qualities?

On Saturday in November, the two couples went promenading together. This time, they walked alongside their respective sweethearts. They found one empty bench, and the ladies sat down while André and Hermann went for some treats. André could not let the opportunity pass. "So, Hermann, are you prepared to be a father?

It's a wonderful experience. Ana Dee and I have a little girl already before we are even married."

"*Bitte*, André. If you are trying to bait me, forget it. I knew you would figure it out after the tea incident, which Nadia told me about. I am just hoping that you'll be enough of a friend to keep it to yourself."

As he advanced to join the ladies, he said, "*Excusez moi, s'il te plais*, Hermann. You can be sure to trust *moi*."

CHAPTER 39

If you would be a real seeker after truth,
it is necessary that at least
once in your life you doubt, as far as possible, all things.
—René Descartes

Ana Dee was very busy the following weeks between helping with Nadia's wedding arrangements and the Las Posadas school project. The schoolchildren were excited with the preparations. The whole town was involved through the church. The parents committed to making the pilgrims' costumes, learning the litanies in Spanish and offering their homes as posadas.

Most of the homes playing the part of posadas would deny the pilgrims entry. The last home visited on each evening had to be a welcoming one, meaning they would provide much of the food and refreshments for the pilgrims.

The class spent hours making nine piñatas filled with candy in the shape of a seven-pointed star; each point represented the breaking of the seven deadly sins when the welcoming posadas granted Mary and Joseph a place to stay.

The holidays were getting closer, and there was only one more spiritual discourse to attend before the end of the year, coming up on November 22.

On the evening of Saturday, November 20, while checking the church hall for Nadia and Hermann's wedding decorations, André said, "As soon as we are married, I want to see about formalizing our guardianship of the children."

"That's a wonderful idea. We won't have any problem with David. He was old enough to know if he had any family left. By now, they would have claimed him. But my little Mary is a different story."

"How long do we have to wait do you think?" André's impatient tone told her something was different.

"I don't know, but we'll probably have to convince Father Murphy first."

There was tension in his voice as he briskly walked ahead, leaving her behind. "Ana Dee, I am not one to enjoy a fight, but if anyone tries to take my baby girl away, I think I would kill them."

She could not believe the way her sweet André was behaving. He would not look her in the eye. She tried to calm him down by explaining, "My darling Père, we are both very attached to her. It would not be easy for me to see her go either. It would break my heart. But think about it. There might be a good reason for someone not to have come forward before now. She certainly had been well taken care of before we knew her. They must have loved her as much as we do. We must trust Spirit to have her best interest at heart."

He turned around, realizing he had left her behind, and rubbed his forehead. "Je ne peux pas être d'accord avec toi." André seemed frustrated as he raised his voice. "We've had her for almost three months now! She would not want to leave us, and it would cause her permanent damage if they took her away. Three months! The same amount of time we've known each other. I could not give her up any more than I could give you up. Don't you see, she brought us together." He held Ana Dee's hands in his.

Ana Dee wondered if something else was causing André's unusual agitation. It was so unlike him to assume an angry tone with her. "André, mi amor, you are too emotional. Calm down. Why don't we go back to the house?"

Pouting, he said, "Yes, let's. I don't understand how you can be so unemotional about this."

Once they were settled in the living room, watching André tapping his finger on his armchair, Ana Dee broke the silence. "There is something else bothering you. No?"

"Ana Dee, yes, you are right. I am sorry for the way I have been behaving. I have to tell you how I really feel about your 'path.' I didn't know how to tell you, but here it goes. I won't be attending your next class this coming Monday. I don't want to follow a teaching that says one must be resigned to accept whatever Spirit decides. Surrendering does not sound good to me. I want to make my own decisions. You probably think it is my mind deciding and not Soul. But you do believe we have 'free will.' I love that you are so trusting and good. I can't be that way. I can't trust that Spirit, as you say, decides what is best for our Mary. I don't believe I am ready for your teachings."

"André, please believe me, I won't stop loving you if you do not accept my path. That is what I like about it. We are not here to convert or convince anyone of our beliefs. We respect each other's paths and beliefs. I love you for yourself. I love you as you are. You are sincere and good. I will take you as you are if you'll love me as I am."

"Ma chérie, thank you for understanding. Knowing you has made me a better person. I was reborn when I met you. I don't need any more rebirths right now."

They sat holding each other in the quiet of the night for a little while. Then standing up, Ana Dee took his hand and led him to the door and embraced him before he went out into the cold November night.

On Sunday morning, André picked up his little family, and they went to church together. The children were excited about the upcoming Christmas festivities. Ana Dee and André were happy to enjoy the children and spend a full day together. Manuela served tamales for dinner and proudly announced they were made with the children's help, to everyone's admiration.

Later during their nightly tête-à-tête, the young couple discussed their wedding plans. Sunday, December 26, would be a good day if Father Murphy and Fray Francisco were available. They needed to confirm with them before announcing it to the children and Tios Manuela and Pedro. Other than them, Ana Dee only wanted to invite André's uncles, Sean and girlfriend, if any, and the Meyer newlyweds. She was sad her mother and sister would not be there and would write to them as soon as she and André spoke to the priest.

On Monday morning, André picked up Ana Dee, and they went to the church after the 6:00 a.m. Mass to speak to Father Murphy before going to work. The priest was surprised at how soon the couple wanted to get married. André explained, "We are actually waiting till then because Ana Dee is too busy right now with the Posadas festivities. Otherwise, we would do it this week."

The priest shook his head and said he would check his calendar and let them know because he too was busy. Ana Dee explained she just wanted a very simple ceremony like her sister's. Squinting his eyes, he said, "I don't believe that you are compromised like her, no?" Ana Dee assured him that was not the case. The priest had them sit down while he went to check his schedule.

André asked his fiancé, "Does everyone in this town 'compromise' before wedlock?" He gestured quote marks and winked at her. "There must be something wrong with us!" Ana Dee punched him lightly on the shoulder and asked him to be silent.

Father Murphy agreed to December 26 as long as it was in the evening. The couple thanked him effusively and left the church before he could change his mind.

That night after dinner, Fray Francisco and Ana Dee retired to the library for their discourse.

"I suppose you are wondering if André is coming tonight," Ana Dee said.

"My dear child, he just about told us last time that he was not interested."

"What do you mean?"

"He is uncomfortable with the concept of surrendering."

"You are right. How are you always right?"

"André is a beautiful Soul. A free spirit, much like your father."

"He does remind me of Papa."

"In his youth, your papa behaved very much like André. The difference was that Anthony was an introvert, whereas André is an extrovert. I am not surprised that he conquered your heart in such a short time."

"He is very different from Hermann. I could never get close enough to him."

"Yes. Hermann is very traditional, rigid in his concepts. He is comfortable with an orthodox religion, which frees its members from social injustices, not from karma." After a pause, he went on. "Nadia, on the other hand, has often rebelled against her cultural ties, though she is used to dealing with traditional concepts even while not abiding by them. Nadia understands Hermann and can possibly help him be more flexible. They complement each other. For you, however, it would have been extremely hard to deal with Hermann's unbending beliefs. You have been brought up to question and inquire and even study ideas opposite to yours. That was your papa's gift to you—an open, inquisitive mind."

"I feel that André is the same way."

"He is. That's why you understand each other. It matters not that he doesn't follow our teachings. He is also on the same track. There is no hurry. We each will return to God in our own time. When the pupil is ready, the Master will be there."

"Thank you, Fray Francisco. I knew that it didn't matter if André and I don't follow the same path, but it's nice to hear another's perspective."

"Ana Dee, your love for each other is a gift from Spirit. You will learn so much from each other! Think of how much good you are doing for your two little ones. You are providing a safe and loving home for them."

"By the way, our wedding is the evening of December 26. I want you to be there to witness our union and give me away."

"You honor me, my dear! I would not miss it." The monk was touched by Ana Dee's words and took a minute to compose himself. "Now, should we cover some of the virtues that are required for our journey to mastership?"

"Yes, of course."

"Please take note of them, and we will later discuss each in more detail: self-restraint as opposed to lust, forgiveness as opposed to tolerance, contentment as opposed to greed, discernment as opposed to poor choices, detachment as opposed to attachment, and humility as opposed to vanity."

Their meeting went on for a full hour. They agreed to wait until January to continue with the classes.

The next morning, Ana Dee was in good spirits, ready to tackle her hectic schedule. She and André would announce their wedding date to Manuela, Pedro, and the children at dinnertime.

She told Manuela that André would stay for dinner because they had something important to talk about with the family. Manuela knew what it was about, but she could not wait to find out the date.

When André revealed the date of the wedding, everyone started talking at the same time. Pedro said it was too close to Christmas and there was too much to do, Manuela agreed there was too much to do with all the posadas preparations and she would not have time to put on a nice reception, David wanted to know if they would go away from home, and Mary didn't understand what the big deal was and kept asking if they were going to get the presents for Christmas that David had told her.

Ana Dee tried to calm everyone down to no avail until André stood up and said loudly, "Attention, *s'il vous plaît*!" Once there was silence, he pointed at Ana Dee to speak.

She said, "Nothing will change. It will be a simple ceremony in the evening. Only family and those we consider close friends will be attending: Fray Francisco, Hermann and Nadia, André's two uncles, and Sean. So a regular family dinner will be fine, Manuela. I am sure you will have tamales left from the holidays, and that should make the cooking easier. Oh yes, the only difference is that Père André will be living here afterward."

They all sat in silence absorbing the news and afraid of being yelled at by André, except for little Mary, who got up and climbed on her Père's lap to make sure he wasn't angry with her.

In her mind, Manuela was already planning the meal and thinking she was glad she had started sewing a Christmas present/ dress for Ana Dee with the embroidered fabric she got from the Youssefs' store. She only needed to work on a veil to match.

As they got up from the dinner table, everyone was again in good spirits and making plans for the future.

CHAPTER 40

True love is not known for what it
demands, but for what it offers.
—Jacinto Benavente

It had been decided. Teresita, who was thirteen years old, would play the role of the Virgin Mary; and eleven-year-old José, appropriately named, would play Joseph. Little Omar, Nadia's three-month-old nephew, would be little baby Jesus on the last night of the Posadas, to be celebrated at the church hall after midnight Mass. There was less than a month left for the Posada nights to start. The children were now working on a manger stage inside the church's hall. This was a large room between the church and the parish house where Father Murphy resided.

Once into the month of December, Ana Dee and the students worked on their Posadas project. Nadia's wedding reception was also going to take place in the church hall so all decorations had to be appropriate for both events. This caused a bit of chaos. Eventually, the parties compromised on a Christmas wedding theme.

For Nadia's dress, her mother had ordered a beautiful whitework linen from Mexico, a fabric made by nuns whereby selected threads are drawn and pulled from the ground fabric, leaving the rest to be bound and reinforced in decorative stitches, with designs of hearts, flowers, and doves. It was a one-of-a-kind wedding dress worthy of Nadia's diet.

On the afternoon of December 15, Nadia entered the church on Sharif Youssef's arm. Admiring his enchanting bride, Hermann wore a sheepish smile throughout the ceremony, not believing his luck.

Once Ana Dee and André had placed the *lazo* around the wedding couple's shoulders at the proper time during the wedding ceremony, André exhaled, relieved. He had never witnessed a wedding ceremony as elaborate as the Mexican Catholic one. Ana Dee explained to him that they actually got away with one of the easiest sponsorships and to be glad they did not have to come up with the thirteen gold coins for the couple's savings or the wedding rings. She was, of course, kidding him since most of the gifts—seven in this case—were actually provided by the bride and groom who gave them to the sponsors to present during the ceremony.

Ana Dee was exhausted and told André they should leave the reception by eight o'clock because she had to be rested before the hectic schedule of the Posadas the next day.

On the walk home, André told Ana Dee, "That was a nice wedding, perhaps a little complicated and long. You were right in saying that ours was the easiest sponsorship although I would not have minded donating the flowers for the Virgin."

"You are so funny, André. That is always the maiden of honor's responsibility. But you are right, the ceremony was really pretty, but it had too much pomp and symbolic rituals for me. Nadia and Hermann obviously enjoyed that."

"I am so glad that we agree. You and I are simple people, of simple taste, *ma chérie*." He looked at little Mary asleep in Ana Dee's arms as he carried a tired David.

"Yes, very simple." They both laughed softly.

CHAPTER 41

We need to help students and parents
cherish and preserve
the ethnic and cultural diversity that nourishes and
strengthens this community—and this nation.
—Cesar Chavez

The pilgrim parade was to start at 7:00 p.m., but by seven fifteen, the participants were barely arriving at the point of departure. At the head of the entourage, a monk carried a large candle inside a *luminaria* candle bag. The procession followed with Teresita who had on a white tunic covering her large cushion belly and a blue rebozo covering her head. She rode a stubborn donkey that young José pulled with a rope tied to its head. The three other older students wore turbans and finer robes than José's, representing the three wise men; they each carried the make-believe containers of gold, frankincense, and myrrh. The other thirteen children depicted shepherds, angels, and veiled girls carrying poinsettia plants. Little David took his role seriously, walking very straight with his shepherd's cane. The students were followed by a band, some goats, a calf, and about twenty other parishioners, some dressed in period clothes. Most of the pilgrims carried lit candles.

The group stopped to sing the litanies at the first designated home.

They sang the first litany at an unwelcoming home: "*In the name of Heaven, I request you grant us shelter, given that she cannot walk, she my beloved wife.*"

The uninviting home and its family answering sang, "*This is not an inn. Please continue ahead, I cannot open, you may be a robber.*"

The group moved on to a second home and sang, "*In the name of Heaven, I request you grant us shelter since the King of Heaven will prize you for that.*"

The unwelcoming innkeeper answered, "*You can already go away, and do not bother because if I get upset, I will beat you up.*"

And so on. The pilgrims went to different assigned homes singing similar litanies and being refused shelter until the last home of the evening: "*In the name of Heaven, I request you grant us shelter. I am Joseph the carpenter, my wife is Mary.*"

The welcoming inn responded, "*Are you Joseph? Is your wife Mary? Come in, pilgrims. I did not know you.*"

The pilgrims answered, "*May God pay, sirs, your charity, and may Heaven bless you with happiness.*"

The welcoming innkeeper lets them in: "*Joyful be the house that this day hosts the pure virgin, the beautiful Mary.*"

These or similar litanies were sung for nine nights as they visited the different homes. Each night, the home that welcomed the pilgrims served food, drinks, and broke one of the nine piñatas. Once this was done, prayers would be said as the participants sat or stood around a Nativity scene.

On the twenty-fourth of December, the entourage ended at the church hall for the welcoming Posadas festivity. At midnight, almost the whole town attended midnight Mass, after which all the Posadas participants went back to the church hall where Teresita and José sat in the *nacimiento* with little Omar, who portrayed baby Jesus. Music and singing continued until late into the night.

After Ana Dee was praised for the wonderful job her students had done, André dropped her off at her home with her dear ones around two in the morning.

Christmas Day the children were up by eight in the morning, ready to open the presents baby Jesus had left them by their small homemade Nativity scene. When Ana Dee came out in her robe, they begged her to let them open the gifts, but she reminded them Père needed to be there. Mary started screaming in jubilation when she heard the knocking at the front door knowing it was her Père. As soon as he walked in, the children dragged him to where the gifts were laid.

André asked, "Did everybody have breakfast already?"

Manuela said the kids had eaten already, but Ana Dee hadn't and she would be glad to bring him and Ana Dee some breakfast tacos into the sitting room so they could eat while the anxious and impatient children opened their gifts. Acknowledging that the children didn't want to wait for the adults to finish breakfast in the dining area, André thought it was a great idea and went to cuddle on the couch with his fiancée.

The children immediately started opening their presents. They got a porcelain doll, two paper dolls with paper wardrobes, small cast metal soldier figurines, a small cast-iron horse and wagon, and a series of board games.

Manuela and Pedro got lots of different-colored yarn, pieces of fine leather, and craft-making materials for their artistic endeavors.

They were all happy with their presents, but Ana Dee was especially grateful to Manuela for sewing her a beautiful dress she could wear the next day for her nuptials. After noticing Ana Dee's sapphire birthday brooch and finding out what the blue gem meant to her, André gave her a pair of sapphire earrings he had ordered from the town's jeweler. The gesture endeared him so very much she was teary-eyed.

Her gift to him was Descartes' *Passions of the Soul* from her papa's collection. She had dedicated the inside cover" *"A mon amour passionnées selon Descartes: Passions are intrinsically good, and all we have to avoid is their misuse or their excess."* André stared at her and whispered, "You know me so well."

It was a relaxed Christmas Day with the family simply enjoying their gifts and each other. After lunch, they sat around playing board games. The children particularly liked the Mexican *loteria* pictures.

Before André left for the evening, he agreed to bring a suitcase with his belongings the next morning since he would be moving in. Ana Dee could not believe her days as a single independent woman were coming to an end, but she knew she was ready for the next step.

Once André dropped off his personal possessions in her bedroom, she asked him to leave and meet her at the church by seven o'clock. She could not possibly get ready with him in the house, and she also needed to do a contemplation to clear her mind.

He picked up his wedding suit from the bedroom and winked at her. "I will also do a soothing HU this afternoon so that I can be restful for tonight."

CHAPTER 42

I learned with you that there are
new and better emotions.
I learned with you to know a new world of illusions.
—Armando Manzanero

Late in the afternoon, after a relaxing and prolonged bath, Ana Dee put on her new pretty dress, left her hair loose under a lace veil, and wore her new sapphire earrings. The children said she looked like a princess from a fairy tale.

The whole family was dressed in their best attire as they left the house. They met Fray Francisco at the entrance to the church who walked Ana Dee down the aisle toward the altar where André waited surrounded by their friends. Everyone sat down as Fray Francisco placed Ana Dee's hand on André's.

The service was sweet and short. Father Murphy asked them to exchange rings, and they both said, "We already did," to the amusement of those present. Shaking his head, Father Murphy said, "Take them off so we can do this properly." So the couple took the bands off and pronounced the bonding words "with this ring I thee wed" to each other before putting them on under the priest's approving eyes. At the end of the ceremony, André took Ana Dee into his arms and, doing a deep bend down, kissed her unceremoniously until she grabbed hold of his unruly hair curls and pulled them both back up. Everyone clapped.

They all walked back to Ana Dee's house, now the Fournier home, together. André's uncles, Pierre and Louis, had never visited the house before although they had seen the inside of the clinic, being the apothecaries who provided the medicines to it.

The uncles admired the interior courtyard with the small mesquite tree and the large flowerpots. Pedro had decorated the place with decorative *luminarias*. The children pulled out their Christmas presents to show their guests while the food was served buffet-style since there were not enough sitting places at the dining table. By ten o'clock, all the guests had left. Ana Dee and André tucked the children in bed. The kids were so tired they didn't even ask Ana Dee to read them bedtime stories like they were accustomed to.

Now alone, the couple walked hand in hand to their now shared bedroom. They entered the room each carrying their chamberstick candleholders, which they placed on their corresponding nightstands. Ana Dee went behind the side screen to change into her nightgown. When she came out, André was already in bed under the covers waiting for her. Ana Dee got in bed and blew out her candle. She asked, "Aren't you going to blow out your candle, André?"

André answered, "I want to see you, my beautiful bride."

She said, "Please, André, blow it out."

"Why?" he asked.

Ana Dee covered her face. "I am embarrassed."

After a few seconds of staring at his wife, André pulled her hands away from her face, kissed them, and blew out his candle. "You needn't be shy, ma chérie, we are finally married. But I don't need my eyes to see you."

As he reached his hand out for her, she drew closer to him; and finding his lips, they yielded to the entwining dance of lovemaking.

The Christmas days off were a gift to the young couple. They were able to have some time to adjust to each other's daily habits before retiring to their honeymooning nights.

Accompanied by the children, they took rides in the buggy carriage pulled by Lumen. They rode around the town and around the surrounding countryside. They made crafts under Pedro's directions, who also took the opportunity to show them steps to the Adai Caddo rain prayer dance. The whole family got involved in milking the goats and making cheese. Every day was a new adventure.

CHAPTER 43

We all have a duty of love to fulfill, a
story to do, a goal to achieve.
—Gioconda Belli

After sharing dinner one evening, they sat in the living room where André was teaching Ana Dee to play chess.

"André, we should invite your uncles for dinner sometime this week before school starts again."

"They were just here for our wedding, ma chérie."

"Yes, but we really haven't socialized much with them. I would like the children to get to know their granduncles better."

"Fine. How is tomorrow evening? Do you think Manuela won't mind cooking?"

"Actually, I was thinking of cooking myself anyway."

"You are such a good homemaker! I will stop by tomorrow morning and invite them."

"You resemble your uncle Louis—you know, your eyes, bushy hair, general features."

"They did name me after him: Louis André Fournier. I never liked that name. I prefer André because there are too many Louises in the family."

"Uncle Pierre, however, does not look at all like his brother."

"Why should he? He isn't a Fournier."

"What do you mean? They had a different father?"

"No, sweetheart, they are partners."

"I know that—of the apothecary."

"No, love partners."

"You mean . . . Oh. Everyone in town thinks they are brothers."

"You are so naive. People know. They just don't say anything because it is not socially accepted. In my country, that practice between consenting adults was decriminalized in 1791. I hope you still want them over."

"Of course. Mama Catherine explained to me that type of intimate relationship a long time ago. She has a male cousin who is attracted to other males. She never believed her cousin was sick like the doctor said. Papa explained to us that that practice is openly accepted in some cultures, and people are just born with such preference. Part of one's learning experience, or karma, you could say."

"I wish I had met your parents, Ana Dee. Their open-mindedness is the reason you grew to be what you are, such a caring and broad-minded human being."

"Your parents must have been broad-minded as well. You are a very tolerant, caring, and accepting person, André. Those are some of the traits I love about you. The more I know you, the more I feel that we are kindred souls. I dare say that we would love each other in this life even if we had been born of the same sex."

"I'll have to think about that one. Right now, I am happy that I am a man married to such a beautiful woman."

CHAPTER 44

Friendship is the salt of life.
—Juan Luis Vives

The nights felt chilly to the locals in January of 1849. There was no actual promenading during the colder season. To André and Hermann, however, they seemed perfect for strolling; and both insisted on going to the plaza on the weekends. Ana Dee and Nadia had no choice but to bundle themselves up a couple of Saturdays and venture into the cold breeze to please their husbands. After the second time they took a cold stroll, the husbands felt sorry for their wives, and André suggested visiting inside the Fourniers' courtyard where the ladies sat close to the grand old clay potbelly *chimenea* that burned mesquite logs. Much to the ladies' enjoyment, that became the norm throughout the winter. It also pleased the husbands who were then able to share a periodic glass of imported wine. Ana Dee, who didn't drink alcohol, and Nadia, who was not used to it, drank nice cups of hot Mexican chocolate with cinnamon sticks.

Evening promenades didn't pick up again until March.

Life continued in the little town of Santo Tomás as to the surprise of most, Nadia gave birth to a premature but quite healthy baby in June.

Hermann was very proud of his little Hans Ali Meyer. Nadia brought him to the clinic during her work hours, but her mother put a stop to that. Nadia said her mother was already busy with her other grandson, little Omar, but her mother claimed that Omar was old enough for his own mother to take care of him. Believing the first months were the most important in Hans Ali's care, the pampering grandmother insisted on watching the infant. She brought him to the clinic for Nadia to breastfeed every three to four hours. The baby's comings and goings turned out to be somewhat disruptive to the running of Hermann's medical practice so they arranged with Manuela for Nadia to go into the house side to feed the baby.

During one of those half hours Nadia was gone, André stopped by to bring Hermann some supplies. There were no patients, and the young men were able to speak privately.

"The baby's schedule is wearing me out. Nadia is in and out of the clinic all day, and we hardly sleep at night. We haven't even been intimate in months, which is good because I don't think I could handle a second child right now."

"*Mon Dieu, mon ami*, you can use *condons*, you know! We have some made from lamb intestines at the apothecary. They are quite comfortable and feel most natural."

"*Bitte*! Frenchie, to use those things is against the Christian teachings."

"*Incroyable*, Hermann! Are you a fanatic? Other choices are not very reliable, comfortable, or convenient."

"You are right there. I might just think about it. I'll consult with Nadia and see what she thinks, *ja*. How reliable are those things?"

"If used properly, quite good."

"Are you using them yourself?"

"Hermann, shame on you. You know the honor man's code: don't kiss and tell." And he walked out.

Of course, he confided their friend's situation to Ana Dee, and she immediately reprimanded him.

"I would think that their decision on this private matter is none of our business, André. Hermann is very devoted to his religious principles, and you shouldn't criticize him or interfere. We have to respect one another's spiritual paths."

"But, my love, he brought it up. I was just giving him scientific information."

"André, he's a doctor, you know."

"And I am a medical professional who makes his medicines and apparently knows more about remedies than he does."

"I never knew you to possess such vanity!"

"How can you call me vain when you know it's a matter of experience? I do have more experience in that area than he does. I bet Dr. Moore would have agreed with me."

"I supposed that he would consider Hermann to be inflexible as far as his religious beliefs."

"Exactly. Can you imagine yourself in Nadia's place?"

"But I am not. I chose not to be, remember? I am sure she agrees with him. That's why they make such a good couple."

"We'll see."

"Now that we are on the subject, don't we want to have children sometime in the near future? Why are we avoiding it?"

"I guess we haven't discussed that possibility."

"No, we haven't. So what do you want?"

"We already have two youngsters. I figured we could wait. I would like to take you to Galveston next summer for your twenty-first birthday. It would take us over a week to go and come back. So we would be away for two to three weeks. The children will be old enough to stay with Manuela and Pedro then. If we had a baby, we would have to wait years to be able to travel."

"When were you planning to share your plans with me?"

"I wanted to surprise you. You don't like the idea?"

"I'm not sure. I would love to take a vacation just the two of us, though I don't know if it's wise to be gone so long."

"Think about it, ma chérie. It would be like a *voyage à la façon anglaise* we haven't had."

CHAPTER 45

Before you speak, ask yourself if
what you are going to say
is true, is kind, is necessary, is helpful.
If the answer is no, maybe what you are
about to say should be left unsaid.

—Bernard Meltzer

With school back in session, Ana Dee stayed home Saturday afternoon working on her lesson plans while André took the children to the plaza to play with their friends. He was sitting on a bench watching the kids running around the gazebo when he saw a couple sit on the bench across from him. He noticed that the young woman had an uncanny resemblance to his little Mary.

He started to panic thinking he should grab the children and slyly rush back home. Then he thought of Ana Dee's disapproval and knew what she would want him to do. He took a deep breath, walked across to the couple, and introduced himself. "Good afternoon. I am André Fournier, from the apothecary. I haven't seen you around town and wanted to welcome you to Santo Tomás." He extended his hand to the gentleman. Shaking his hand, the newcomer introduced himself as Edward Smith and his wife, Camille.

André then asked what brought them to town. Mr. Smith explained he was in the army and headed for the border fort (later named Camp Crawford and subsequently Fort McIntosh) to guard the Texas frontier. The river crossing in Laredo was a strategic one.

When he asked if they had family here, Camille said she had lost everyone to cholera except for her little sister. With apprehension, André then asked where her sister was. Camille said she had traveled to Texas with Edward's parents on their way to Laredo about a year ago. But they stopped receiving letters from his parents. They had inquired with different stagecoach companies about the older couple and a little girl, but they weren't very helpful. From what they understood, the stagecoach companies could not guarantee a safe trip because they were often attacked on the road.

By this time, André was convinced Mary was Camille's little sister and wondered how to approach the situation. It wasn't long before little Mary came running to him and said, "Père, David won't let me play with them because I don't know the snake game. I want to play, Père."

André picked her up, and as she buried her head on his shoulder, he saw Camille's baffled expression. He said, "We need to talk. Would you care to follow us to our home?"

He turned to call David who came running and tried to explain that Mary was not abiding by the rules of the game. Père interrupted him, "Never mind that. That's not why we are going home."

André walked to the house with the children, followed by the wide-eyed couple. As soon as Ana Dee saw Camille, she stopped working on her school plans and invited the couple to sit in the living room. She could tell how upset André was and asked him to take the children to the kitchen with Manuela.

Ana Dee introduced herself to Camille and Edward and told them how they came upon little Mary the previous year. She explained how they had tried to find out who the little girl belonged to without any luck.

André came back to the living room with the guardianship papers. As he showed the papers to Camille, he explained how many children had been abandoned because of Indian raids and others left orphaned by the war. He further explained that the families in Santo Tomás were used to taking in the deserted youths because they did not have an orphanage in town.

Camille seemed confused and stared at the papers André was showing them. Somewhat baffled, Edward exclaimed, "My parents must have been killed. They would never have abandoned the child. Did you hear anything about an attacked stagecoach?"

André could not wait any longer and asked, "What do you intend on doing?"

Ana Dee took his hand in hers. "Sweetheart, this is too much for them. You need to realize that he just found out about his parents' probable death. We need to give them some time to digest it all." She turned to the couple and said, "We probably should go talk to Father Murphy. He might have some information that we don't know about."

Camille said, "Yes, please. We need to calm down and process the situation. If you could take us to the priest, I would be most obliged."

Ana Dee was puzzled by Camille's reaction and asked herself, *Why didn't she ask to talk to Mary?*

Father Murphy was getting ready for the evening Mass and told them he only had a few minutes. When Ana Dee explained who the couple was, he gave Camille a quizzical stare and furrowing his forehead said, "I am sure Ana Dee has told you everything we know. You certainly look like little Mary, but you would have to prove the relationship if you want to remove the child from her now perfect home."

To everyone's surprise, Camille said, "We have no such intention. We merely want to know what happened. If Edward's parents were killed and didn't make it here, who brought Mary to this town?"

André turned to Ana Dee, and she could see he was holding back an exclamation of joy. She felt relief as well upon hearing Camille's words, but was perplexed by her attitude and unsure as to her intentions.

Impatiently, Father Murphy explained he had no more information. An older couple had not arrived in Santo Tomás when the child had appeared. For all he knew, the stagecoach drivers abandoned the child at the plaza expecting someone would take her in. He suspected Edward's parents had died on the way before reaching Santo Tomás. It was all speculation, but he had no other explanation. In any case, Father Murphy had to get ready for Mass and excused himself.

Ana Dee asked the couple if they were staying at Andersons' inn and how long they planned to stay because she wanted to invite them for dinner the next evening. Edward said they would gladly accept the invitation since they had a couple of days before the next stagecoach left for Laredo.

On the walk back home, André told Ana Dee that if Camille went with them to the notary and relinquished her rights as Mary's sister, they could now obtain permanent guardianship of little Mary. More cautious by nature, Ana Dee was not celebrating yet. Camille's behavior puzzled her.

The next evening, they were ready to welcome Mary's relatives. They told Mary her sister was coming and she could visit with her for a while.

To everyone's surprise, Edward Smith came by himself. André had a hard time hiding his consternation. Edward hastened to explain she was not feeling well.

Everyone proceeded to the dining room, and little Mary asked when she would be seeing her sister. Mr. Smith looked at the child and said, "We'll see how she feels tomorrow. But I can tell you a little about your family if you like. My parents raised you before you came to live here. Do you remember them?"

Vaguely remembering an older couple, Mary asked, "Where are they?"

André ventured to say, "They went home after they left you with me." That seemed to appease the child, and the conversation at the dinner table changed to Edward's family hometown—Dandridge, Tennessee.

Once dinner was over, the children were excused, and the adults remained in the dining room drinking coffee. Ana Dee asked, "Now that Mary has gone to her room, would you please explain Camille's lack of interest in her sister?"

André was taken aback by his wife's tactless manner, so unusual for her. He realized she was just as dismayed as he was.

Mr. Smith too was up front. "Camille's parents didn't die of cholera. Mary is a thorn in Camille's life. When she was born, Camille was twelve years old. Their mother died in childbirth. Shortly thereafter, their father committed suicide. Camille's mother was my mother's distant cousin and only living relative. Hence, my parents took the girls in.

"Camille blamed Mary for losing her parents. When I came home on furlough last year, Camille and I fell in love and got married. My parents decided to travel to Laredo and find a home to be close to us once I was assigned to the border camp in Laredo.

"I have a paper here that Camille wrote, which should facilitate your guardianship of her sister."

André took the paper and read it aloud.

> *I, Camille Smith, maiden name Taylor, am the sister of Mary Lee Taylor, who was born in Jonesborough, Tennessee, on May 21, 1843. I hereby relinquish all guardianship rights of Mary Lee Taylor to Mr. and Mrs. André Fournier.*
>
> *Camille Smith*
> *20 of September of 1848*

After hearing it, Ana Dee asked Mr. Smith if Camille could stop by the alcaldia the next morning to have the paper recorded. Edward didn't think Camille would object and, after getting directions to the town government offices, agreed to meet them there at eight o'clock the next morning.

The two couples met at the alcaldia as planned, and all signed the papers for their proper recording. Ana Dee had to go to her school afterward, but André invited the couple to join him at Guadalupe's Cafe for breakfast.

Edward promised to write to André once they were established in Laredo. He felt they needed to keep in contact for little Mary's sake. Camille did not contribute much to the conversation. As they parted ways, she did, however, thank André for providing such a loving home for her sister. André thanked them both and wished them a safe trip.

CHAPTER 46

*Magic is a bridge that allows you to go
from the visible to the invisible world. And
learn the lessons from both worlds.*
— Paulo Coelho

André went back to the alcaldia and talked to the in-house *notario*, Mr. Carlisle. He discussed with André what the possibility of adoption was. When Ana Dee got home, André explained to her that because he was over twenty-five, as a couple, they now could adopt the children by signing a "private bill," basically a "last will and testament" naming the children their legal heirs. André wanted to do it before they left on their trip to Galveston. Ana Dee said it was a good idea even if they didn't go on the trip.

That week, the Fourniers officially became a family of four.

As they promenaded around the plaza that October evening, the young family enjoyed the wild sunflowers in bloom. The plaza was nicely decorated for the feast of Our Lady of the Rosary weekend. The vendors carried little wooden figurines of saints and mangers, mother-of-pearl embossed missals, religious relics, and of course, rosaries made of different kinds of materials like silver, gold, and semiprecious stones.

There were also some wooden toys that attracted the children. After much begging, Mary and David both got a little wooden figurine for their manger. Preparing the Nativity scene was one of the family activities popular in Santo Tomás. Every year, some new addition was made to it, and they competed for the prettiest and most realistic manger set. The Fourniers supported their children's endeavor in building their little manger but left the decorations entirely up to them, so the figurines were mostly of little animals.

As they strolled around the plaza, André asked his wife, "Are you happy, love?"

"How could I not be? I have the best husband and children I could ever imagine."

"I don't think I ever told you, but the first time I saw you, I tried to avoid looking at you because it felt as if you put a spell on me."

"You mean when I walked into the church?"

"No, at the alcaldia. I saw you as I was leaving. You were sitting down waiting for your turn to talk to the regidores, and Fray Francisco was standing behind you."

"Fray Francisco was with me? I don't recall him being there."

"I remember well because I wondered why he stood behind you when there were plenty of empty seats. I thought 'if there are angels on earth, you must be one.'"

"I knew you needed help, mon chérie." Although she was sure the monk was not with her on the day in question, she didn't want to reveal Fray Francisco's bilocation abilities to André. She didn't want him to think she was trying to promote her spiritual teachings.

"By the way, I haven't seen Fray Francisco lately. Didn't you have class planned for last month?"

"He is not in town right now. Sometimes his duties take him to other places, and he might be gone for months at a time."

"He is an odd one. I like him nonetheless. He seems to care for you as if you were his child."

"My padrino is very dear to me, André. Like a father figure, you know."

"I understand there is a strong spiritual connection between you. I know he has been your constant base of support through all the losses you have suffered. Ana Dee, I admire how you look at what life has given you instead of what it has taken away. You always look at the positive side of things, and I know it has to do with your spiritual path."

After their promenade, they went home, and she went to the library to do her daily meditation. André stayed with the children, helping them set up a stand for their religious figurines. When Ana Dee came back from the library, they put the children to bed and sat by the chimenea drinking warm tea.

"I should follow your example and do the HU chant more often. It does relax me."

"I didn't know you were under stress, my love."

"Not stress, more like concern. I keep thinking of the revolutions ravaging my native home. I imagine my relatives suffering the consequences. There has been unrest all over Europe. Hermann is also concerned about his relatives. It seems like we go from one political upheaval to another. Just as our war with Mexico was over at the beginning of this year, the revolts in Europe started. Many of my compatriots are coming to this new land escaping hardships of the Old World."

"There is actually a gold rush headed for California, which probably seems like mana to those immigrants. I didn't think you had much family left in France, André."

"I still have some distant relatives in Paris. My relatives aren't poor by any means and decided to wait for things to get better. But being well off hasn't made much difference. Everyone is affected by the revolts. I am glad I cashed in my investments, took my capital, and left when I did."

"You've told me before that you left because you sensed what was coming."

"Ma chérie, I think you were calling me from afar. I was wandering aimlessly without a purpose until we crossed paths."

"I know you are joking now, but it's possible. This town, André, was calling you. It is a tranquil oasis in the midst of chaos."

"You have never been out of Santo Tomás and have nothing to compare it to, yet you understand its worth. You know more about life's true values than someone who has traveled the world."

"I did learn a lot about other places in the world with Papa, you know. I don't think our little town can escape the outside influences headed our way. You know Mama's letters always have information on current events and how the world is becoming smaller. Perhaps it is time that I experience other places to prepare for the future. I have been meaning to tell you I will go with you to Galveston next summer."

"Ana Dee, that's great news! I can't wait."

"I feel better now about leaving the children since we prepared our wills. Besides, you are right—we haven't spent much time together, just the two of us."

"Most couples start that way. We had a built-in family before we married. And yet, no matter who is or what happens around us, I feel at peace when you are with me. Ma chérie, you mean so much to me."

"*Cariño*, sharing our lives makes me happy. I think I am strong and can manage on my own, but truth be told, I feel safer with you by my side."

Christmas holidays were coming up. All the preparations for the Posadas festivities were ready. Ana Dee and André were strolling by themselves when they came across Nadia and Hermann.

"Well, if it isn't the Meyer couple with their young offspring."

"Good evening to you too, André."

"We haven't seen you promenading in a while."

"Can you believe little Hans Ali is sleeping through the night, allowing us to rest? So we can enjoy our time off work."

"It's so good to see you strolling. May I hold little Hans?" Ana Dee picked up the baby from Nadia, and they walked together with their husbands following behind.

"Carrying the baby suits you, Ana Dee. I thought that you would be expecting one of your own by now. Look how my baby loves how you rock him."

"I would love to have a baby, but André wants to wait until next fall so we can enjoy our trip this coming year."

"How can you be so sure of not conceiving? I don't imagine you are abstaining."

"I don't believe that is in André's vocabulary." They both laughed at her comment while the men wondered what was so funny.

"Seriously, how are you doing it? I have been trying the pessary of gum arabica, but I am afraid I am pregnant again. I asked Rosa, the *curandera*, you know, the old woman healer, about some herbs to prevent pregnancy; but she wanted to give me one to get rid of a pregnancy. I could never do that."

"So you think you are pregnant, Nadia? How do you and Hermann feel about another baby so soon?"

"I suppose it's a joy and a burden at the same time. Honestly, what method are you and André using?"

"I am pretty sure André talked to Hermann about it. You know André and I are not as religious as you are. You might still want to discuss it with Hermann."

André approached his wife just in time, thought Ana Dee, and asked if he could hold little Hans for a while. The baby smiled at André and snuggled up against his chest.

Tilting her head in admiration, Nadia said, "He loves Uncle André."

Hermann squinted his eyes and added, "You should have a baby, André. Children love you."

"Right now, yours will do, Hermann." He held up the baby. "Tell them you agree with your uncle André, Hansali." To everyone's glee, the baby let out a big burp and laughed. Ana Dee couldn't help but look adoringly at the picture of her husband cuddling little Hans.

As it turned out, to Nadia's relief, she was not pregnant at the time. She and Hermann had a serious talk about the topic and must have come to some kind of solution because for a while, they avoided another pregnancy.

The holidays went by without much change. Letters came from Catherine and Elizabeth telling of their new home and of James's new position in the navy. His new schedule allowed for more time with his family. Catherine found a nursing job, and little Billy was now in school.

CHAPTER 47

Do not dwell in the past, do not dream of the future,
concentrate the mind on the present moment.
—Buddha

By the new year, 1849, the California gold rush was in full swing, bringing immigrants from all parts of the globe promoting the westward movement of population to territories ceded by Mexico to the United States as per the Treaty of Guadalupe Hidalgo in July 1848—Texas, New Mexico, Colorado, Nevada, Utah, parts of Arizona, and California. Mexican citizens in Texas then had to decide if they would become United States citizens.

In Santo Tomás, school was back in session, and Ana Dee had three more students register for the new year. Expecting the fall registration to be even higher, the councilmen were considering renting one of the houses facing the plaza and turning it into Santo Tomás Public School. It also meant hiring a second teacher. Fortunately, a few tutors in town regularly hired by the wealthier families for their children were available. The councilmen appointed Ana Dee to help in the selection of the new teacher from the experienced tutors. She was excited at the prospect and started planning the division of students into two groups by age and learning levels.

Meanwhile, André was making preparations for their trip to Galveston. Mary and David were not so happy about it, so André talked to Pedro about giving the children lessons on the different art crafts during the summer to keep them occupied. He also convinced Nadia to bring Hansali to play with the kids daily during the time he and Ana Dee were gone. Little Mary loved to play with baby Hansali. After André started blending the two names Hans and Ali, it became popular. Nadia thought it was cute, in spite of Hermann's disapproval, who thought, "Leave it to a Frenchman to use French in English."

Ana Dee's concerns about her trip were alleviated by the fact that Fray Francisco was back in town and promised to visit the household daily and help with its needs. He had been with the masters of his spiritual path at the remote monastery in Kulkanzin, Mexico, sharing information of their service around the world with students of the teachings who resided in the monastery, Colegio de Teología de Kulkanzin, until they were ready to go onto mainstream life and serve mankind.

Fray Francisco remembered when he took Robert Hughes, then around five years old, to live and study at the monastery. His parents, a Protestant missionary couple, had lost their lives at the hands of religious fanatics. The orphan child had been hidden by an old indigenous woman who was a disciple of Fray Francisco's spiritual path. When little Robert met Fray Francisco, he immediately recognized him as his spiritual teacher since the monk had visited him in his dreams.

After eleven peaceful years living in Kulkanzin, Robert came back to Tejas, where he had been born, with Fray Francisco. He had a mission then, to protect the innocent from the rages of raiding and warfare. To better help his people, he went into the lion's den itself by joining the Texas Rangers.

Fray Francisco felt the same responsibility for Ana Dee as he did for Robert. He was her spiritual adviser. Before she departed to Galveston, he sought a private moment to talk to her. "Your life seems to be going well with Louis André Fournier. I find you in better spirits. I thought you would never get over my protégé."

"I must admit that my heart was torn for a while. Thoughts of Robert always saddened me. I found myself crying over his memory, whereas Louis André makes me smile. He brings joy to my heart. I chose to be happy. Isn't Soul supposed to be happy?"

"You are right, mija. Contentment is a virtue and a blessing. In your travels, always know that I am with you spiritually and remember that whatever happens in this life is simply part of your greater spiritual journey."

CHAPTER 48

If you don't climb the mountain, you will
never be able to enjoy the landscape.
—Pablo Neruda

Ana Dee and André decided not to take much luggage since they would need the space for the many things they planned to buy in Galveston. When the day of their departure arrived, they left the house at the crack of dawn, having said their goodbyes the night before. Manuela had insisted they eat breakfast before leaving and was the last one to wish them a good journey.

They picked up the Celerity wagon, pulled by four mules, in front of Andersons' pensión, which was to take them to San Antonio.

Two men sat inside the stagecoach across from them: a rough-looking cowboy and an elderly, slightly better-dressed man wearing a vest with a gold pocket watch. André leaned close to Ana Dee's ear and asked, "Did you put the small pistol I gave you in your handbag?"

She answered in a soft voice, "Yes, but you know my aim. You think I'll protect you, but I might end up shooting you! Besides you are already carrying your Aston."

André laughed and looked at the pair of passengers in front of them. He introduced himself and added, "This is my wife, Ana Dee. It's her first trip outside of Santo Tomás."

The older gentleman shook André's hand and introduced himself, "Henry Smith at your service." Then looking at Ana Dee, he added, "It's a rough trip, little lady. Don't worry, we will be below the dangerous Indian territory, the *Comancheria*. Between here and San Antonio, there are rarely any raids. In any case, we are prepared."

Mr. Smith looked back at André. "I am headed for Helotes where my vaqueros will be moving cattle back to the ranch. My *hombre* here"—he pointed to the man next to him—"Gabriel, is not a big talker." The cowboy nodded his head to acknowledge the couple. "But he is a great sharpshooter. He always travels with me when I carry my cattle-purchasing hard cash."

Ana Dee whispered under her breath, "So we might get attacked by bandits instead of Indians!"

André took her hand and held it tightly. He kissed it and said, "Monsieur Smith, please, you are scaring my bride."

Mr. Smith exclaimed, "Oh, so you are newlyweds! How nice. Where are you headed?"

Ana Dee looked lovingly at her husband. "We are not really newlyweds. But you could say we are still on our honeymoon. We plan to travel all the way to Galveston. San Antonio will be a nice stop, though. We do want to tour the town, right, André?"

Mr. Smith warned, "Oh, you shouldn't risk it. The cholera has been spreading there this year. Besides, the town is not what it used to be. Why, with all the raids and wars and now the cholera, San Antonio's population has been greatly reduced."

André asked, "It seems you travel this route often. How do you avoid contracting the disease?"

Mr. Smith explained, "Once we reach the stagecoach stop for the Matamoros route, I switch to the north route to reach Old Houston Road, which will take me to Helotes, avoiding the town. The coach will make a stop at the Pajalache Mill. From there, y'all should continue west to Seguin, where the accommodations are better at the Magnolia Hotel."

André smiled at Ana Dee and thanked Mr. Smith. "I appreciate the information. We are glad to be traveling with a person as knowledgeable of the area as you are."

They moved through the countryside for five hours before coming to an unmanned water hole stop. The terrain was arid with spots of amber florae, except for the prickly pears of red, purple, and yellow blooms of the nopales cacti. They got out and stretched their legs, refreshed themselves, and got coffee, all in about fifteen minutes. Mr. Smith and his vaquero went behind an adobe wall to relieve themselves and then asked if Ana Dee and André wanted to do the same. Once they were all done, the group got back on the Celerity wagon and rode for six more hours before coming to the Pajalache Mill in San Antonio. Ana Dee and André bade farewell to Mr. Henry Smith and Gabriel and then were fortunate to obtain passage to Seguin in the next Concord stagecoach leaving that afternoon.

This time, four other people traveled with them, and although the coach was bigger than the previous one and was more attractive inside and outside, it was slightly cramped. The one advantage was this stagecoach was being pulled by six horses; it would make the trip in less time.

Ana Dee got into the carriage first and sat next to the window so André could sit between her and another passenger. The other four riders were all males. Three of them dressed in the regular western outfits but the older gentleman, sitting across from Ana Dee, wore a Brummell style suit, riding boots and a regency top hat.

In the dim light, the older gentleman boldly stared at Ana Dee, eliciting André's reaction of extending his arm around his wife's shoulders in a protective and possessive manner.

Ana Dee felt her husband's discomfort and tried to ease it. "André, this is going to be a seven to eight-hour-long trip. We should introduce ourselves to the rest of the riders."

André replied, "It's almost midnight, dear. These gentlemen are probably tired and sleepy. *Ne les dérange pas.*"

The man in the suit exclaimed, *"Tu es Français!* My name is Emilio Galvez Alcazar at your service." He extended his hand to André.

André was too polite not to respond, so while still frowning, he shook Mr. Galvez's hand, introducing himself and Ana Dee. He then asked, "May I ask where you are from?"

The gentleman answered, "I am from Spain. I came to Galveston from Veracruz, Mexico, by ship. I thought I would check out San Antonio as well. I am on my way back to Spain."

Ana Dee couldn't help but say, "Mis abuelitos eran Españoles."

Emilio Galvez smiled and said, *"Claro.* I knew that your beauty had to be *de sangre Española."*

Ana Dee blushed and turned to see if André understood what Don Emilio had said. From his solemn appearance, she knew he got the gist of it. She said, "If you would like to turn off the lantern, I think I am ready to nap now."

André stared at the gentleman across from them and with a warning look said, *"Buenas noches,"* as he put out the flame.

They arrived at the Magnolia Stagecoach Home Station in the early morning hours. The Spaniard hurriedly got off and extended his hand to help Ana Dee get out of the coach. Half asleep, she accepted his help and as they entered the hotel were directed to the breakfast dining area. Although André did not appreciate the Spaniard's attention toward Ana Dee, he let them go ahead of him. André knew he needed to check on the accommodations first and foremost so they could stay comfortably in the town until the next stagecoach to Houston made its appearance in Seguin. Otherwise, they would need to continue their journey after breakfast in the same uncomfortable basswood curved-body Concord coach they had arrived in. So he let his wife go on to breakfast and went to secure their lodging for the day.

Once he got the last room available—at the time, the Magnolia Hotel consisted of only three rooms—he went back out to the stagecoach to unload their trunk. By this time, Ana Dee was wondering what happened to him, but she was starving. After Don

Emilio assisted her with a heavy pitcher to cleanse their hands at the washstand, she allowed him to sit next to her.

By the time André came for breakfast, Ana Dee and Don Emilio were enjoying a lively conversation in Spanish and enjoying fresh bolillos with *huevos revueltos con jalapeños*. André sat across from them, politely bearing it. He asked the waitress to bring him tortillas instead of bread rolls.

Don Emilio commented, "I much prefer bread to tortillas. You know, in Spain, tortilla means omelet."

André replied, "I prefer the Mexican flavor cuisine myself," and shared a loving smile with his wife.

As they were finishing their breakfast, the stagecoach driver came in to announce its departure. André looked at the Spaniard and asked if he was not leaving. Don Emilio sat twirling the ends of his handlebar gray mustache and said, "Oh no. I am spending the night here at a boardinghouse around the corner. I will be here until the next stagecoach going to Houston comes in a couple of days."

André couldn't figure out how the Spaniard had made his arrangements so fast, so he questioned him, "How did you manage your reservations in town?"

Seeming very pleased with himself, Don Emilio Galvez Alcazar answered, "I spoke to the coach drivers before leaving San Antonio. One of them knew Seguin well and offered to help me when we got here—for monetary compensation, of course. Anyway, he will be back with my information before the coach takes off to Houston."

Sure enough, the coach driver approached Don Emilio at that moment and informed him that his luggage had been taken to the boardinghouse and gave him the directions to it.

André stood up, took Ana Dee's hand, and said, "Let's go to our room and rest before taking a walk around town."

She answered, "Good idea." She excused herself with Don Emilio, who also stood up and, bending over, quoted Antonio Ros de Olano as farewell: "*Musa de mi dolor . . . tuyo es mi canto . . . Solo el suspiro que te mando es mio.*"

Ana Dee felt André's grip tighten around her arm and without saying another word walked away with him, afraid to look up at his face.

Their good-sized private room was in the back of the property. It had a comfortable double bed; a washstand with towel racks holding the ceramic basin bowl and two water-filled ceramic pitchers, two ceramic chamber pots, which the servants emptied daily, with lids; a nice dresser; and a good-size armoire.

Ana Dee entered the room and sat on a Windsor-style chair next to the window. She waited for André to cool off before saying anything.

André sat on the bed, took off his shoes, and lay down. He asked, "Aren't you going to lie down for a little while?"

She answered, "I am not sure it's safe."

"Why? You don't really think I would hurt you!? I might have wanted to slap Galvez's face, but never you. Besides, I didn't really understand what he said, except that you are his Musa or Muse. Ridiculous old man!"

Ana Dee laughed, then taking off her shoes, slipped into the bed with her husband. "I don't know whether I like your jealousy or not. I certainly don't want you to get into a fight over it. Besides, you know that I love only you. How can you doubt that I am yours mind and soul, just yours?"

"If that's so"—he opened his arms—"then may I have the pleasure of your mind and soul?"

"You may."

By the afternoon, the young couple was ready to take a walk around town.

"The lady at the registration informed me that we are only a block away from the center of town, where there is a courthouse and a central park."

"I hope we can find a nice restaurant as well."

They crossed Crockett, the street in front of the Magnolia Hotel, and walked one block down Center Street. The concrete courthouse building was on the block to their right, and the public square was to the left on the block facing it.

"Isn't it interesting that the center of town has a courthouse instead of a church like we have in Santo Tomás?"

"America believes in a secular government, ma chérie. The rule of law is most important. Besides, it was founded on the principle of religious freedom, and no one church is supposed to be the center of the community."

"I do appreciate that concept. I am just noticing the differences. I don't see many Tejanos here, you know, like me of Spanish and Mexican descent. The little we saw of San Antonio was more like home. Here they are mostly immigrants from the North—White and Negro."

"We might find some good Mexican food, though. Let's stroll around the center and find a restaurant. After that, we can check out the park."

They passed a barbershop, a general store, and a butcher shop before finding a small Mexican restaurant. They were seated and reading the day's menu when Don Emilio Galvez walked in.

"Well, if it isn't the lovebirds! May I join you?"

André was about to say who knows what when Ana Dee kicked him under the table and, smiling, said, "Please do. Perhaps you can enlighten us about the town's history."

To André's surprise, Don Emilio sat across from Ana Dee and next to André on the four-place square table. André would have thought Don Emilio would prefer to sit next to Ana Dee, but then again, he had a better view across from her.

"I don't really know much about the history, but I am really impressed with all the concrete construction in town. I found out that the community was originally called Walnut Springs and founded by a group of Texas Rangers. With the troops here, more settlers came, feeling it was more secure."

The waitress brought Don Emilio a menu.

"I had the nopales tacos here before when I stopped on our way to San Antonio. I can vouch for them. *Pero bueno* . . . I am sure you've had those before."

"What did you think of San Antonio? We were told to avoid it because of the cholera outbreak."

"Yes, my timing was most unfortunate. They were apparently coming out of it when I first got there about three days ago, but I did shorten my trip. I barely got to see the Alamo and the *Concepción/ Pajalache Acequia*. Of course, the aqueduct does not compare with the Roman aqueducts, like the one we have in Segovia. I did appreciate the town's Spanish heritage, though."

André began to feel more comfortable with "the ridiculous old man" and asked him, "You never told us what was your interest in coming to Galveston, Mr. Galvez."

"I actually had business dealings in Veracruz. Once there, it would have been a pity not to come the extra mile and visit Galveston. As a relative of Bernardo de Galvez, viceroy of New Spain, the viscount of Gálveztown and count of Galvez, I always wanted to visit the town named after him."

Excitedly, Ana Dee said, "Yes, Galveston was named after him, a hero of the American Revolution for independence. He assisted the American revolutionaries with supplies and soldiers. He freed the lower Mississippi Valley of British forces and relieved the threat to New Orleans, their main port of entry. The United States would not have won the war against the British without his help, as per my papa's words."

"I am impressed by your knowledge of history, Señora Fournier!"

"Thank you, my parents taught me about your ancestors' contribution."

"You have made my wife a fan. She is a history *fanatique*."

After their tasty meal, the three tourists toured Seguin's downtown. André bought a bag of pecans at the general store and afterward suggested they sit on a bench at the park to enjoy the view. Don Emilio said his goodbyes and walked over to the barbershop to trim his carefully manicured handlebar *moustache*.

"Cariño, I wonder how you would look with a *moustache*!"

"Horrible! Well, possibly a goatee?"

The following day, the Fourniers were able to catch a large-size Concord stagecoach going to Houston, with a couple of waterhole stops and the home station stop in Columbus. This track of the trip took approximately thirty-seven hours. It was a strenuously long stretch, but they were anxious to get to Galveston and did not want to make any more overnight stops. By the time they arrived in Houston, they had eaten some pinto beans, bread, and coffee at a couple of water stops after their meager meal in Columbus. Beans were the staple cowboy meal, as long as they weren't in their chili.

Upon arriving at the Houston port, the Fourniers caught the steamboat ferry and, in less than twelve hours, crossed the Buffalo Bayou and landed in Galveston.

CHAPTER 49

Fascism is cured by reading, racism is cured by traveling.
—Miguel de Unamuno

A horse-pulled carriage took them to the General Boardinghouse on Market Street. It was within walking distance of the Strand Commercial Area. The room was comfortable, not unlike the Magnolia, and breakfast was included.

After resting for a couple of hours, Ana Dee said she wanted to see the ocean. They decided to take off their shoes and put on sandals so they could walk on the sand. They stopped at a cafe and had a light meal then took a horse-drawn buggy cart to the shore.

"It's just like my dream, even the birds!" she exclaimed as they viewed the Gulf of Mexico. They got off the cart and walked along the shoreline.

"Ever since you told me about your dream, I have wanted to show you the real ocean. So is it the same as you imagined?"

"It is."

"I think it's amazing that you imagined it before actually seeing it."

"Dreams can be real. They can transport you to places you've never seen. Didn't you imagine America before you came?"

"Yes, and it turned out to be quite different."

"Well actually, the people here are different from what I envisioned. Both in Seguin and here, I have noticed a large number of Negroes. We don't have that many Negroes in Santo Tomás although we do have mulattoes. Also here in Galveston, I hear other languages, especially German, like in Seguin. It is a pretty mixed community, don't you think?"

"Yes, there are many immigrants from Europe, and there is a lot of trading going on with Europe. Cotton is the main export. But you do know that the majority of Negroes and mulattoes you see are slaves, no?"

"I thought so, but wasn't sure. Of course, we don't have slaves in Santo Tomás, so it's hard for me to absorb that reality." Her mood changed from happy to somber.

Wanting to change the topic of conversation, André asked, "I still can't understand how one can have dreams that can be useful in dealing with our daily lives. Are there techniques that you can teach me to help me remember my dreams and interpret them?"

"You have to work with your dreams. I mean, like writing them down, keeping a journal, with details about the dream. If you do that, they will eventually become clearer. Abuela taught me that."

"But that does not make them more real."

"If you could not imagine —that is, see images with your inner vision—you would not be able to dream. So you start by using your imagination. It can be trained and used as a step to see reality in the inner worlds like you see it in the physical world around you."

As they walked along the beach wetting their feet, Ana Dee stopped and picked up seashells. "I'll take these for the children, also for my classroom. Not many of them get to see the ocean."

"I wonder, did you ever dream about me before we met?"

"I didn't. I think Abuela did, though. I've never had prophetic dreams about myself. In most of my dreams, I am just like an eye on the wall, watching events happening. I am really me, that is, Soul, watching what's happening."

"You mentioned spiritual or inner guidance before. Do dreams help you with that?"

"Yes, of course. When I was studying with Papa and Mother, I remember asking for help in my lessons before I went to sleep.

Oftentimes, I would resolve problems, especially math problems, in my dreams."

"Now that sounds worthwhile! I definitely want to learn how to remember my dreams to exercise the muscle of my imagination. We'll buy a journal book while we are here."

"That's great, love. When we get back to the hotel tonight, we can do some mental image exercises during contemplation that will help you with your dream worlds."

André pointed to an elongated wooden structure. "Look, there is a small pier. A couple is sitting on this side of it. Why don't we go sit on the other side?"

They walked to the end of the small pillar-supported platform and sat down, their dangling legs almost touching the water. André held Ana Dee's hands in his and staring into her eyes said, "Ma chérie, I am reminded of some lines from Shakespeare's sonnet when I look at you here, a bright vision against the summer light reflecting from the water. Let me see if I can remember a couple of lines."

> *Shall I compare thee to a Summer Day?*
> *Thou art more lovely and more temperate.*
> . . . Uh
> *But thy eternal summer shall not fade,*
> . . . Uh
> *When in eternal lines to Time thou grow'st.*
> . . . Uh
> *So long as men can breathe, or eyes can see,*
> *So long lives this and this gives life to thee.*

"I am sorry I don't recall all the lines."

"That's so romantic, *mi amor*. It doesn't matter that you skipped some lines, it's lovely. If we weren't out in public, I would kiss you."

"If we weren't out in public, I would do more than kiss you."

As they watched the sunset beyond the blue horizon, the enamored couple walked across the road to a seafood restaurant with an ocean view. Ana Dee ordered the famous gulf red snapper and André the gulf shrimp smothered in garlic butter, but they shared each other's dishes with gusto. Not having had fresh saltwater treats before, the food tasted heavenly to Ana Dee's palate.

André commented how he was enjoying sharing new experiences with Ana Dee and how he wanted to visit new places with her in the future.

They hired one of the horse-drawn buggy carts parked along the road for the tourists' convenience. The driver took a different way back to the boardinghouse, going through Church Street before turning into Twenty-Third and up to their destination on Market Street.

Ana Dee felt dizzy and said she was very tired. André thought maybe the unusual food hadn't settled well with her. After they went inside their room at the boardinghouse, André said he would go out to find an apothecary and get her some medicine, but she said there was no need since she was already feeling better.

The following day, André wanted to show his wife the commercial center of Galveston, the popular Strand District. They visited several shops and bought some gifts for the children. At noon, they went into a New Orleans' flavor restaurant. As soon as they walked in, they ran into Mr. Galvez. "What a pleasant surprise! Please join me." He pointed to his table.

"It is good to see you here," Ana Dee said. She kissed Don Emilio on the cheek and then sat down on the chair André pulled out for her.

"It is a pleasure to find you here." Shaking hands with Don Emilio, André took his seat. "I was wondering why you didn't take the stagecoach with us from Seguin?"

"I spent another night in Seguin. My arthritis was acting up, and I needed to rest."

"You know I can get you something for that pain. I think I saw a Labadie Pharmacy close by, probably owned by a compatriot. If you will permit me, I can check it out after lunch."

"André is a very knowledgeable apothecarist."

"*Estupendo*! Let's have lunch first. I understand the gumbo is their specialty."

They placed their lunch orders, and while eating, they compared notes about the civil wars between liberal and absolutist factions taking place in Spain.

"Well, my friend, I am afraid that if we were in Europe, you and I would not be good friends. But in this country, we can converse amicably."

"That is true. Look at you. You are married to a beautiful Spanish señorita. What do you think about the slavery situation, though?"

"We are fortunate that so far it is nonexistent in our small town. We were talking about that yesterday, and I am afraid it has spoiled Ana Dee's enjoyment of our vacation."

"I see that you are not eating much, my dear child." He looked at Ana Dee's plate. "The shrimp gumbo is really delicious."

"I don't have much of an appetite."

"Try and eat a little more, Ana Dee. When we are done, you and Don Emilio can go to the little shop we just passed where they have paper goods and books while I go to the pharmacy."

Following André's suggestion, Don Emilio accompanied Ana Dee to the bookstore while André went to Dr. Labadie's office and pharmacy. His mission accomplished, he went back to meet Ana Dee and Don Emilio who were browsing through the quaint paper shop.

"Look, André, they have these journals with printed quotes on them. They would make great presents, don't you think?"

"Pick out some good ones while I give instructions to Don Emilio about this herb mixture."

André found Don Emilio sitting in a corner reading a book.

"I am glad you are back. My pain is bothering me and I want to go rest, but I didn't want to leave Señora Fournier by herself."

"*Je suis désolé*. Dr. Labadie was nice enough to let me make my own mixture of herbs. Of course, he kept a copy of my *recette* in exchange. It's basically Curcuma longa tubers with a couple of other more common herbs. I have written the ingredients and portions for you to take to your pharmacist back home. When you get back to the boardinghouse, just brew a tablespoon in a cup of hot water."

"Thank you so much. How may I repay you?"

"Mais non. It's my parting gift to you. I hope it helps."

Don Emilio Galvez said his farewells to André and Ana Dee and, after exchanging addresses, slowly made his way back to his boardinghouse.

"So what journals did you find?"

"Quite a few actually. The owner of the store is Persian, and he had some journals made with translations of quotes from the poet Rumi! Do you remember him from Papa's manuscripts? Look at this journal's quote, it should be for Fray Francisco: 'Old age and passage of time teach all things. By Sophocles.' What do you think?"

"That is perfect, ma chérie. What did you find for Hermann?"

"Let's see, how about this one by Saint Teresa de Ávila? 'Truth suffers, but never dies.'"

"That should work for him."

"This one, by Rumi, is my favorite for you: 'Wherever you are and whatever you do, be in love.'"

"I love it. I shall start using my journal tonight."

After buying several journals, André suggested getting Ana Dee a swimming gown so they could enjoy the beach and actually go in the water.

"Walking on the wet sand at the beach was lovely. But I don't want to go in the water."

"Why not? You go in the river with other ladies in Santo Tomás."

"Exactly. The women go at one time during the day and the men at a different time."

"You know, that is why I said we could buy you a proper gown. They make them of a heavier material so they won't float up when submerged in the water."

"That sounds like it would be too hot in this weather. I prefer just to wet my feet. If you want to go swimming, go ahead. I'll watch you from the pier."

"*Quel dommâge!* I actually brought my latest-style red-striped trunks. But I won't get in the water if you don't."

They continued shopping in the Strand the rest of the afternoon.

After dinner, they worked on techniques for André to remember dreams. André also started writing in his journal about their experiences and impressions from the honeymoon trip. Ana Dee had taught him to write down the daily events that he recalled; they would help with understanding his dreams as well.

The following morning, they were both ready to go to the beach again. While riding across town, Ana Dee was taciturn, her mood improved at the sight of the ocean. Walking hand in hand barefooted along the beach, André asked, "What would make this trip more enjoyable for you, *mon cher coeur*?"

"Why do you ask? I don't seem happy to you?"

"You seem to have lost your enthusiasm. Do you miss home?"

"Yes and no. I like having you all to myself. To be honest, I thought I would like Galveston more. I guess I am just a small-town girl after all. Right now, though, I like strolling along the beach with you."

"You know what they say, when we share our happiness, we double it."

"At times you are so corny. But I know you are sincere, and romantic, and I love you for it."

They spent the day at the beach. It was Ana Dee's favorite place. Her appetite came back when they ate the fresh seafood. She acknowledged she would miss that part of their trip. After a full day, having had enough of the sand, sun, and salty humidity, they hired a horse buggy to take them back to the boardinghouse. As they crossed through Church Street, Ana Dee felt once more dizzy and started rubbing her wrists and ankles. André carried her down from the cart and helped her climb the stairs up to their room. As soon as they were inside the chamber, he checked her temperature and her pulse.

To their surprise, she was fine again. "Cariño, I think I know what's wrong with me."

"Please enlighten me."

"I am experiencing someone else's pain."

"I don't understand."

"I had never experienced it before, but Fray Francisco explained to me that because I was sympathetic to people in distress, it might happen. That is, I would feel as they did. I could feel another person's suffering. People's emotions often remain in the place where they are affected."

"So you are saying that on our way here from the beach, we passed a place where someone had been hurt, perhaps tortured or abused?"

"I believe so. The state of anguish I was in was not mine. I have no reason to feel that way. Besides, it quickly went away."

"Mon dieu, what a cross to bear! I have a million questions, but right now I want to know how to prevent your absorbing such misery."

"I don't know. It has never happened this strong before that I can remember."

"We know that the route coming back from the beach was the same as yesterday's. We also know that it happened not long before we got here while we were crossing the street about three or four blocks from here."

"I guess we can figure out the place where those horrible feelings came from. Something bad must have happened there. We could walk that street again and—"

"No, you can't go through that again. You stay here, I will go and see what's there."

André left before Ana Dee could stop him. She did a contemplation while André was gone. She wanted inner guidance about her recent experience. She saw people in chains and shackles and understood the suffering brought by centuries of oppression. The vision only took seconds, but left her in a state of exhausted stupor.

When André came back, he found Ana Dee sitting on a chair fast asleep. He picked her up and laid her on the bed.

Ana Dee woke up in the middle of the night to find herself embraced by her husband's loving arms. He probably thought he could protect her. From what, her own inner perceptions? All she needed from him she already had: his loving heart. She looked up at his face. There was just a streak of moonlight coming through the window, and she could see he was smiling in his dream world.

Not wanting to disrupt his sleep, she refrained from stretching and stayed snuggled up against him until she dozed off.

In the morning light, André woke up to find Ana Dee dressed for the day, coming into the room with a cup of coffee.

"Here you are, cariño, just like you like it." She offered him the mug.

"What time is it? I didn't notice you leave the bed."

"It's almost eight o'clock. You were sound asleep when I got up, probably tired from walking around town doing your investigation."

"Well, let me tell you what I found out." He took a couple of coffee sips before he went on. "The name of the street where you experienced the 'disturbance' is Church Street. Ironic, no?"

Before he went on, Ana Dee interrupted him. "It had to do with slavery."

"You are right! How did you figure it out?"

"I saw an image of slaves with shackles on their wrists and ankles. That's why my wrists and ankles hurt yesterday."

"Yes, I remember now, you were rubbing them." He put his coffee cup down and taking her hands in his, he said, "There is an auction house, a slave auction house, McMurry and Winstead, on that street."

"It's closed now, no?"

"I am afraid not, ma chérie. The public sale of slaves is still going on in this country."

"So all that misery is still going on? André, what can we do?"

"Ana Dee, you can't seriously think we have any power to do anything, especially here, where we don't know the system or anyone, for that matter."

"But why, then, did I have that experience? Spiritual messages happen for a reason."

"Could it be just for you to be aware of what's going on outside of our town? This might be meant just to open your eyes. You have lived a sheltered life. Yes, you have lost dear ones, but death is not the worst thing that can happen to man."

"I hate this. I feel so helpless."

"You might be helpless here. But you have a voice in Santo Tomás. We can fight that loathsome institution from home. The abolitionist movement is growing throughout the country. We can find out ways in which we may be able to help."

"That's probably why I had to take this trip with you. I needed to open my eyes to what is going on around us. I've been so naive, André."

"Ana Dee, you do a lot for our town. You especially help the young ones, not just ours, but the school students. We have a school where children of all races can go. There is no better way to teach acceptance of each other's differences than through educating young minds. And that is happening because of thee. I fall in love with you every day, because every day I witness your kindness to your fellowman."

"I love you, André. I don't say it enough. You are my rock."

"It's true, you don't tell me you love me often enough. I would gladly hear it several times a day. You know I feel the same way about thee."

Ana Dee embraced her husband. "How much longer do you want to stay in Galveston?"

"I am getting the feeling that you've had enough. We can leave whenever you are ready."

On the last day, they toured the Strand, bought a few more gifts for the family, and booked passage back home for the following morning.

CHAPTER 50

Life and death are one thread, the same
line viewed from different sides.

—Lao Tzu

After a day crossing the bayou back to Houston, they stayed at the Houston House Inn until the next morning when they hoped to catch the next ride to Columbus.

From the group of people waiting for passage to San Antonio the next morning, the stagecoach driver had explicitly chosen the Fournier couple to ride with his other two customers. Ana Dee and André were glad to secure their fare and didn't question the reason for their selection.

The other two passengers to Columbus were a dignified fifty-some-year-old man in a Livingston-style white high collar with a squarish bowtie, and a soldier wearing his white pants uniform and blue cloth fatigue cap.

The travelers barely greeted one another when the stagecoach took off, followed by a team of six horseback-riding soldiers. It was apparent that they had an escort.

André reached for his pocket watch and was immediately stopped by the soldier who pointed his gun at him. Ana Dee stared in horror as André raised his arms. The older man said, "Don't be a fool, Dan, the gentleman is just checking the time."

The soldier put down his arm and said, "Sorry, sir. One can't be too careful."

After catching her breath and wiping André's sweat from his brow with her embroidered petite handkerchief, Ana Dee asked, "What on earth is going on?"

The older gentleman said, "I've had a few life threats, so Dan is extremely cautious. Please forgive his zealousness."

André held Ana Dee's hands and, looking at the gentleman, asked, "I take it you are Governor Wood? It is an honor to meet you, sir." He turned to Ana Dee. "Isn't it, my love?"

With wide eyes, Ana Dee responded, "Yes, of course, Governor. It's our pleasure although I can't feel the same about your friend."

"Ana Dee, please, it was an understandable mistake," André said, patting his wife's hands."

In an orotund voice, she said, "Not if he had shot you."

Governor Wood laughed. "You got a wild filly there, young man. I dare say she is as protective of you as Dan is of me."

"So, sir," asked André, "may we ask what you are doing traveling this way?"

"Oh, surely I was on business in Houston, but now I'm headed back to Austin via Columbus. I hear they have a nice racetrack there."

"That sounds exciting. I did enjoy that sport in France. As a matter of fact, my family owned several *Orientales* . . . Arabian horses that we would race."

When Ana Dee commented he hadn't mentioned that hobby before he said, "It was so very long ago, ma chérie, a whole other life." He turned back to the governor. "I would love to stop in Columbus and check it out." But before Ana Dee could intercept again, André turned to her and continued, "Never mind, I know you are anxious to get home."

Changing the conversation, Governor Wood said, "I am also visiting Robert Robson in Columbus. I understand he built a three-story castle in concrete. I am especially interested in the piped-in running water provided by a cistern in the roof."

With a sigh, Ana Dee exclaimed, "Indoor running water!"

"Yes, there are several homes and hotels in Paris with indoor water."

"Now that I remember, my mother mentioned that the Tremont Hotel in Boston had indoor running water. Papa wanted to have a cistern at home for that purpose, but then he became ill and nothing was done."

The Fourniers enjoyed conversing with the governor throughout the trip. They covered several topics: the five million Texas debt, the state school system, and information about the town of Santo Tomás.

The stagecoach made two waterhole stops where they had coffee and some sweetmeats the governor shared with them. Once they arrived in Columbus, the governor and his entourage left the stagecoach. As he said his goodbyes, Governor Wood mentioned that the ride back to Seguin shouldn't be too dangerous since they were in Texas Rangers' territory.

André exclaimed, "That should keep the Paducah away."

Governor Wood laughed and said, "Not Apaches, sir, the Penateka, better known as Comanches."

André was glad to hear that the long ninety-mile trip, from what he could remember, would be relatively safe. On the other hand, Ana Dee was more worried; if it was Rangers' territory, it must also be Indian territory!

Their military escort was gone; and they were joined instead by an elderly man, Mr. McDonald, and his eight-year-old granddaughter, Lucy.

It was midafternoon when they stopped at the first water hole where they were offered unsavory biscuits and unappetizing greasy meat. Across the blooming field of Mexican hats and Indian blankets, André noticed black smoke signals.

One of the stagecoach drivers called out, "Them Indian signs! Everyone back in the coach. Let's hope the Rangers also notice the signals."

They first heard the sounds of galloping horses approaching and then the raved howls and whooping war cries. The driver who had sounded the alarm dropped to the ground, an arrow puncturing his neck.

Everyone raced to the coach. Another arrow pierced the older man, leaving him gasping for air. The howling grew louder as the raid party got closer. Lucy ran to her grandfather, and a raider reached out to grab her. When André ran after the little girl, shooting at the raider, two crisscrossed arrows pierced his chest, dropping him to the ground. As the Indians got closer to the coach, the other stagecoach driver began shooting at the Indians. He started to say, "The Rangers are—" when he was pierced by a lance.

Ana ran to André's side. She cradled his head in her lap, sobbing, "Please don't leave me, mon chérie. Help is coming."

André barely whispered, "Je t'aimerai pour l'éternité," and stopped breathing.

Two Rangers on horseback dashed in front of Ana Dee and Lucy and told them to hurry and climb onto their mounts. Ana Dee cried, "I can't leave him here!" She kept holding André.

The Ranger yelled, "Our team will bring him with the coach later. Right now, we need to get you out." In a daze, the Ranger pulled her up onto the horse behind him while a second Ranger picked up little Lucy. The two horses raced away as other Rangers kept fighting the Indians.

CHAPTER 51

Goodbyes are not forever, are not the end;
it simply means I'll miss you until we meet again.

Ana Dee held on to the Ranger as they sped through the prairie. The painful sadness in her heart seemed unbearable. She hummed her sacred word within for comfort and inner guidance.

After three hours of riding, they arrived at the Magnolia Stagecoach stop in Seguin. The Ranger dismounted and held his arms up for Ana Dee to get down. It was the first time she looked at his bearded face, suddenly recognizing his steel-blue eyes. Anger rose within her, and she started punching the Ranger's chest with her fists. He didn't try to stop her. Someone tried to pull her away, but Robert held them back. He alone understood her resentment and grief.

After a brief tirade expressed through her eyes and fists, she turned around and, seeing little scared Lucy, held out her arms to her. The child ran to her, and together they walked into the station.

After a deep sigh, Robert asked the other Ranger to explain to Ana Dee how his team of Rangers would bring the stagecoach to Seguin later on. He sat alone on a board outside the station and pulled out a blue kerchief with the initials *ADP* from his pocket. He buried his face in the blue cloth, trying to inhale its long-gone bergamot scent while silent cries shook his body.

Shortly after their arrival in Seguin, Lucy's parents, the McDonalds, who lived there, were informed of the tragedy. When they picked up their daughter, Lucy's mother invited Ana Dee to stay at their home for the evening. Wanting to be there when the stagecoach arrived with André's body, Ana Dee thanked her but declined the invitation.

No other stagecoaches were scheduled, so Ana Dee sat alone in the waiting room. The station manager asked her to join the dinner crowd, but she had no appetite. After everyone had gone to bed, she stayed on the bench with only the light of an oil lamp as her companion.

Robert and the other Ranger, Luke, had gone to the small Mexican cafe downtown for dinner. After they parted ways, Robert also wanted to be at the station when the stagecoach arrived, hopefully later that evening. He didn't know how Ana Dee would react, but he had no intention of leaving her alone to handle what was coming.

He walked into the Magnolia waiting room and sat down across from Ana Dee. She appeared to have calmed down. She said, "I am sorry for blaming you. It probably makes no sense to you."

The Ranger leaned his head on his arms and let out a long exhalation. "I understand, Anita. You think that if I had stayed in Santo Tomás years ago, none of this would have happened."

Thinking he understood her better than she herself did, she nodded her head. In a measured pace, as if pondering her words, she confided, "I know it makes no sense, but I would not trade my time with André for anything in the world."

Robert replied, "I am sorry we didn't get there on time. I know. I am sorry you are going through such pain. I am sorry I wasn't able to avoid you going through that experience. Spirit will often give us what we need although it may not necessarily be what we want."

Ana Dee begrudgingly agreed with his words. Had they been able to prevent what happened, she would have been warned by her Voice or told in contemplation.

They were silent for a while. Robert noticed that Ana Dee's body was slowly leaning forward. She seemed to be asleep and about to fall off the bench. Robert knelt in front of her and sat her back up.

"I'm fine, I'm fine," she said, pulling away from him.

"No, you are not. You are tired and falling asleep," he said as he sat next to her. "Here, lean on my shoulder." She shook her head and tried to open her eyes wide. Robert just sat silently watching, and soon Ana Dee dozed off again. He tenderly laid her head on his shoulder.

In the early morning hours, the sound of an approaching coach was heard. Robert opened his eyes and saw that Ana Dee was still asleep. He gently awoke her. "They are here, Anita."

Ana Dee jumped up and rushed to the door with Robert behind her. Six Rangers accompanied the stagecoach. A rough-looking man called out to Robert, "Sorry we took so long, Captain. Had to replace two horses."

Some of the Rangers were unloading the luggage. Holding Ana Dee back, Robert replied, "Thanks, John. I take it the bodies are inside the coach? Did we lose any men?"

John answered, "No, sir, no Rangers were lost. The coachmen and two travelers' bodies are inside." He pointed to the stagecoach. "We need to take them to the undertaker. The summer heat has not helped. Thank God most of the trip was during the cooler night."

Robert gave the order. "Please go on to the undertaker. We have already ordered four coffins."

Because of the fast decomposition, especially in the hot summer, the bodies had to be buried as soon as possible since embalming was not an option in those days.

Ana Dee struggled to get away from Robert. "Why can't I see André? Let go of me. I want to take him home."

"Anita, listen to me," Robert said, trying to calm her. "We will go to see him shortly. Give the undertaker a chance to set your husband in a coffin. In the meantime, tell me which is your luggage. We also have to send someone to inform Lucy's parents."

Once the luggage and notification was taken care of, Robert knew he had to tell Ana Dee how taking André's body all the way to Santo Tomás was not feasible.

She asked, "May we go now to the undertaker?"

He said, "Let's go. Lucy's parents are probably there by now."

They walked across town to the undertaker's carpenter shop. Robert had often visited the undertaker in Seguin, where many Rangers ended up. The undertaker had just finished placing the last of the four corpses inside one of four wooden boxes and was talking to the McDonalds. Lucy's mother came over to greet Ana Dee. She said, "I understand that your husband gave his life protecting our daughter. Please allow us to take care of the burial expenses. We have burial plots at the Riverside Cemetery here in Seguin. You can pick out a headstone to your liking, and we will gladly have it placed at the gravesite when it's ready."

Ana Dee was taken aback by the woman's words. She didn't know how to respond. Thinking André was not going back with her struck her as unreal.

Robert stepped in and addressed Mrs. McDonald. "That is very generous of you. Moving the body to Mrs. Fournier's hometown would probably take at least two whole days, if we were to find a coach that would take it." Seeing Ana Dee's perplexity, he explained in a low tone, "We need to give her some time to understand the situation."

Mrs. McDonald went to Ana Dee's side and took her by the hand. "Mr. Grave, the undertaker, was nice enough to let us see my father-in-law before he closed the coffin. I imagine you would like to see your husband?"

Ana Dee followed her in a daze.

Mr. Grave was getting ready to wrap the body with large pieces of gauzy cloth and stopped when he saw Ana Dee. As she looked at André in the wooden box, she saw that the two arrows that had pierced his body had been cut down and could hardly be seen. She stared at André's colorless but handsome countenance and fainted.

Robert caught her. He picked up her light body, cradled her like a baby, and walked back to the Magnolia.

The staff at the hotel fixed the one available room for her. It was smaller than the room she and André had stayed in before. Robert laid her on the bed, and one of the servants brought her some smelling salts. When Ana Dee came to, Robert asked the servant to please bring her a cup of chamomile tea.

Ana Dee appeared disoriented. Robert explained, "You fainted at the undertaker's. I brought you back to the Magnolia Hotel. I know the owners, the Calvert family, and they are pleased to have you. They'll be bringing you some tea and your luggage. I will wait for you in the front area. I am not going away, but it's not proper that I stay in the room with you. Please come out when you feel better, and we can get something to eat." As he walked out of the room, the servants were bringing her the tea and luggage, as well as a pitcher of water and clean towels.

Robert went to the hotel entrance and told his team of Rangers that he intended to stay until the situation with Mrs. Fournier was settled, so they could go back to Columbus ahead of him. When they left, he got himself a cup of coffee and sat outside, knowing he had no intention of going back to Columbus. He could not let Ana Dee travel alone back to Santo Tomás. Though his feelings for her had not changed, and he knew they could not be reciprocated, he felt a need to protect her, borne from his affection, if not from brotherly responsibility.

Robert's mind went back to a night in September of 1847, after the Chapultepec battle, when he was in Mexico; and for a few seconds, he had imagined seeing Ana Dee. It was as if she was asking him to come back. The desire to go to her kept pulling at his heart, but he kept hearing "it's not time yet." Had he left the war, he would have been branded a deserter. Besides, his mission wasn't over. In vain, he had hoped the peace treaty would be signed in time to answer Ana Dee's call.

A few months later, the Treaty of Guadalupe Hidalgo was officially signed, and the war with Mexico was over. He intended to leave the Rangers then and move to Santo Tomás, excited at the prospect of courting Ana Dee. To his chagrin, Fray Francisco let him know she had married Louis André Fournier that December. Without hope of pursuing his love, Robert remained with the Texas Rangers. Now, so many years after their meeting, destiny brought her back into his life. Fray Francisco had reached him through inner channels to warn him of her peril. Without a second thought, he had gathered his team of Rangers patrolling the path from Columbus to Seguin. Seeing the black smoke signals set his men into action.

It was obvious to him that Ana Dee adored her husband and was hurting so much. Robert couldn't bear to see her anguish. He was torn because as much as he loved her, he knew he had to keep his distance and not be the one to comfort her. The best and only solution was to take her home where she would be with her family and under Fray Francisco's guidance.

Knowing she had to make plans and talk to Robert, Ana Dee rinsed her face and washed as well as she could before changing her clothes. After braiding her hair, she did a spiritual contemplation, singing the HU to herself for a few minutes. Then she spoke to André in a soft cracked voice with loving tones as if he were there. "I know you are continuing in your spiritual journey. Perhaps you can come to me sometime and let me know if you are happy. I will try to do my best explaining to the children where their loving Père is now. I miss you terribly. Who is going to keep me laughing, mon chérie?" Ana Dee felt a wave of love surround her as the tears rolled down her cheeks.

A short while later, she walked toward the dining room where Robert was waiting for her. As soon as he saw her, he thought she looked like the innocent fifteen-year-old he had first met in the plaza years before and later taken to the ancient stone circle, Tlazolia Occepa. Just like then, he told himself, "Be still my heart," as they walked into the dining area.

Ana Dee picked at her lunch, eating it ever so slowly. Robert kept eating and avoiding the obvious dilemma. Gently he said, "I hope you are agreeable with Mrs. McDonald's offer. I don't see how you—that is, we—can transport . . . your husband to Santo Tomás."

Ana Dee let out a sigh, shuffled her food around, and at last said, "I am afraid I was very rude to the lady. She made a very kind offer, and I know I need to accept it. I am so sorry. Please excuse me." Abruptly, she got up and went back to her room. A pensive Robert sat alone finishing his lunch and giving thanks for Ana Dee's change of mind.

Everything fell into place that afternoon as arrangements were made for the burial. Ana Dee was glad Robert offered to take care of passing on the information to the undertaker and the McDonald family.

Standing alone by André's burial site, Ana Dee remembered Rumi's words and recited them:

> *Goodbyes are only for those who love with their eyes.*
> *Because for those who love with heart and soul there is no*
> *such thing as separation.*

She leaned down and placed a yellow rose on the dirt covering her beloved.

CHAPTER 52

*I was made and meant to look for you and wait for you
and become yours forever.*
—Robert Browning

The stagecoach to San Antonio left the next morning with two cowboys and an uncoupled pair. Robert insisted on taking her all the way to Santo Tomás in spite of Ana Dee's protests. He didn't tell her he intended to make Santo Tomás his home and resign as a Texas Ranger. He knew deep in his heart "it was time."

When they got to the Pajalache Mill Station in San Antonio in the late afternoon, they had to wait at the stagecoach stop overnight in order to catch the coach to Santo Tomás the following day.

Ana Dee was glad Robert was with her then. He took her to the only open eating place nearby, Cantina La Clinica Mexicana, across the street. It was obviously not the right place for a lady, but no one dared bother the companion of an armed rough-looking Texas Ranger. Robert was almost six feet tall and had become more muscular than she remembered. Plus, his beard gave him a rugged menacing look. The cantina turned out to be a good place to wait for morning since it was open all night, and she didn't want to go to a hotel. She knew she would have plenty of time to sleep on the coach ride back home.

It was a good time for them to catch up. She managed to start a conversation. "Fray Francisco has told me about your spiritual mission as a Texas Ranger. Are you happy serving in that way?"

"I wouldn't say I am happy as a Texas Ranger, but I am happy serving. How about you? I understand you have adopted two beautiful children."

"Yes, they are a joy. They both loved their Père very much."

"You mean their father, Monsieur Fournier?"

"Yes, they called him Père. What did Fray Francisco tell you about him?"

"Not very much. I know he was French. He was a good person. Had to be to adopt two abandoned children. Most importantly, he made you happy."

"He did that. He had a jovial personality. You know, I told him about you. About having had a crush on you when I was fifteen, and you know what he said?"

"What?"

"He said that if you came back to Santo Tomás, he did not want to meet you! I guess he was jealous. Can you imagine, jealous of a childhood crush?"

Robert thought he would have felt the same, but just smiled and didn't say anything.

"He came to a couple of spiritual discussions with Fray Francisco and me, but then decided he was not interested in our paths. He was a free spirit, you know. I guess he still is." Tears fell down her cheeks.

Robert remembered how he once kissed her tears goodbye. He wanted to wipe them away, but he didn't dare touch her. Instead, he said, "I should get us coffee refills," and he called for the waitress.

Ana Dee filled him in on her family's doings and Santo Tomás in general; he talked to her about some of his adventures as a Ranger. They passed the time exchanging stories until the crack of dawn, when they walked back to the stagecoach station.

Ana Dee was comfortable with the brotherly relationship she now had with Robert; Robert welcomed any way she could accept him in her life. This made it possible for him to move to Santo Tomás without constraint.

CHAPTER 53

Love is so short, forgetting is so long.
—Pablo Neruda

They arrived in Santo Tomás around seven the next morning. The heavy hard canvas trunk and one large carpet bag were left at the Andersons' pensión to be delivered later to the Fournier home. Robert insisted on carrying the other carpet bag for Ana Dee and walking her to her home. They shook hands goodbye before he left her knocking at her front door. Manuela opened the door and yelled, "They are home!" Looking for André, she asked, "Where is Père?"

Ana Dee walked into her home and embraced the dear woman. With a knot in her throat, she just shook her head. Pedro joined and immediately understood André wasn't there. He picked up the carpet bag, and the three of them went into the living room where Ana Dee sat down and in a shaky voice told them about the raid. Manuela cried and Pedro stood dumbfounded, shaking his head. He voiced what they were all thinking. "How do we tell the children? Thank God you were spared." These were words Manuela repeated.

Before the children were awakened, there was a knock at the door. Pedro went to open, and Fray Francisco walked in. Ana Dee stood up and hugged her spiritual guardian. "I just talked to Robert. I am so sorry, my child." He looked at the three grief-stricken people in front of him. "I take it that the children don't know yet?"

Ana Dee was grateful Fray Francisco was there to help her explain André's death to David and Mary. She noticed he was walking with the help of a cane, but didn't ask why. Her concern right then was little Mary's reaction upon hearing the news. Although she knew it was wrong, she was relieved when the little girl didn't believe André was dead and kept waiting for her Père to get back.

Her luggage was delivered in the afternoon, and she slowly unpacked and gave everyone in the family their gifts, telling them how André had personally picked them out.

The Fournier brothers offered a Mass in André's memory. Friends and family gathered afterward for a memorial service. The Meyer couple hosted André's memorial gathering, giving Ana Dee the welcomed support she needed.

Ana Dee told the story of how André gave his life to save little Lucy. She heard comments such as, "He would do that," "Just like him," "He loved children," all the while Mary hid in her room and refused to see anyone. David held back the tears, assuming he was now the man of the house and needed to act accordingly. Hermann patted him on the shoulder, acknowledging his maturity.

Hermann already missed old Frenchie's playful temperament, knowing he had lost his best and dearest friend. He gave a heartfelt eulogy that brought everyone to both tears and laughter about his best *amigo*.

For Mary, when the realization of Père's death sank in later in the week, depression took over. Ana Dee felt useless to help her adopted daughter, being in a similar state herself. She knew time would help heal her own heart, but her child's sense of loss seemed to grow, not diminish.

Ana Dee sought Fray Francisco's help. He told her he would talk to the child and contemplate on the best course of action. He knocked on little Mary's door and asked if he could enter her room to talk.

"If you have to."

Fray Francisco took her response as a yes and walked in. She was hugging a stuffed toy dog.

"Did Père buy that for you?"

"Yes. He knew I would take care of it."

"Oh. Like he took care of you?"

"Like we took care of each other."

"Well, Mama Ana Dee takes care of you too."

"Mama takes care of David because she found him, so he takes care of her. Père found me, so I took care of him."

"I see. Well, you are doing a good job taking care of the puppy Père gave you. I believe Père will send you someone to take care of. But you have to be ready to receive a gift from Spirit because Père is Spirit now."

"I know. Mama said Père is Spirit now and he is still taking care of me, but I can't take care of him."

"Don't worry about it. Père is safe now. I have a feeling that you will love his gift."

Fray Francisco went back to see Ana Dee and asked her if it would be all right to get Mary a small pet she could take care of and love. "You know that animals are Souls too. They can provide comfort to us when we need it. It's an unconditional love like with David and the horse Lumen."

After the family's experience with Periquito's loss, Ana Dee wasn't convinced a pet would be a good idea. She trusted her spiritual guide, though, and was desperate for a solution to Mary's melancholy. Reluctantly, she agreed when he explained he knew the perfect pet for Mary and would bring it in about a week.

Before he left, Ana Dee asked him about his use of a cane. The monk told her about a dear friend, old Don Octaviano Sánchez, who had suffered a heart attack and fell to the ground, landing on top of the monk who was trying to support him. His friend died, and Fray Francisco was left limping.

After explaining this to Ana Dee, the monk took his leave, knowing the pet he had in mind for Mary was not only a good idea for her, but it also helped solve one problem for him. His deceased friend, Don Octaviano, had lost his entire family and lived alone near the monks' homes, a series of one-room adobe sheds near the river with vegetable and herb gardens surrounding them. The old man didn't possess many material goods, but he did have a little companion dog, whom he had brought from Coahuila, Mexico, two years prior. Fray Francisco was left taking care of the sweet creature. The little dog was one part of the solution.

The second aspect of his plan had to do with Robert who should be back in a week. The monk wanted to encourage his protégé's relationship with Ana Dee and her family. What better way to get Robert acquainted with Ana Dee's children than by having him deliver the gift to Mary?

Fray Francisco knew Robert's heart and his desire to help Ana Dee and her family. If he could be an instrument to either one of his pupils' happiness, why not? To bring happiness to others is part of spreading divine love.

After resigning as Texas Ranger and picking up his personal belongings from Columbus, including his guitar, Robert came back to Santo Tomás. He met with Fray Francisco upon arrival and explained he intended to run for the sheriff's position coming up in Santo Tomás. Many Rangers became sheriffs after retiring, the most famous being John Coffee Hays, who became the first sheriff of San Francisco when he moved to California.

The monk was glad to hear his protégé's intentions. "Yes, I was waiting for your return so I could send you on an important mission."

By the end of the week, Robert visited the Fournier home. Ana Dee opened her front door to find a clean-shaven Robert wearing a vest with the Texas Ranger badge and holding the cutest small dog she had ever seen.

Robert said loudly, "I have a gift for Ms. Mary Fournier." With a lower voice, he said, "Fray Francisco sent me."

The children came running out when they heard Robert's announcement. Mary let out a joyful shriek and cried out, "It's Père's gift!" After showing her how to hold it, Robert placed the puppy in her arms.

Young David's eyes were wide open, staring at the man in front of them. "Are you a real Texas Ranger?"

Robert unpinned the five-pointed star he had made himself from a Mexican peso and gave it to David. "I used to be. Would you like to save my badge for me, you know, in case I ever need it again?"

David took the rounded insignia and said, "Yes, sir," as the man shook his hand and introduced himself.

"Captain Robert Hughes, at your service."

The puppy licked Mary's face, making her laugh. Ana Dee was grateful watching her daughter become her usual lively child. She looked at beardless Robert, who seemed so much younger than a couple of weeks ago. She knew that sending the puppy was Fray Francisco's doing, but giving the badge to David so he wouldn't covet his sister's gift was definitely Robert's doing. She wondered if he was truly leaving the Rangers and what his plans were. He hadn't come to the memorial service, and she had thought then he had left town for good.

Robert turned to leave the premises when Pedro came out. "Ah, if it isn't the man who brought our girl safely back home! How are you, sir?" The men shook hands, and seeing Ana Dee's questioning look, Pedro explained, "Fray Francisco introduced us before Mr. Hughes went back to Columbus to resign from the undesirable job of rinches."

Mission accomplished, Robert walked back to the front doorway and, tipping his hat, waved as a way of saying goodbye to everyone. They all waved back goodbyes and thanks as he left.

Once Robert was gone, Mary asked Ana Dee if little "Paco," as she immediately named him, could sleep in her room. Ana Dee promised to find a basket with a pillow to use as his bed in Mary's room.

The Fournier household began adapting to its new stride. Throughout the following summer weeks, the children bounced back to a healthier approach to life. Ana Dee knew the importance of staying strong for her family and, in spite of her depression, hid her sadness from them.

She began to work on the new school-year plans. The remodeling of the new schoolhouse was almost finished. Once the second teacher was selected, together with Ana Dee, they started taking enrollment forms from the prospective students. As they expected, attendance that year would be around thirty-some students.

Having turned six years of age, Ana Dee felt Mary was old enough to start formal schooling. Since the students were to be divided into two groups according to age and skill, Mary would be in the first group with the new teacher, and David in the second group, which Ana Dee would be teaching.

Except for the fact that Mary wanted to take Paco to school with her, the children were excited about the upcoming school year. They were tired of being home all day. Occasionally, Nadia brought Hansali to play with them, or they went to the plaza to play with their neighbors if Manuela had some free time and could take them. Pedro was too busy helping at the clinic to take the children out, and Ana Dee claimed to have something to do all the time.

In reality, the plaza brought her too many memories of André. Almost every bench in the plaza held a remembrance of him. She had names for each bench: love, gratitude, compassion, humility, patience, contentment, listening, etc., all qualities her André possessed.

In the evenings, she would open his journal and caress the embossed golden words on its cover: *"Wherever you are and whatever you do, be in love."* Some nights she would read all his writings, other nights different sections. He addressed his journal as if he were writing to her. Several pages described their trip experience.

He wrote that at first, he did not like Don Emilio Galvez because of how he flirted with Ana Dee, but later he got to like the fellow. After all, how could he blame the man for admiring his beautiful wife?

The most endearing feature was how he started each page with a note to Ana Dee: "You are the center of my Universe," "My heart beats for you," "Each day with you is a treasure." It was as if he knew she would read them someday.

Only one dream got recorded:

> *Ma Chérie,*
>
> > *I did have a vivid dream last night. I was sitting on our favorite bench at the plaza waiting for you. You know, the one we named "Love." Fray Francisco appeared and sat by me. The aroma of sandalwood was in the air. He handed me a glowing book in silver binding and said, "It holds your spiritual journey. Do not be afraid of the future. You are reborn through love." I opened the tome to see your smiling face. I then woke up.*
> >
> > *I am writing the dream down because you said that way, I won't forget it and can interpret it. However, I don't think I'll ever forget it. As far as its message, well, it is obvious that I was spiritually reborn when I met you.*

In retrospect, to Ana Dee, the Franciscan's words "Do not be afraid of the future" seemed to imply André's departure from the physical world. It gave her some comfort to know Fray Francisco was with him. She thought of consulting the monk about it, but sharing the dream could mean letting go of André's last consoling secret, and she wasn't ready for that.

While she had sought solitude, Robert Hughes was attending most of the town's social activities in Santo Tomás, becoming more and more popular.

When he first arrived in town, Robert had gone to the constabulary and was hired straight away as deputy sheriff because of his Ranger experience. They all knew he would be the sheriff after the election in the fall, not just because of his skill, but because no one would run against him. In the meantime, the town would have a chance to get acquainted with the prospective head of law enforcement in Santo Tomás.

In the evenings, he was on duty at the plaza, walking about, making sure order was kept in Santo Tomás, not unlike he had done six years before when he had first gone into law enforcement and encountered Anita.

Robert attracted the attention of young promenading señoritas, but wasn't interested in pursuing a romantic relationship with anyone other than Ana Dee. Being near her was enough for now. He was convinced that in time, she would come to care for him. When he sought Fray Francisco's opinion, the monk said, "We shall see. A heart has to mend before it can truly venture into another intimate relationship. You have been loyal and constant in your affection toward Ana Dee. It is too early for her to recognize it, though. You are right in giving her time to deal with her mourning. I know she trusts you, and that is a big step."

Robert knew his guardian was his ally. Why else would he send him to deliver the puppy to Mary? It was a good introduction to the children who became his friends and often conversed with him when playing at the plaza. He made it a habit to ride his horse around the plaza in the afternoons and on several occasions, with Manuela's permission, had David mount in front of him and ride around the square.

Once school started, though, the children stopped coming to play at the plaza in the afternoons. He did see them on some weekends promenading with Pedro and Manuela.

Sometimes Robert played his flamenco guitar in the gazebo to the delight of the townsfolk and the young sweethearts strolling by.

As expected, Robert won the November election and became the proud sheriff of Santo Tomás.

CHAPTER 54

Before you conquer the mountain, you
must learn to overcome your fear.
—Isabel Allende

Teaching the schoolchildren again gave Ana Dee a sense of purpose
and satisfaction. She also enjoyed comparing notes with the other
teacher. Her only other social activity was when she invited Nadia
and Hermann for dinner, after which they sat in the courtyard
watching their children and Paco play.

Fray Francisco did visit frequently. On one of those occasions, she
was able to relate André's dream to him. She asked if he remembered
the meeting with André in the dream world. Fray Francisco explained
he could not recall all the dream experiences he had with his students,
but he did know he had visited André in his dreams. He wanted
to let André know, at some level, he was on a spiritual journey
and protected, not to be afraid because more spiritual growth and
enlightenment was coming in future earth incarnations.

Her guide's explanation helped her understand how the Holy
Spirit worked through him. She was certain her presence in André's
dream meant she had somehow helped him in his spiritual journey.
Was that all it meant? Only time would tell.

Nadia was pregnant anew, and this time, she ate a lot. She said she was making up for her last pregnancy. She and Hermann occasionally promenaded around the plaza and often took Hansali, David, and Mary with them.

During the feast of the Virgin Mary, in September, the children asked Ana Dee to go with them to the plaza to select the figurines they added yearly to the nacimiento. Nadia convinced her to come along as well.

The little group was strolling around the plaza when Professor Eduardo Salazar, the other school teacher, asked if he could join them. Eduardo was a single man in his thirties, originally from Laredo. He had wide sideburns and bushy eyebrows. Eduardo had studied at the prestigious National Autonomous University of Mexico, the oldest university in North America, founded in 1551. He was relatively good looking but did not have good luck with the female gender because he had a way of turning every conversation into an erudite discussion.

Ana Dee could tell the children weren't too excited at the prospect of strolling with Professor Salazar, but she, as well as Nadia and Hermann, were too well mannered not to invite him to join them. Nadia sensed how discomfited Ana Dee felt, already knowing how her friend tried to dissuade Eduardo from anything more than a work relationship. Seeking to help Ana Dee, she linked arms with her and the children, leaving Hermann with no choice but to walk behind with Professor Salazar. Hermann caught the hint and to avoid embarrassing the teacher started asking him questions about the new school.

The plaza was busy that night. Mary and David were ready to pick out their manger figurines but had to first check out all the vendors. It was the Meyers' first time putting up a manger, so Hansali got several figurines. Mary was busy inspecting her choices when she saw the sheriff. She immediately ran to get him so he could help with her decision. David too was asking for Robert's attention.

Ana Dee was surprised watching her children's familiarity with Robert, as well as the time he took helping the children make their decisions.

After they'd made their choices, Mary grabbed Robert's hand and asked him to promenade with them. Ana Dee was embarrassed, not knowing how to explain to the children it would not be right for two men, Professor Salazar and Sheriff Hughes, to promenade with her.

Exchanging looks with her, Robert said, "I am sorry, but I must get back to my job of patrolling the plaza tonight." He said goodbye to the children, tipped his hat, and walked away.

Hermann had noticed Ana Dee and Robert exchange looks. Recalling his history with Ana Dee and his talks with Pedro. he said to himself, *Perchance the sheriff was the one.* Just then, Nadia brought him out of his reverie. "Please pick Hansali up, dear. I think he is tired and getting fidgety."

Ana Dee took advantage of the situation and said it was time for her children to retire as well. The professor offered to accompany her and the children to their door, which to her relief was just across the street.

As luck would have it, Hermann had a chance to question Robert about his relationship with Ana Dee the very next day.

Robert walked into the clinic and asked Nadia, "Would it be possible for the doctor to come over to the jail this morning?"

"What's the problem, Sheriff?"

"I believe a prisoner has a broken or dislocated arm."

"As you can see"—she pointed to the three patients in the waiting room—"he is quite busy right now. Could he come by around noon?"

"That would be appreciated. I prefer not to bring the prisoner here."

"I'll let the doctor know."

"Thank you, Doña Nadia." He took his leave.

Nadia was impressed he recalled her name from the previous night encounter at the plaza. She went into the examining room where Hermann was taking care of a tonsillitis case and told her husband about the prisoner.

At noon, Hermann begrudgingly forfeited his siesta plans and went to the jailhouse, where Robert was waiting for him. "I appreciate you coming over, Dr. Meyer. The man has been groaning and moaning every time he moves."

"*Gerne geschehen.* What exactly happened?" he asked as they walked over to the cell.

"The man was being rough with one of the children at the plaza, and when I pulled him away, he thrust a knife out on me. I had no choice but to punch him and twist his arm to grab the knife."

"Why was he attacking a child?"

"A case of mistaken superiority. It was Juanito, Mr. Pérez's grandchild. I understand he was buying the last pan dulce from the vendor, and the Texian—out-of-towner, of course—decided he wanted it instead and thought nothing of beating up a little mulatto child out of the way."

Hermann went into the cell, and after a short examination, during which the prisoner cussed him out, he pulled on the dislocated shoulder with Robert's assistance and straightened it out.

As he was getting ready to leave, he shook Robert's hand and said, "I'll send you the bill, *gut*? That was some punch you gave him! By the way, aren't you a Texian too?"

"No, sir. I am a Tejano. I came from Mexico." He didn't give any more explanations, but Hermann was not done asking.

"You seemed to have known Ana Dee from a while back. Were you her friend back in '43 or '44?"

"Yes, I had the privilege of knowing her before you courted her." He smiled at Hermann, who swallowed hard.

"*Ja*, well, I guess you know more than I thought. I am not interested in getting one of your punches, so I will take my leave in peace."

They both barely restrained a laugh at that, and the doctor left thinking he had a story to share with Nadia and some questions for Pedro.

Nadia was privy to Ana Dee's first love, but she never knew who he was. Hermann's suspicions about the sheriff struck her as possible, knowing Robert Hughes had left Santo Tomás some years back and had just recently come back. People remembered the cowboy flamenco guitar player! Not satisfied with Nadia's incomplete information, Hermann thought he would ask Pedro what he thought.

She said, "If you are so curious about your old heartthrob, why don't you just ask her?"

He turned on the defensive, afraid of Nadia's jealousy. "You know that we were never serious. Nevertheless, I consider her our friend and would like to help. Don't you think it's our duty?"

"How exactly will this help her?"

"Well, she brought us together. Perhaps we can bring them together again."

"Precisely why you should ask her first. She might not be interested in him anymore, if it is him, and you are just going to start trouble behind her back."

"Fine, I'll leave it alone. I am certainly not going to ask her about an old sweetheart." But his mind was made up. He intended to approach Pedro; after all, Pedro was the one who told him about the man originally.

Ana Dee's twenty-first birthday had gone on quietly. Everyone knew celebrating it would only stir up memories of the trip to Galveston, which had been André's gift, and it would sadden her more. Instead, her attention was drawn to the schoolchildren's preparations for the holidays.

It seemed the whole town was involved in the Posadas since many more students and their families were participating. Afterward, Christmas Day, however, was spent quietly by the Fournier household at home. The children enjoyed opening their presents and Christmas dinner with Manuela's famous tamales. Fray Francisco, their one guest for dinner, came in the afternoon to check on the little family and ask if Ana Dee wanted to continue the spiritual discussions toward the middle of January since she still showed no interest in social activities. The monk wanted to provide some kind of diversion and help uplift her mood.

Ana Dee said yes, she wanted to renew the discussions; she looked forward to their meetings.

Hermann, Nadia, and Hansali visited the day after Christmas to exchange gifts. When he had the chance, Hermann asked Pedro if he could help him find some bandages at the clinic. This wasn't unusual since Pedro took care of storing a lot of the inventory at the clinic. Nadia was not fooled, though, and tried to catch Hermann's eye to give him a stern glance; but he avoided looking in her direction.

Once inside the clinic, Pedro pointed to the questioned bandages. "I don't know why you couldn't find them, this is their usual place."

"*Ja*, never mind that. I need to ask you a question."

"What about?"

"You know the sheriff, right?"

"You mean Robert Hughes?"

"Ja, him that used to be a Ranger."

"Of course. He saved Ana Dee from the Indian raid that killed André."

"Ja, ja. Did he?"

"He also brought her home safely."

"Ooh, that's why they seemed to know each other well."

"Why are you asking?"

"I wondered if he was the one you told me Ana Dee was in love with when we broke up."

"You mean when you stopped courting?"

"Ja. I remember you said he was away at the time."

"It might have been him, now that you mention it. But—"

At that moment, Nadia walked into the clinic. "Just what I thought." She turned to Pedro. "Not you too. It does not matter if the sheriff is the person y'all think he might be. What matters is that Ana Dee is just barely getting over losing André and does not need you meddling in her affairs."

"*Meine Liebe*, we just wondered if the sheriff is Ana Dee's past love. We aren't conspiring about anything."

"I know you, Hermann Meyer. Besides, you already suggested, 'Perhaps we can bring them together again. Ja,'" she said, imitating his voice.

"Don't bring me into this. I am not planning anything. My girl is still mourning her husband's parting. If he is the one, time will tell."

Ana Dee peeked into the room. "Why is everyone in the clinic? The children are waiting to open their gifts."

They all gave some excuse about the bandages and walked back into the house where Manuela and the children were distributing the presents.

CHAPTER 55

We have to laugh. Because laughter, we already know,
is the first evidence of freedom.
—Rosario Castellanos

The second phase of the Industrial Revolution was taking place. Locomotives, telegraph, photo cameras, typewriters, etc., were making life easier for a large part of the country although few advances had reached Santo Tomás.

Catherine kept her stepdaughter informed of the latest events by sending her newspaper articles. Ana Dee told Manuela about the new stitching machine that saved seamstresses a lot of time while they worked on the new silk plaid fabric of bright colors, the latest in fashion for a special school celebration where the students would read their essays on the Industrial Revolution.

Ana Dee said perhaps they would be able to buy one of the new stitching machines in the near future. Manuela was all for that.

In the meantime, plans for settling the dispute on the land claimed by Texas after the annexation to the United States started early in 1850, though it would be September before a settlement was agreed on. None of this made much difference to the remote town of Santo Tomás, but it had to be taught at school so Ana Dee tried to keep herself and her students informed on current events.

Fray Francisco and Ana Dee resumed their spiritual discussions, and once more, she began to feel involved in life.

On a cool Saturday morning in February, the children were busy with their chores. Pedro mentioned he was going to take Lumen out for a ride because the poor horse hadn't been on a regular run in a few days. Ana Dee said she would take him. She needed to get some fresh air. Pedro was glad to hear her say she wanted to go out and saddled up Lumen for her.

She rode him around the outskirts of Santo Tomás, realizing how the town was surrounded by more *jacales*. She didn't remember that many mud and stick shacks. Poor peasants had moved closer to town as the old haciendas they'd squatted in were divided and sold. If not with pesos, they probably used chickens or piglets to settle with one of the regidores in order to build their sheds in the small *solares*.

As Ana Dee got close to the river, she heard another horse approaching. She turned her head to recognize Robert, who galloped up alongside her.

"Good morning, Sheriff."

"Good morning, Doña Anita. It's nice to see you out and about."

"As you can see, I am not riding away from the town but staying within its borders."

"I wasn't implying otherwise." They were both remembering the day long ago when they had gone galloping together. "Would you be uncomfortable if I kept you company?"

"Why would you ask that?"

"Well, you seem to be avoiding me since I came back to Santo Tomás."

"If I had, it wasn't on purpose. I just don't care to go out very much."

"Oh? You did go promenading with your fellow teacher, Alberto."

"Robert . . ." Ana Dee was going to correct him on the professor's name and the fact that she was not really accompanying him, but then she thought Robert knew better and was just baiting her. She gave him an annoyed sideways glance and set her horse on a faster gallop.

Her use of his first name stunned him. It was music to his ears. Thinking that they were on a first-name basis again was encouraging, but then he realized she was galloping away. He thought, *Could she be upset?* He sped his horse to catch up with her. Lumen seemed to be enjoying the quick run. When they got close to the river, Ana Dee got off him and led him to drink the cool water, petting his neck.

Robert caught up with them and dismounted his horse as well. He joined Ana Dee sitting on a wide boulder by the river shoreline.

"If the water weren't so cold, I would dip my feet in it."

"The water is actually warmer than the temperature in the atmosphere. You can tell by the mist above it. I think I will take my boots off and check it out."

After a while of listening to Robert's comments about how nice the water felt, Ana Dee ventured to follow his lead and dip her feet in the water. They laughed like carefree children.

"It's so good to hear your laughter." Robert summoned up the courage to ask her, "Would you mind if I join your next spiritual discussion?"

"I guess I should not be surprised that you know about my meetings with Fray Francisco. As long as he is in agreement, it is fine by me. Our next meeting will be the last Friday in February at seven o'clock."

"Thank you, I'll be there. Now, shouldn't we be getting back to town? I'll have to dry my feet first."

He jumped down from the boulder and walked over the sparse grass to his mount where he kept a piece of cloth in his horse satchel bag. When he returned to offer it to Ana Dee, he saw she was already drying her feet with a kerchief similar to the one he had kept from her years before.

"I see that you come prepared," he said and proceeded to wipe his feet with his cloth before putting on his socks and boots. "Do you always carry one of those bandannoes with you?"

"Yes, they are very practical. I always keep one in my pocket. I used to embroider my name on them because both Mom and Elizabeth had the same kind."

They got on their horses and rode back to town, both with their own quiet thoughts. Robert touched his pocket, where he kept the treasured kerchief. In his fancy, holding on to it replaced her presence all those years, as if part of her was everywhere he went. Now she was near, and yet remained physically intangible.

On the other hand, Ana Dee thought she could enjoy Robert's company. She felt at ease with him. His friendship took the place of an older brother, which she never had. After all, they were studying the same spiritual teachings, and he was her spiritual brother. If at any time she thought he had more than a sisterly interest in her, she refused to acknowledge it.

He helped her take Lumen back to the stable, the same way he had done so long ago. This time, there were no tears to kiss; he was feeling apprehensive to even shake her hand. He was afraid to make any gesture denoting the slightest romantic interest hindering their relationship. So he tipped his hat, waved goodbye, and took his leave.

Ana Dee thought that was odd. She had been ready to give him a goodbye hug. Their friendship was strong enough to warrant it. Maybe after they met for the spiritual studies he would feel more at ease with her.

A letter awaited her when she went inside the house. Elizabeth wrote she was expecting another baby, which caused Ana Dee to worry. She remembered how hard the pregnancies had been on her sister and was glad Catherine was with her. Nadia's baby was due around April and she was doing fine this time around.

Knowing both her closest friend and her sister were soon to have a 'bundle of joy' reminded Ana Dee she, too, would probably be expecting by now if André were still alive. At least that's what they had planned. It was a depressing thought and she tried to push it out of her mind. She took comfort in the two little souls who enriched her life.

She wrote to Catherine and Elizabeth about her trip, about the loss she was feeling since Andrés' death, about her thoughts on slavery, and asked how it was up North.

Mary and David were the center of her world and she enjoyed teaching them about the world such as Papa Moore had done with her. So every day after school the three of them went into the library where she helped them with their homework and did research from Papa Moore's books relevant to what they were studying in school.

The month went by and the day of the spiritual class had arrived.

CHAPTER 56

I want to die being a slave of principles, not of men.
—Emiliano Zapata

Friday evening, Fray Francisco arrived earlier than usual. He wanted to visit with the children and catch up on what they were learning in school and at the same time play with Paco. The little dog was so excited to see his old friend, he kept jumping up and down.

David said, "He must have been a cat in his previous life!"

"Very possible," said the monk.

After dinner, the children stayed in the dining area where they were going to play *loteria* with Manuela and Pedro. Once Robert got there, he retired with Ana Dee and Fray Francisco to the library.

"Good evening, Roberto. Glad that you could join us."

"Thank you for having me, Padre. It reminds me of my days in the Colegio de Kulkanzin, which I truly miss."

Ana Dee raised her eyebrows. "Excuse me, where was this?"

"It is a remote place in the mountains of Mexico where we are able to enjoy the sacred teachings. Roberto grew up there. As a young child, he was under my tutelage in the monastery."

"You grew up in a religious monastery?"

"It is a spiritual center where we are taught to contemplate and use the necessary spiritual tools to deal with our daily living while progressing in our inner journey to God. Of course, basic school subjects, like reading, writing, arithmetic, and theology are taught as well as the arts. Once our forming years are over, we go out into the world to serve others while maintaining our inner communication with our teachers and guides." Robert looked at Fray Francisco and added, "Fray Francisco has been my guide since I was five years old. You are very fortunate, Ana Dee, to have been under his tutelage as well. After I graduated, I joined him here. That's when I first met you, Anita." His wistful eyes directed at Ana Dee as if asking, *Do you remember the first time we met?*

"I see," she answered. Memories flooded her mind, recalling every detail of their first encounter at the plaza seven years before—Abuela Brau's fear of him, the bread he brought her, his playing the guitar, and the current she felt run up her arm when they touched. Unconsciously, she rubbed her arm. Wanting to wipe away the stirring thoughts, she turned to the monk. "So what is the topic tonight?"

"These classes are meant to help you achieve an understanding of the larger picture so that you may understand your part or purpose in the grand scheme of life. I know that is a lot to expect from our humble class, but consider it from the opposite view—we can learn what is not expected from us as well.

"Now, the reason I am bringing this up is because I understand that you, Ana Dee, have felt somewhat powerless since you came back from your trip. Could you enlighten us as to what happened to make you feel that way?"

"It never ceases to amaze me how you can read my feelings. Yes, . . . well, . . . I had a strange experience in Galveston. As a result, André and I were planning to help with the abolition movement once we got back home. Without him, I feel lost and can't seem to gather my thoughts as to where to begin or what to do."

"Could you share that experience with us? I understand if it's too painful to talk about. But it could help you process it."

Ana Dee related to them how she had felt sick the two times they had passed the slave auction house and later her vision about it. When Fray Francisco went to comfort her, he noticed she was trembling.

Once she stopped, he stood up and walked out of the library saying he was going to get her some water.

Robert took the opportunity to share with her, "Anita, you have a lot of compassion for others' suffering. I can relate. When I first started as a Ranger, I witnessed such horrors I wished my life to end. The only thing that kept me going was the knowledge that I was on a spiritual mission and . . ." He was about to say "your memory," but instead he went on. "I had to build up my stamina to bear it and do what I was able to do to help those innocent souls whenever possible."

"Humankind can be so cruel, Robert."

"Yes it can," he answered, "but it is slowly learning to be better."

Fray Francisco came back and handed Ana Dee a glass of water. He waited until she drank some before going on. "That brings us to man's spiritual progression. Slavery has existed since man has been on this planet, for economic reasons more than anything else. Only very remote cultures like the indigenous people of the Arctic or Australia did not practice slavery. It might be said that they were closer to their spiritual life than other societies. Those societies were rather isolated from the rest of the world, and its members had to depend on each other for survival. Love and caring for one another in such communities is a natural response."

"It is true, Robert, that those virtues would be easier to practice then. In the end, though, they are lessons learned from karmic experiences then or before. Nonetheless, we should take comfort in the growing opposition to slavery around the world. It comes with the raising of spiritual awareness of the world in general.

"Already in the southern part of our continent, many countries have legally abolished slavery. So that even if not yet in full practice, it will happen. Some countries such as Uruguay and the Llanos of Venezuela have compensated, with land and other benefits, those who previously had been enslaved. I dare say that we might see emancipation in our country within our lifetime."

He took a deep breath and after a pause went on. "Forgive my long lecture. I hope, though, that it helps you with your quandary, my child. But I wanted to share my observations before we continue with our class."

"I am beginning to understand where we are going with this. So the elimination of slavery has to do with man's spiritual awareness or growth and how, in general terms, it is taking place?"

"That's right, Ana Dee. Let's not forget other significant advances in our spiritual progress, such as women's rights, that are also emerging, though other humanitarian concepts have yet to see the horizon. Roberto, what do you think we should discuss in reference to humankind's awareness of the spiritual laws?"

"Perhaps we should discuss some of God's messengers throughout time."

"That is a good approach. I am leaving it up to you both to do some research on that topic for our next meeting. You have Dr. Moore's library to help you, Ana Dee. I would like you, Robert, to go within and review your notes from the *colegio*, and if Ana Dee is agreeable, you could also avail yourself of some of Dr. Moore's wonderful library."

"Of course, you are welcome to come by anytime, Robert."

"Thank you, Anita. I will try and not impose too much upon your generosity."

"Well, unless you have any questions, we shall meet again on the fourth Friday of March at the same time. That should give you ample time for your research. I will leave you with a hint, and that is not to forget the 'common link.'"

The spiritual discussion meeting ended. All three parted after friendly hugs, to Ana Dee's satisfaction and Robert's disconcerting but pleasant feeling.

Two weeks passed before Robert mustered enough courage to visit the Fournier family library to do his research. He was welcomed by Mary, David, and Paco, who kept running in circles around him.

"Let's let the sheriff come inside without trampling all over him."

"But, Mama, we haven't seen him in a long, long time."

"Yes, he doesn't come over ever."

"Come and play with Paco, Sheriff Heeus."

"Just for a little while, Mary." He tossed the dog's ball around the courtyard with the kids and Paco running after it.

Watching them play, Ana Dee admired how well Robert got along with the children. She thought about how much the children missed playing with André and was grateful for their friendship with Robert. After a short while, Ana Dee interrupted the game. Remembering Robert's endurance during their trip back home, she knew he would not easily tire out; at all times, he had been alert while she slept most of the time, feeling safe under his care.

"I think that the sheriff is here to do some research. Be nice and let him go into the library."

Robert took out two *piloncillos* sugar bars from his satchel and asked Ana Dee if he could give them to the children. When she agreed, he also took out a small piece of hide for Paco to chew on. Happy with their treats, the children let go of his arms, and he was able to follow Ana Dee to the library. He thought she would leave him to figure things out on his own, but instead, she proceeded to explain how the books were organized. He tried to listen to her instructions, but he was distracted by how her hair kept getting in front of her eyes as she bent up and down pointing out the different shelves and how she kept pushing it back. He wanted to hold her hair back, caress it, catch a whiff of its fragrance, twirl a curl around his fingers—in short, bury his face in it. This went on for a couple of minutes until she took hold of her semiwet mane and rolled it into a bun on top of her head.

"I am sorry. I let my hair loose to dry up, but it keeps getting in the way. So that is about it as far as the categories by which the books are organized. Do you have any questions?"

"It's clear as a bell." Then he thought better. "May I ask you again if I forget?"

She noticed he looked somewhat confused, like a schoolchild who had been caught not paying attention.

"Surely, if you are as good a pupil as Fray Francisco claims you are, you should have no problem figuring it all out."

Thinking he had been caught in flagrante, he turned to check inside his satchel for paper and pencil. As Ana stepped out of the library, she heard him mumble, "Darn! I forgot my writing paper."

She turned around and said, "I'll get you some."

Ana Dee went to her bedroom and picked up a new journal then returned to the library and handed it to Robert.

"I can't accept this. It must be quite expensive," he said, seeing the golden embossed letters on the journal's cover, "*I am not this hair, I am not this skin, I am the SOUL that lives within*" by Jalāl ad-Dīn Muhammad Rūmī.

"It is meant for you. You are a Soul brother. It's for all the help you have given me since the raid and for which I have never properly thanked you."

"Thank you so much. It is beautiful. I will treasure it. May I ask how you came upon it?"

"André and I bought several journals in Galveston. He was going to start writing his dreams. I actually gave one each to Fray Francisco, Hermann, and Pedro. I started to use André's myself because he hardly got to write in it. So this one was extra. I think the quote fits you, don't you?"

"Yes, it is perfect. You know, Rumi is probably one poet worth mentioning in our next class."

"I agree with you. His writings are so inspiring. I will leave you to do your research now." She walked out of the library.

Ana Dee's next letter from Catherine let her know Elizabeth was not as weak as she had been in her previous pregnancies and was staying in good spirits. Catherine mentioned she was involved in the suffragette movement, which was gaining momentum in New York. She also wrote that she and fellow activists subscribed to W. L. Garrison's abolitionist paper, the *Liberator*. She could send Ana

Dee some newspaper copies if she was interested, as well as the book, *A Narrative of the Life of Frederick Douglass*, the abolitionist who had himself escaped slavery. Ana Dee wrote back immediately to please send her the book and copies of the newspaper on a regular basis, if possible, as she was unable to acquire it in Santo Tomás. She wanted to share the papers with Fray Francisco and see if he had any suggestions on how to make the best use of them. Besides, they would be a good addition to Papa's library.

Ana Dee felt it her duty to add interesting books and reading material to her father's collection. She had brought some new volumes from Galveston: Jane Austen's novels, Alexandre Dumas' two famous works, *Wuthering Heights* of Ellis Bell (Emily Brontë), and journals on the Lewis and Clark Expedition.

The next spiritual discussion meeting was coming up though Robert had not revisited the library for his research. Ana Dee had found enough information on different world prophets and couldn't wait to share it. The collection of mystical and philosophical material was substantial in her papa's library. Dr. Moore had been a product of the Renaissance philosophers, seeking enlightenment through science and opposing religious dogma. But he also accepted the personal inner guidance that one could acquire through direct communication with his own "Higher Self."

The gift of healthy skepticism had been ingrained in Ana Dee. Dr. Moore used to tell her, "Prove it for yourself, not because they say so or tradition dictates it. Always respect and tolerate others' point of view, but beware if it doesn't feel right."

This was a fine line to tread as a teacher. She felt the need to inculcate in her students introspection rather than accept ideas at face value, not easy to do in a small town like Santo Tomás. A job easily accomplished with her own kids, though, who questioned her every command with their favorite word *why*.

She was ready for the spiritual discussion of God's messengers.

CHAPTER 57

A path must demonstrate divine love if it's
to be a true path for its followers.
—Harold Klemp

Winter was coming to an end, but it was still cold enough for Ana Dee to wear her favorite sweater, an off-white Aran-style turtleneck Catherine had knitted for her while she shared her Welsh ancestry with her daughters. Ana Dee wore with it a khaki-colored split riding skirt to keep her legs warm along with her comfortable tan moccasins. Fray Francisco joined them for dinner. He wore his raw wool jorongo over his monk's habit and tall moccasin boots.

After dinner, Ana Dee and Fray Francisco retired to the library and waited for Robert to join them. Robert visited with the children briefly and then came in. Attired for warmth in his blue jorongo, he brought his treasured new journal with him.

"Buenas noches, Padre, buenas noches, Anita."

"Good evening, *mijo.*"

"Glad you could join us, Robert. We weren't sure your schedule would allow it. I understand there was a family quarrel that got out of hand."

"Yes, a love triangle. I don't know who started it, so we locked up the two men on drunk-and-disorderly charges and are holding them until Monday for the council to see the case. Fortunately,

Deputy Iturbide is on duty this weekend. He likes to do the *Sereno* watchman."

"Well, we have to have some kind of excitement in town occasionally besides our fiestas. I am sure it will be the talk of the town during tonight's promenade."

Not wanting the conversation to turn into town gossip, the monk said, "Why don't we start tonight's spiritual discussion with what you found out, Roberto."

"Yes, Padre. I went back, as you suggested, and wrote down some notes on material I studied while attending the classes at the monastery."

"Excuse me, Robert, how exactly did you do that? Just from memory?"

"It's a technique I learned, where I can go back and see in my mental screen what I have studied or read before."

"So you carry your reference library inside you!"

"I suppose so. Anyway, what I can remember, as I wrote in my journal"—he showed Ana Dee the journal—"are words used by different religious prophets to express what we know as the Golden Rule.

"Christ taught as per the Bible: *Do unto others as you would have them do to you.*

"Buddha taught as per the Udanavarga: *Do not treat others in ways that you might find hurtful.*

"Judaism from the Old Testament: *Thou shalt love thy neighbor as thyself.*

"Hinduism, Krishna Dvaipāyana from the Mahabharata: *Your duty is not to do unto others that which would cause pain if done to you.*

"And lastly, Zoroastrianism from the Shasta-a-shayast: *Whatever can cause you injury, do not do unto others.*"

"Good recall. What about you, Ana Dee? Did you go in the same direction, and if you did, did you find other quotes besides the ones Robert mentioned?"

"Oh my! I should have gone first, he took most of my quotes. But I do have a couple more.

"From the Analects of Confucianism: *Practice loving kindness and do not do to others what you would not want done to yourself.*

"From the Hadith of Islam, Mohammad says, *Not one of you truly believes until you wish for others what you wish for yourself.*

"On Jainism as per Mahavira from the Sutrakritanga: *One should treat all creatures in the world as one would like to be treated.*

"Taoism by Lao Tse: *Regard your neighbor's gain as your own gain and your neighbor's loss as your own loss.*

"And Sikhism by Guru Granth Sahib: *I am a stranger to no one; no one is a stranger to me. Indeed I am a friend to all.*"

"Excellent job, Ana Dee. I see you made good use of your father's notes."

"You got me! Papa had already done some research on this and I took advantage of it."

Robert shook his head. "Totally unfair!"

"Well, you just repeated what they had taught you in class!"

"Really, you are both acting like children. The point is, you are both on the same direction. Now, let's expand on your findings. Ana Dee first, since you probably have some views from your papa's notes. Tell us why you think these apparently similar messages in different scriptures have a bearing on man's progressive spiritual development."

"I think for two reasons. First, the message, or supposedly God's revelation, kept coming over and over throughout time via the different prophets, while secondly, man's enlightenment, in general, progressively grew or is still growing."

"In other words, you think God's voice, in whatever form it had reached the prophets, whether through the spiritual light of an image or the sound of the Holy Spirit, was seeking to raise the general awareness of humankind?"

"Well, yes. It addresses different cultures with different words, but the message is still the same."

"What do you think, Robert? Please share your conclusion."

"I agree with Anita about the message and its purpose. I would add, however, that the meaning, although meant to be the same, is interpreted differently by the different peoples. It is not always understood to include all humankind. Such as in the use of the word *neighbor* instead of *mankind*.

"Also, the message is sometimes presented as 'what you should do' and other times as 'what you should not do.' That can lead to different interpretations, let alone the influence of social traditions and its perceived needs.

"Therefore, my conclusion is that the spiritual awareness resulting from the message was interpreted in its most enlightened form only by a few recipients. As a consequence, the universal awareness progression has been ever so slow."

Holding Robert's eye contact, Ana Dee commented in a firm tone, "I can agree with that. In other words, the message is there, but the general population maturity is not."

"So, Ana Dee, you have answered your own question. Is our country spiritually mature enough to eliminate slavery?"

"Apparently not."

"So then, can you tell me what is missing when people hear the Golden Rule?"

"It's possible they don't want to understand it because of economic reasons, like you mentioned before."

"But what is missing?"

"I write down something I read in the library that might address that. It is a quote by the poet Rumi: *Words are a pretext. It is the inner bond that draws one person to another, not words.*"

Her eyebrows rising, Ana Dee exclaimed, "Robert, I have misjudged you. I didn't think you got much from the library. Rumi's quote is perfect. Man needs the inner communication to fully grasp Spirit's message. Papa always said to look within. Is that what's missing, Father?"

"Very true. The practicality of the outer world consumes our society's mind. Personal and survival needs force humans to be that way, thus ignoring the inner communication. Also, societies as human groups have to deal with karma. But there is another ingredient that can help man with caring for one another. This word appears in only a couple of your quotes."

Both Ana Dee and Robert replied, "Love," and gave sideways glances to each other.

"I think we have touched upon the most important aspects of tonight's discussion. We may bring more questions on this topic next time we meet. My hope is that this has helped you understand why the abhorrent practice of slavery still exists, Ana Dee."

"I do have one more question tonight before we adjourn, if I may?"

"Yes, of course, dear."

"Rumi was not considered a prophet, more of an interpreter of the Koran. Was he a spiritual master?"

"He was definitely spiritually aware and knew divine love. I will tell you a lesser-known truth. His mentor Shams-i Tabrizi was a spiritual master."

As they parted that evening, Ana Dee thought she had been blessed by always having loved ones in her life. After every stone along her path, there came a gift to compensate. The only love she missed was the kind her best friend Nadia had—a life companion.

CHAPTER 58

Only love can sew the hole of absences.
—Sandra Barneda

Nadia's baby was due in late April. She had gained so much weight Hermann called her his *lieblings ente* or "darling duck" because of the way she walked. On Thursday after work, she came to see Ana Dee.

"I need to find someone to help at the clinic. My feet are so swollen I can hardly walk."

"I noticed that Tio Pedro has been working double time at the clinic these days."

"Yes, he's had to help me with organizing supplies, cleaning equipment, really anything that requires me to get up from my desk. Do you know anyone who could take my place for at least two to three months?"

"I heard from Manuela that our old friend Carmen was looking for a job. But you would have to give her some training. Do you think you can continue coming to the clinic until you have the baby?"

"I have no other choice. Hermann wants me there in case I go into labor early. He doesn't think I will make it till the end of April!"

"I can go now and talk to Carmen."

"Thank you, dear. Go before it gets dark."

Ana Dee grabbed a sarape and headed out to the Pérez residence on the other side of the plaza by the stables' street. As she was crossing the plaza, she ran into the sheriff. He was concerned to see her by herself at that hour and asked if he could be of service. When Ana Dee explained the situation, he said he would accompany her as it was already dusk. Robert waited at the stables, checking on his horse and visiting with Don Juan while Ana Dee went inside the Pérez residence to talk to Carmen.

Carmen was home making dinner for her dad, Juan Pérez, and her two boys. She had grown into a strikingly attractive woman, a product of her black father and mestizo mother: a smoky topaz complexion, high cheekbones, the almond-shaped Olmec eyes, and tight curly hair she wore braided down to her waist. She had married a mulatto vaquero in her early teens and had the two boys, now six and seven years old. Her husband worked in one of the large ranches now owned by an Americano and came home only twice a month. For that reason, Carmen preferred to live with her dad. She had moved back with him three years before, shortly after her mother's death.

Carmen was excited about the prospect of working at the clinic now since her two boys were in school. She had learned to read, write, and speak some English when Ana Dee and Catherine had their adult classes in their home. Ana Dee knew her to be a smart and fast learner.

Once it was agreed that Carmen would start work the following day, Ana Dee left the Pérez's household and met Robert who was waiting to accompany her back home. She wanted to thank Robert. It was already dark, and being in the middle of a winter week, the plaza was empty.

"I appreciate your walking with me. I didn't realize it was so late when I left the house. Nadia just sounded so desperate."

"Anita, whenever you need me, don't hesitate to ask. You know I'll always be there for you, you and your family."

"I have no right to beckon your assistance," she replied, snapping her fingers. She turned toward him. "I know you think of me as a younger sister. Please don't say you are my spiritual brother. In fact, if you were to marry, your wife would not accept that. I know André would not have accepted it."

"But André isn't here, nor do I have or intend to have a wife."

She gave him a quizzical look and decided to end their little parley.

"Good night, Sheriff."

"Have a pleasant evening, Anita."

After she closed the door, she leaned against it for support and took a deep breath. Why did Robert's deference to her needs make her self-reproach? It was unnerving! She knew she had overreacted.

The sheriff walked away thinking he probably should not have referred to her husband's absence nor to his present unattached status. It was too soon; not even a year had passed since her loss. What was he thinking? On the other hand, maybe it was time to be up front about his feelings toward her. She obviously suspected it. How could she not? Was it possible she hadn't until now and thus her sudden annoyance with him? Fray Francisco had warned him to give it time. He decided he would give her some space and stay low until their next spiritual discussion.

When Ana Dee went to bed that night, she tossed and turned in vexation. Her state of disquietude was hard to comprehend. She had been miserable since André's death. She was resolved to stay miserable and simply continue dealing with life's responsibilities for the children's sake. The reason why Robert felt the need to continue protecting her didn't matter. She would not admit to herself it did.

The next morning, Ana Dee woke up with bags under her eyes from the unrestful night. On her way out to school, she stopped at the clinic; and to her satisfaction, both Nadia and Carmen were there already. Upon seeing her, they both suggested she stay home because of her tired appearance. Ana Dee disregarded their recommendations, picked up her kids, and headed to school. She was glad not to see the sheriff, who ordinarily would be doing his morning patrol around the school at that time. Her first thought was, *He is avoiding me. Good.* She went into the building.

Because the next day was Saturday, she was able to stay home and rest. Manuela noticed her depression and tried to comfort her with warm herb teas and blankets. Ana Dee didn't even read to the children as she usually did. Manuela told Pedro how worried she was about Ana Dee's sudden mood change. Pedro decided to have a talk with his niña.

"Mija, what's going on? You were doing so much better. Did something happen?"

"Oh, Tio, I am so confused." She leaned on Pedro's shoulder and in between soft sobs asked, "I think Robert might still love me."

Pedro almost jumped up from the couch; it took some effort to pretend calmness. Hermann had been right in his suspicions! He decided to act as if many years ago Abuela Brau had confided Robert's identity to him.

"Of course he does. Anyone can see that. The question is, how do you feel?" When she didn't answer, he went on. "It's been almost a year since André's demise. You are still young. No one expects you to bury yourself in his memory. He certainly wouldn't. Is it possible that your feelings for Robert are coming back?" He pulled his handkerchief out of his pocket and handed it to Ana Dee.

She wiped her tears and blew her nose. "I don't know, Tio. Robert has such a heart-loving halo. But when he is around, especially if he is attentive to my needs, I tend to lose my composure. I get irritated, not really by him, but with myself."

"Ana Dee, you are obviously feeling guilty, disloyal to André. Don't do that to yourself. I too have seen the light that surrounds Robert, and he is worthy of your love. That anger will go away. Give yourself some time to sort out your feelings. Do your spiritual contemplations. They will bring you peace and understanding."

Ana Dee spent the rest of the weekend mostly quietly in her room. She contemplated, read, and wrote in her journal. By Monday, she seemed in a better mood. She walked to the school with the children, and as the previous Friday, did not run into the sheriff.

Mary and David, who were used to seeing the sheriff every day on their morning walk, wondered where he was. Ana Dee told them he was busy doing his job and not to expect to see him every morning. Mary put her hands on her hips and, facing Ana Dee, said, "Mama, I think you scare him away."

Ana Dee was taken aback by her daughter's observation and would have inquired why, but pointing at his sister, David said, "Nobody scares the sheriff, silly girl." By then they were inside the school grounds and the youngsters ran to meet their classmates.

Robert did not make his morning appearance the whole week. Nonetheless, they would have to eventually meet for the spiritual discussion. That couldn't be avoided.

As promised, Catherine sent a package with the abolitionist material. Ana Dee couldn't wait to share it at their meeting and get suggestions as to the best use of the newspapers.

It was the last week of March when Carmen, barely getting used to her new job, had to assist Dr. Hermann with the delivery of his new offspring, who saw fit to join the world three weeks early. This time, it was a premature delivery. Nadia couldn't be more relieved.

When Ana Dee came to see her, she found a strong, healthy newborn baby girl. After Nadia breastfed her, she held the infant and rocked her.

"She is beautiful, Nadia. How wonderful! You now have a boy and a girl. Have you planned her baptism? What are you going to call her?"

"That's what I wanted to talk to you about. We are naming her Esra Marie, and we would like you to be the godmother."

"It would be an honor, but isn't it traditional to choose someone in your family? Will your parents agree to it?"

"This time I am putting my foot down. I will not have their antiquated ideas on women's behavior influence my daughter. I want her to grow up secure in her rights as a human being, and you are the perfect role model. Please say yes."

"Of course I will accept. But let me tell you, you are one of the strongest women I know and a perfect role model for your daughter. You are always able to keep such a positive attitude, and your determination to keep the peace even while bending the rules amazes me."

"Let's not get mawkish. It is only in case something were to happen to me. I want Esra Marie to have someone like you to turn to."

"It is set then. Let me know when you've arranged things with Father Murphy. I imagine one of your brothers will be the godfather?"

"Most likely. I have to discuss it with Hermann. By the way, he is delighted that you will be the godmother."

"Really? I'm a little surprised at that. He always thought I was too much of a freethinker."

"Goes to show you. When it comes to his daughter, he admires that quality."

CHAPTER 59

He who would be no slave must consent to have no slave.
                                                    —Abe Lincoln

Ana Dee served as godmother at Esra Marie's baptism. Being light skinned, the baby favored Hermann more than her mother. Already the apple of his eye, Hermann was so enamored of his little girl that it was obvious she would be spoiled as such.

Since Carmen was helping at the clinic, Nadia decided she would take a month off to recuperate and care for her newborn and Hansali, after which her plans were to go back to work on a part-time basis. This was music to Carmen's ears, who wanted a permanent job.

Carmen also got to visit with Ana Dee more often. Her boys came back from school with Ana Dee every day to go home with their mother. The brothers, Juanito and Gilberto, followed David around as their leader. This annoyed David, except when he got to boss them around.

Late April, the evening of the spiritual discussion, Manuela invited Carmen and the boys to stay for dinner. They enjoyed a lively conversation with Fray Francisco.

Ana Dee could not wait to tell Fray Francisco that the copies of the *Liberator*, the abolitionist weekly newspaper, had arrived. Carmen became curious at the mention of the abolitionist paper and wanted to know more about it. She had come across some underground papers about Josiah Henson, a former slave who was now in Canada. Henson would later be recognized as the character who inspired *Uncle Tom's Cabin* by Harriet Beecher Stowe. Ana Dee said she would be glad to let Carmen read the papers her mother sent her as long as they remained in the library. They made plans for Carmen to see them after work the following day, which was Saturday and the clinic closed early.

Carmen and the boys were on their way out when Robert came in for the spiritual discussion meeting.

As he walked into the library, Robert asked, "Who was the beautiful damsel leaving as I came in?"

Ana Dee answered in a slightly petulant tone, "Excuse me, she is a married woman." Seeing Fray Francisco's raised eyebrows and odd smile, she clarified, "Anyway, her name is Carmen, and she is one of my childhood friends. She is Mr. Pérez's daughter, and you went with me to hire her for the clinic, remember?"

"Yes, of course." Robert quietly sat down, amused by her reaction and thinking, *I'll be darned, could she be jealous?*

"I think we should postpone our spiritual discussion and just review some of the literature that Ana Dee received from Catherine. Ana Dee wants our help figuring out the best way to share the newspaper information with our community."

"That's fine by me." Browsing through the material spread out on the desk, Robert picked up the book. "I would love to read about Mr. Douglass. I had heard about him before."

"That's fine, but I prefer that the book stay in the library for now until we figure out a lending system."

The monk looked at Ana Dee and said, "Mija, I think you can trust Robert to take care of it."

Ana Dee let out a big sigh and nodded her head. "I suppose so, if you promise to be really careful."

"Ana Dee, you offend me. What have I done to earn your mistrust?"

Feeling ashamed of her irrational behavior toward Robert, Ana Dee blushed.

Trying to spare her embarrassment, Fray Francisco said, "We'll have to excuse Ana Dee from being overprotective with this material. Reactions have a way of running amuck when it comes to this topic."

Feeling unrealistically guilty for embarrassing Anita, Robert said, "I am sorry, Anita. I didn't mean to upset you."

His asking for her forgiveness, when she was totally at fault, only made her more ashamed of herself. Knowing she was not in control of her mood, she decided to remove herself from the discussion.

"Could we possibly meet next week about this? I don't feel well. Please take the book with you, Robert. Padre, please take some of the papers with you as well."

Fray Francisco and Robert both stood up as Ana Dee made her exit.

"Padre, I am worried about her. She has acted strangely every time I've seen her lately."

"Yes, she has, but only when you are around. I'd say that is a good sign. I think it is time to declare your true feelings to her."

They both walked out into the night, Fray Francisco wearing a worldly-wise smile and Robert looking bewildered, thinking about the monk's advice.

As planned, Carmen visited the next day. They perused eighteen copies of the twenty weekly papers Ana Dee had received, avidly reading and sharing the stories and comments. Carmen wanted to make it available to everyone in town, but Ana Dee explained that state forces were determined to eliminate the copies and do harm to those who spread them. She told Carmen about the planned meeting with Fray Francisco and the sheriff for ways to safely spread the information. Carmen left, promising to be of help whenever Ana Dee made a decision on how to best use the material at hand.

CHAPTER 60

*Read and you will drive, don't read
and you will be driven.*

Fray Francisco, Robert, and Ana Dee met the first Friday in May. It had been drizzling all day. They sat by the warm hearth in the library.

"I have given this some thought and have a suggestion."

"Please share it with us, Padre."

"In our path, we best serve others by helping them find their way to a higher consciousness. That is not a political mission. Our message is always one of love, spread by words, not by violence. Do you not agree?"

Both Ana Dee and Robert nodded.

"I know you would both agree that slavery is contrary to the Golden Rule as it applies to all human beings. Slavery goes against the spiritual laws, and it is thus an impediment to achieving a higher consciousness.

"Now, the best way to spread the spiritual message is to teach our youth positive moral behavior. As a teacher, you have a perfect opportunity to spread this message to your students so that they grow up with proper moral values. Why not make this literature available to the students?

"As you are aware, when our youth reaches fourteen to sixteen years of age, many are leaving Santo Tomás. Our town is not growing, and there are not enough jobs for the new generation. Those men and women who leave Santo Tomás will be emissaries of the teachings they receive."

"I am in agreement with that approach," said Ana Dee excitedly.

"There is just one point that we must consider."

"Pray tell, Roberto."

"Ana Dee should not take this literature to the school."

"Do you think there will be some opposition?"

"Not by the students or even the teachers. However, if it's known outside Santo Tomás, the district might lose the promised state financial support. Worse yet, you might be in danger from bigots."

"That is true. Then we make the material available through the use of this private library."

"In other words, I can make the library accessible to the students, and they can even have tertulias here," Ana Dee offered.

"Hold on. You can't have people trotting into your house whenever they want."

"How about if you assign a time and day of the week for access to your library?" Fray Francisco suggested.

"I'm not sure that Ana Dee should take that risk."

"I can handle it."

Aware of Robert's concern for Ana Dee's safety and how it was starting to upset her, Fray Francisco excused himself, hoping Robert would take the hint.

"While you two discuss this, I am going to talk to Pedro about something else." He winked at Robert and walked out of the library.

Robert closed his eyes in exasperation, thinking, *He wants me to tell Ana Dee about my feelings for her.* He swallowed hard and decided to go for it.

"I have no doubt you think you can handle it. But I know it would be more dangerous than you realize."

"Is that the lawman speaking?"

"For one thing."

"What's the other thing?"

"I care what happens to you . . . and your family, of course. What the hell, I love you. There, I said it. I am in love with you."

Aghast, she asked, "How long?"

"How long what?"

"Don't play with me. How long have you known you love me?"

"Since the day I kissed your tears or before, since the day I met you at the plaza in 1843. I never stopped loving you."

"I don't believe it."

"My love has been constant." He approached her and confessed, "Yes, I tried to court other women after you got married, but I found that only you can quench my thirst for love."

Robert pulled out the treasured blue handkerchief with her initials and placed it in her lap. He went back to sit down at the other end of the room, where the darkness from the burned-out candle enveloped his countenance, where he observed her reaction.

She examined it and saw her initials, knowing full well it was one of her very old ones, realizing he carried it all those years. The current of his love emanated from the familiar piece of cloth, not unlike what she had experienced from his touch. Not even his heartfelt words could have expressed his love better. She sat dumbfounded, caressing the kerchief and smiling at the memory of their ride to the eternal love site, Tlazolia Occepa. Her thoughts went back to the time she twirled in a contemplative dance inside the circle of sparkling stones dreaming of Robert as her life companion.

Fray Francisco came back, wondering if they had cleared the air or if they needed a referee. They were silently sitting on opposite ends of the room, absorbed in their own worlds. He thought it might be appropriate to leave.

"I have to tell you I plan to go back to Kulkanzin to retire pretty soon. I miss my true home. I would like to see this situation resolved before then, and I don't mean just the library situation. God sends us gifts of love again and again. We often fail to recognize them."

Addressing Robert, he added, "I hope you shared your feelings with Ana Dee. If you are done, I want to go home, my bones are tired. I'll talk to you later, mija. May you have pleasant dreams tonight." He hugged her good night. Robert didn't.

After they left, Ana Dee went to see Pedro. She asked why the padre wanted to talk with him. Pedro told her Fray Francisco had stopped by the kitchen to say hello, have a glass of water, and eat an *empanada de calabaza.* "You know how much your padrino loves the pumpkin filling."

Ana Dee thought, *He knew what Robert was going to tell me and gave us some private time.* In a way, she was glad Robert admitted his love for her. She hadn't just imagined it all those years. In fact, deep down she knew. The question was, could her love for him come back? She knew her uneasiness in his presence was because of her feelings for him, not his for her.

Once in her bedroom, she placed the old handkerchief in her dresser drawer next to Robert's old letter, thinking, *I kept his letter and he kept my bandannoe.* She went to bed hoping for some answers.

If ever she needed spiritual guidance, it was then. She recalled words by her favorite poet Rumi: "When one is united to the core of another, to speak of that is to breathe the name HU, empty of self, filled with love."

In the quiet of her chamber, Ana Dee did her soothing HU contemplation.

The comforting love and warmth she experienced when hearing the Voice surrounded her: *Trust your heart. Accept the gift of true love again.* In an instant, she was able to come in touch with her true feelings. Her heart had opened, and her inner battle was over. She basked in her newfound solace and slept, her mental exhaustion giving way to peace.

CHAPTER 61

It seemed the more I knew about people the more I knew
about the strange magic hidden in their hearts.
—Rudolfo Anaya

The next morning, Ana Dee kept thinking of ways to approach her beloved. Musing in delight at the word *beloved*, she couldn't wait to see him again. Before, though, she had to talk to Carmen about Fray Francisco's proposed library plans. She suddenly remembered the monk saying he was going to retire in Kulkanzin! How could he leave Santo Tomás? Not only had he been her spiritual teacher, but he had also replaced Papa in her life. Did he have a part in getting Robert and her together, knowing he was leaving? She meant to talk to Carmen first that morning, but instead she decided it was more important to talk with Robert about the monk's plans. Ana Dee walked along the plaza to the jailhouse.

It was a misty morning. The plaza greenery was wet with dew. Without thinking, she had left the house without her sarape. Concern with her mentor's retirement took precedence over the damp air. She walked into the jail slightly shivering and asked, "Did you know Fray Francisco was leaving?"

"My God, woman, you are going to catch a cold." Robert grabbed a blanket from the empty cell and wrapped it around her. "Let me get you some warm coffee."

Ana Dee sat down and took the offered drink. She didn't look up at him until she had finished the warm beverage and handed the mug back to him.

"Well, did you?"

"I did. However, it is nothing new. He has been planning it for a long time. I often wondered what kept him here. I came to the conclusion last night that he didn't want to leave until you were taken care of."

"I don't understand. Taken care of by what?"

"More like by whom."

"You mean you?"

"Is that so bad?"

Ana Dee didn't answer. Her mind went blank, forgetting how she had intended to declare her love. Robert walked toward her and took her hand. She felt the old familiar current run up her arm, leaving a soothing warm sensation.

"I know you don't need anyone to take care of you. But can't you let down your guard on occasion and let me love you and look after you?"

Her barely audible response was, "Love me, yes," and walked out, wrapping the blanket tighter around her in a flurry.

Robert stood in his office in a stupefied state of joy. He pulled out his guitar and started strumming a new tune.

Ana Dee walked into her room and folded the jail's blanket; took off her somewhat damp, cold blouse; and changed into a warm sweater. She went into the kitchen to ask Pedro if he could please return the blanket to the jailhouse because she didn't want to go back there and the sheriff might need it. He gave her a bemused stare but didn't question how she came by the coverlet, suspecting she didn't want to face the sheriff.

Ana Dee went into the clinic to see Carmen. They were discussing the plans for the library when Hermann walked in. He didn't yet have a patient and decided to join the ladies' conversation. They had no choice but to share the plans with him. To Ana Dee's dismay, Hermann shared Robert's concern about Ana Dee opening her home to outsiders. That's when Carmen came up with the idea of putting a door in the library facing Market Street. "That way no one has to come in through the house and the library door to the house interior can stay locked."

Both Ana Dee and Hermann thought it was a proper solution. They would need volunteers to man the library for a couple of hours daily. Carmen said she knew some ladies who would be happy to help. Ana Dee left the clinic excited at the new plans. She went to look for Pedro to discuss tearing a hole in the library wall for a door opening.

Pedro was taking longer than expected delivering the blanket. He had entered the jailhouse to find Robert engrossed in a new guitar composition.

"Good morning, Sheriff. I am here returning this coverlet."

Robert put down his guitar and took the blanket from Pedro.

"Oh, thank you, Tio. Please call me Robert or Roberto if you prefer."

"Well, I like being on familiar terms with the law. I take it that this has something to do with *mi niña*."

"*Bien lo sabes*—you well know. I hope to have your approval?"

"If you can make our girl happy, you have my blessings. If you hurt her, though, may God have pity on you. She seems strong and she is in many ways, but her heart is tender and trusting."

"Tio Pedro, I have waited and wished for seven years to hear Ana Dee accept my love. She has said so this morning. I would never want to hurt her. My heart is hers, and she knows it."

"I don't believe she ever stopped loving you. Yes, she adored her husband. He made her enjoy life. In her loyalty to him, she tried to forget memories of you. She has been feeling disloyal to him since you came back into her life. It is odd how loving you has always caused her sorrow."

"I understand why you are worried. But our separation, not our love, caused our unhappiness."

"What I want to know, then, is that you will remain at her side. Because if you leave her again for another spiritual quest or whatever mission that comes along, she would never recover."

"I can promise you that when we are married, I will cling to her like a limpet."

Pedro shook his head. "If I did that to Manuela, she would hit me with the frying pan."

Pedro left a smiling Robert, whose mind relished the thought, *She never stopped loving me. Tio Pedro should know.*

When Pedro got back, he talked to Ana Dee about the door and said it was feasible. He only needed to check the library's outside wall to find the best spot, and Ana would have to cancel any meetings in the library until the work was done. Ana Dee started making plans to temporarily move the books, manuscripts, newspapers, etc., from the library into the living area until the entryway construction was finished and they could reorganize the shelves and provide plenty of seats for studying and tertulias.

When they were finished discussing the new plans for the library remodeling, Pedro asked, "So how do you feel about Mr. Hughes's marriage proposal?"

"He hasn't proposed yet."

"Well, he will soon. Is he coming over tonight?"

"I don't know. I don't believe he is. Did he tell you something I don't know?"

"Ha, that's why you wanted me to take the blanket to him!" he said, wringing his hands. "I can tell you he was quite cheerful. I thought that now that you are both romantically in tune, y'all would take the next step. I don't know . . . courtship, promenading, dinner together, something?"

"*Ayyy*, Tio, I think we are beyond that."

"What do you mean?"

"We are older now. After he proposes, we'll simply get married as soon as possible."

"I suppose you are right. Why waste time?"

"I have to prepare the children, though."

"They already like the sheriff a lot."

"You think so?"

"Of course, they talk about him all the time. If you ask me, Mr. Hughes was preparing the ground ahead of time."

"You might be kidding, but I think that is true. I believe Fray Francisco and Robert have been conniving behind my back since Robert moved back to Santo Tomás."

"Well, the Padre has known you since you were born, and he has had your best interest at heart. If he trusts Mr. Hughes, I will too."

"Patience. That's what I need, patience. I am just waiting for him to propose."

"Don't just sit around and raise your anxiety. Promenading has started already this year. Why don't you take the children promenading tonight? The rain has stopped. It is a nice night for a stroll."

Ana Dee cherished the idea of thinking she might run into her blue man.

That evening, Ana Dee told the children to get ready to go promenading after dinner. Mary and David were excited about it. Pedro had made a leather leash for Paco so he could accompany them. Promptly at seven o'clock, they were out the door crossing Hidalgo Street.

They were strolling along the plaza when Paco spotted the sheriff and started pulling on his leash in his direction. The children immediately went running to meet him. After exchanging greetings, Robert asked if he could join them. The children looked at their mother pleadingly and she nodded. Robert offered his arm to Ana

Dee, who was delighted to take it, ignoring the passerbys' glances. As they strolled along, Robert kept staring at Ana Dee. She felt his gaze, and her face reddened.

The children pulled on them to buy some sweets. Ana Dee stopped to buy the candy, and Robert rushed to pay, holding her hands away. She looked up at him, and from then on, they could not avert their eyes from each other. Neither knew where they were walking, except for the children holding on to them and leading them. It wasn't long before Robert asked, "Should we get a bench?" and started looking for an empty one. David saw an empty one and ran to get it.

As they sat down, the children sat between them, enjoying the candy and playing with Paco, who kept trying to get a piece of it. Robert extended his arm over the back of the bench, touching one of Ana Dee's curls. She leaned her head and rubbed her cheek against his hand. In silence, his lips mouthed, "I love you." They held each other's gaze, telling endearments without words.

They were in another world, and when the children asked questions, as they often did, they simply answered, "Uh-uh." David stood up and turned his mother's head to the bench. He asked, "Isn't this the Gratitude bench, Mama?"

Ana Dee came out of her daze and said, "How appropriate! We have a lot to be grateful for, right, David?" But she was looking at Robert, who wore a mindless but mystifying smile.

After a while, Mary complained about her stomach, and Ana Dee blamed herself for letting the child overindulge in sweets. It was time to go home and give her some soda water. Robert picked up little Mary, and they all walked across the plaza. He brought them to their front door and hugged the children good night. Once they went inside, he held on to Ana Dee's hand, hoping for a kiss from her. She knew what he wanted because she did too. She asked him to wait while she called on Manuela to please prepare a glass of soda water for Mary. When she came back, Robert was waiting in the foyer by the door.

As he pulled her into his arms, he murmured, "I have been wanting to kiss you all night." As their lips found each other, his kiss was timid but craving; her lips were more assured and her kiss more daring. In the midst of their bliss, hurried steps entered the foyer, and a small hand tugged at her skirt. "Mama, I don't like the soda water."

Reality interrupted magic. The couple let go of each other as Ana Dee bent down to Mary's level and said, "I had better make you a tea. How about a *yerbaniz*? You'll like that."

Robert knew it was time to retreat. Hesitantly, he bade the caring mother and child good night.

CHAPTER 62

Music is the divine way to tell beautiful,
poetic things to the heart.
—Pablo Casals

Ana Dee took off her wedding band. After kissing it, she placed it in a small box where she kept André's band and her sapphire earrings.

She changed into her nightgown and got in bed. She wished Robert had stayed and spent the night with her. She was surprised by her intense feelings for him. They filled her heart with love; she had thought she would never feel that way again.

When Tio had said they were "in tune," he had been right. But Robert had yet to propose to her. Something told her to have patience and try to sleep. He might propose in a dream? Nay, she wanted to marry him in the physical plane. One thing for sure, this incertitude was frustrating. She was now determined to take the first opportunity to set straight their relationship. She turned her Argand lamp down to a soft light and closed her eyes.

About two in the morning, Ana Dee awoke to a light guitar strumming outside her bedroom window. She approached the window and heard Robert's voice softly singing:

Asomate a la ventana
Luz de mi Alma.

Espero que en el mañana
Serás tú mi Dama . . .

Ana Dee didn't open the shutters. Instead, she turned around, grabbed the lamp, and went to the front entrance door. Robert saw her barefooted in her nightgown stepping out to the sidewalk, beckoning him with her hand. He jumped the two long steps between the front bedroom window and the door. Holding his guitar in one hand and her free hand in his, Robert followed her into the foyer.

She quietly shut the front door and took his guitar, which she placed on the entry settee. They entered her bedroom, and after closing the door and placing the oil lamp on top of the nightstand, she led him to sit on the bed.

She took his blue Stetson off and lovingly stroked his auburn hair. She said, "*Mi cielo.* Do you know why you are *mi cielo*?" Robert shook his head, almost afraid to speak. "It's because you are my 'man in blue.' Since I first met you, you are always dressed in blue, my favorite color, the color of the sky. *Sky* means 'cielo,' and *cielo* also means 'heaven.'" She wrapped her arms around his neck as if to kiss him.

Robert started to whisper, "We are not married yet . . ."

Ana Dee bent down to help take his boots off and said, "We are *comprometidos*, no? Our union is sanctified by our true love. Let's not spend another night alone."

She was the self-assured, determined, strong woman he loved. He hid his face in the curve of her neck and surrendered to a night of bliss with his beloved.

In another plane, their alliance was celebrated as they prepared the vessel for a loved soul to enter the world in nine months.

At four o'clock, according to the church bells, Robert crawled around the bedroom floor in the dark, searching for his different apparels, which Ana Dee had thrown around the room. Once dressed, he kissed her on the forehead while she tried to get him back into bed.

Softly, he told her, "I must go, my love, before your family wakes up. I will return with Fray Francisco to perform our wedding at sunrise tomorrow."

Ana Dee sat up on the bed and rubbed her eyes. "Can he officiate a wedding?"

"Yes, my love, he is an ordained cleric. We'll be married in the courtyard with just your family present."

"I'll be waiting for you. What should I wear?"

"In Kulkanzin, the bride and groom simply wear white peasant clothing."

"I think I can do that. But I really hate to see you go. It will be a whole twenty-four hours."

"Just twenty-four more hours."

"Adios, mi cielo," she managed to mutter as she hugged her pillow.

"Hasta luego, querida." With silent stealth, he went into the predawn air.

At breakfast, Ana Dee told her family about the wedding.

Mary wanted to know if Robert would be her father; she wasn't going to call him Père while David said she should call him Papa. He could not wait to tell his fellow classmates his father was the sheriff!

Manuela and Pedro asked about the ceremony being at sunrise. Ana Dee said she wasn't inviting any friends and didn't want any fuss. It would be a Monday, and they would be going to school right after. Manuela said she would at least prepare a nice breakfast.

For the wedding, Ana Dee chose a full-length embroidered white-linen off-the-shoulder peasant-style dress she occasionally wore to church, but decided not to wear a mantilla with it. On a nudge, she picked out a silk blue sash for her waist. In the evening, after she and the children bathed in the big old tub, she told them to go to bed early because they would have to get up about five in the morning.

Manuela set out to bake her delicious pastries with different fruit fillings. Pedro busied himself decorating the courtyard with strings of multicolored festive flags that the children had made and decorated. He also placed luminarias with candles around the courtyard, ready to be lit during the ceremony.

Even Mother Earth contributed; May gave way to a temperate climate, perfect for an outdoor celebration.

Everyone went to bed early, but woke up every hour on the hour wondering if it was time to get up.

Fray Francisco showed up in his usual brown habit, clean and newly pressed shortly after five that morning. He was greeted by Pedro who asked what he needed for the ceremony. They place a small table on one side of the courtyard. On it, Fray Francisco set two bowls, one for water and the other for a small flame.

After dressing the half-asleep children, Manuela brought them to the patio.

When Robert arrived, he took his boots off in the foyer and walked in barefooted. He was wearing white linen pants and a peasant white linen shirt with a stand-up collar and grommet lace-up front. He wore no hat but had a blue sash around the waist.

Fray Francisco had Robert stand facing the east.

Pedro went to get Ana Dee. He found his *niña* contemplating. She saw him and, understanding it was time, went to put on her *huaraches*. Pedro explained Robert was barefooted, so she left her footwear in the room. Her hair was in loose cascades down to her waist. She walked to the courtyard holding on to Pedro's arm. Upon reaching Robert, she embraced Pedro, then let go of his arm and took Robert's extended hand.

In the middle of what looked like a fairy tale garden with the luminarias, colored paper flags, and wildflowers, the couple stood facing each other until the monk asked them to face east in wait for the first sunrays to appear.

Fray Francisco then started. "We are here to witness the joining of two souls, Ana Dolores Peregrino and Robert Hughes, in holy matrimony." He then blessed the couple with water from the bowl by placing his wet right thumb on their foreheads.

After reciting some words in an ancient language, he passed his hands through the flame and pointed at the horizon. "Together as Soul you place your feet upon God's Spiritual Path, Tlazolia Occepa." Anon, as if by command, the sun made its entrance. The blue-and-purple shadows of the night turned to golden pink-and-blue rays spreading throughout the horizon.

Manuela and Pedro raised their hands, welcoming Father Sun. Paco jumped and yelped. Mary and David danced in circles with mirth, sensing it was time to celebrate.

As Ana Dee and Robert leaned in to kiss, Fray Francisco said, "Not yet. Hold hands and repeat these words to each other: 'I have your heart and you have mine. I will cherish and care for it until death do us part.'" They did, and he pronounced, "In the presence of the morning star, on this dawn, you are joined as husband and wife." Fray Francisco then ended the ceremony with, "Go forth, my children—oh wait." Looking at Robert, he added, "You may kiss your bride."

EPILOGUE

Your children are not your children.
They are the sons and daughters
of Life's longing for itself.
They come through you but not from you,
And though they are with you, yet they belong not to you.
—Kahlil Gibran

Mary and David grew up loving Ana Dee and Robert as parents although they kept their last name as Fournier. Mary visited her Fournier uncles often and eventually joined them in the apothecary/ drugstore business. David grew an interest in the science of healing under Hermann's tutelage and eventually moved to New York to study medicine and reside with his grandmother, Catherine. Pedro and Manuela lived to a ripe old age under Ana Dee's care.

Dr. Moore's library became the center of the abolitionist movement in Santo Tomás. Eventually, except for Dr. Moore's special manuscripts, all the literature was donated to the school library.

Nadia and Carmen joined the Hughes family in the spiritual discussion meetings.

Fray Francisco returned to Kulkanzin to retire in peaceful service to his community. He kept in touch with his protégés through inner channels whenever needed. The magic portal was closed, but the circle of stones is still there.

Ana Dee and Robert had their first child, Louis, nine months to the day after their wedding. When he turned three and could make himself understood, the little blond boy asked his mother why they called him Louis. She explained that his papa Robert wanted to honor a dear friend.

The child shook his head and said, "But, Mama, I told you before I don't like that name."

Ana Dee and Robert treasured their love long after the sweet, electrifying current of recognition was gone and until they left this earth within hours of each other.

El Fin—The End

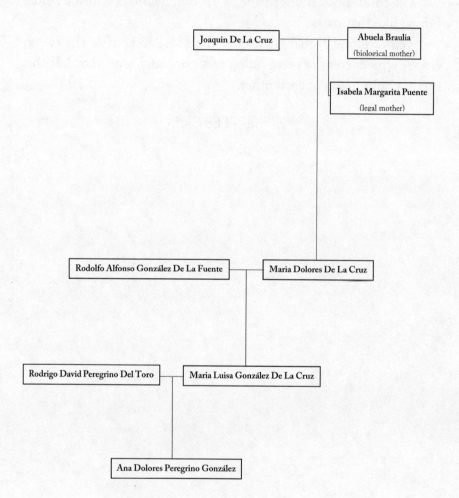

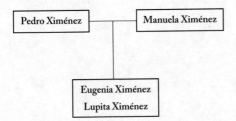

Pedro Ximénez — Manuela Ximénez

Eugenia Ximénez
Lupita Ximénez

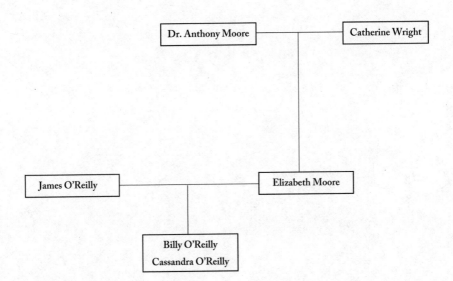

Dr. Anthony Moore — Catherine Wright

James O'Reilly — Elizabeth Moore

Billy O'Reilly
Cassandra O'Reilly

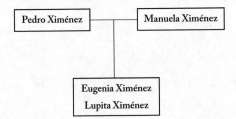

Pedro Ximénez — Manuela Ximénez

Eugenia Ximénez
Lupita Ximénez

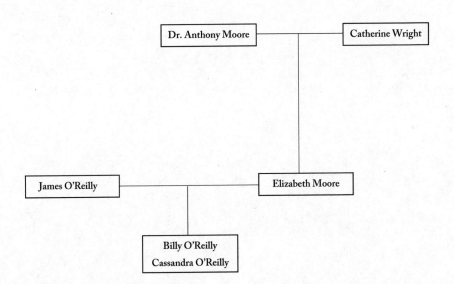

Dr. Anthony Moore — Catherine Wright

James O'Reilly — Elizabeth Moore

Billy O'Reilly
Cassandra O'Reilly